THE
KING'S
KNIGHT

THE
KING'S
KNIGHT

MATTHEW E. BLYTHE
WITH CYNTHIA M. STUCKEY

WESTBOW
PRESS®
A DIVISION OF THOMAS NELSON
& ZONDERVAN

WestBow Press books may be ordered through booksellers or by contacting:

WestBow Press
A Division of Thomas Nelson & Zondervan
1663 Liberty Drive
Bloomington, IN 47403
www.westbowpress.com
1 (866) 928-1240

Because of the dynamic nature of the Internet, any web addresses or links contained in this book may have changed since publication and may no longer be valid. The views expressed in this work are solely those of the author and do not necessarily reflect the views of the publisher, and the publisher hereby disclaims any responsibility for them.

Scripture taken from the NEW AMERICAN STANDARD BIBLE®, Copyright © 1960,1962,1963,1968,1971,1972,1973,1975,1977,19 95 by The Lockman Foundation. Used by permission.

This is a work of fiction. All of the characters, names, incidents, organizations, and dialogue in this novel are either the products of the author's imagination or are used fictitiously.

ISBN: 978-1-9736-2048-8 (sc)
ISBN: 978-1-9736-2049-5 (hc)
ISBN: 978-1-9736-2047-1 (e)

Library of Congress Control Number: 2018902071

Print information available on the last page.

WestBow Press rev. date: 7/24/2018

With heartfelt thanks and deep appreciation
to our parents, Glenn & Linda Blythe,
Who first presented to us the offer of
Pardon from the One, True King

Dedicated to Hannah, Emerson, and Nate.
May you enjoy reading these stories to your children
as much as I enjoyed telling them to you.
My prayer is that you will all be found at the
Front when He calls you home.

Special thanks to Bob Tebow, mentor and friend, who
has taught me over the years what a grand adventure
it is to tell the world the Good News. -M.E.B.

And for Lucy and Abigail. May you both continue to
learn what it means to be a warrior princess. - C.M.S.

Long Live the King!

CONTENTS

BEFORE

A young knight sat on a log by a small, warm fire and bandaged a wounded hand. The fire gave the only light for miles as light snow flurries fell from an inky dark sky. She munched on a hunk of dark bread and a wedge of cheese. Three young and gaunt children, also eating chunks of bread, watched her with fascination. They huddled around her under new, thick wool blankets that were impervious to the falling snow. She stopped every few twirls to tighten the wrap. The knight skillfully wrapped the hand like someone who had done this before. And indeed, she had too much experience dealing with wounds for one so young.

The small band of knights and three children had set up camp in a hollowed out area among jagged rocks and boulders in a forest that was exceptionally thick and dark. An enclave protected the group from the wind, occasional snow, and a host of other dangers known to lurk in these woods. Rocks hid the light of the small fire while trapping the heat and the ridge sloped away dramatically on one side and rolled more evenly down the other. Their position was excellent for hiding yet defensible if they were discovered. In all, it was a perfect camp if one needed warmth, rest, and, above all, to remain hidden from a multitude of ever present dangers.

"Can you tell us how all of this happened?" a young girl named Lydia asked. Bright eyes shone from her dirty face. Her smile was genuine, but the lines on her tiny, upturned face revealed she had known more pain than joy in her short life.

"Well," mumbled the knight between bites, "how much would you like to know?" She twirled the bandage around her hand several times, winced, and took another bite of bread. The knight slurped hot apple cider loudly and wiped her mouth with the back of her hand.

Another knight, barely visible at the edge of the firelight, turned and gave her a frown that cleverly disguised a smirk at her manners. She grinned and held up her cup in a mock salute. The burly sentinel shook his head in feigned disapproval, grinned at the three children with a shrug, and turned back to his post.

Lydia leaned in, pushed her chestnut hair out of her eyes, and replied seriously, "Please tell me everything. I have to know."

"Will you start with your name?" whispered a young boy, Tem, who was as dirty as Lydia and eating twice as noisily.

The knight cinched the bandage one final time and looked up at the children. She motioned and they crowded around her as baby birds snuggled closely to their mother. Wind howled through the thick fir trees above and the fire crackled softly as she began.

"My name is Kal and I am a King's Scout. What I am about to tell you is the truth. Straight out of the Kingsbook. This isn't some bedtime story, you hear? Not all of it is pretty to think about either," she said passionately. There was no anger in her voice, but her words seemed to have an edge to them, as if communicating outside of battle was awkward for her. Her voice softened as she looked at each of them, remembering the three of them knew firsthand that it was anything but pretty.

Kal paused and looked into their eyes as she showed them her well-worn leather book. "Some of it is rather dark. And shadowy." On the front of the cover, a lion's head with two crossed swords was burned into the leather. They all recognized the royal seal of the High King.

Kal, a feisty knight and expert practical joker, was deadly serious when it came to talking about her King. The three now knew two things about her: she was a fierce warrior and she had a fierce love for the One King. Kal opened the pages and began to tell about the beginning of the Dark Times, the period in which they now found themselves.

"The land was tranquil and magnificent. The High King ruled from the seat of the City Beautiful and peace covered the entire land. All of the people who lived in the great land under the King enjoyed the best of all possible things. Every day was like a perfect spring day—warm enough to be comfortable and cool enough to be refreshing. Fires," she added, motioning to the one in front of them, "were more about good friendship than necessity. Everything grew nearly without effort. It was said that if you were to throw away a tomato on the side of the road, in a few short days you had tomato plants that would soon flower and yield beautiful fruit. It was lovely and evergreen. Delicious fruits were everywhere."

"Fruits are real? Truly?" inquired Tem. His eyes were as wide as his hunger. He took another bite of bread and repeated, "Truly?" but his full mouth muffled the question.

Kal grinned and nodded slowly. "Yes, they are."

"There were no black forests, dark mountains, or foul wilds to disappear in. Everything was beautiful and bright, the way it should be," she continued. Her voice trailed off as she thought about it again, as she had so many times.

Elise, the young girl closest to the King's scout, noticed that while Kal had the Kingsbook open, she was not reading it. She was telling the story from her heart.

The night seemed to darken with Kal's story. The wind picked up and flurries of snow surrounded the campfire. The trees, already laden with snow, creaked in the wind like the saddle of her horse.

"Then, one day, in the far reaches of what we now call the Great East, or the Great Shadow Lands by some, in the dark deeps of a valley, something happened." Kal paused for dramatic effect. "Exploring citizens found a cave at the bottom of a steep ravine. In the cave they unearthed an ancient evil that emerged and corrupted the citizens of the King's great lands. A wicked prince led his evil following in revolt. He commanded a host of goblins, foul creatures, and all manner of filth and rottenness. From these depths emerged his champions, one of which was the hideous dragon named Thanatos the Unbeaten."

At the sound of the dragon's name, all three children gasped. They snuggled closer together under the thick wool blanket. Tem strained to look through the tops of the trees as if the dragon might swoop down on them at any moment. They were terrified. Everyone in the land knew of Thanatos.

"The enemy of the One King began to recruit the citizens of the land with a great deception. The evil was so great and complete that entire townships, villages, and even cities united in revolt against the Beautiful City and her King. In a short time, all of the citizens of every province had rebelled. Music faded from the lands which were once alive with its' sound. Beautiful countrysides and rolling hills became desolate. Forests of great beauty and majesty became dark and dangerous. Citizens who once roamed through the forests feared to do so. Many disappeared. Everywhere, and in every way, the land mirrored the shadowy scarring of the hearts of her citizens. Those who had benefited most from the King's goodness forgot about him. All that was good and bright faded into winter and darkness and shadow." Kal spoke sadly and slowly, with great emphasis on the last sentence. "There was not a village or town or city or even a house where that black shadow of treachery did not fall. The air around them was heavy with dread and fear. It was a sickness, a dark ache that spread into every corner of the land.

"And then, to add even more misery to treachery, the dark prince and king-pretender turned his goblin armies on the citizens. Many were slain outright. Ironically, the goblin armies imprisoned the rest under the laws of the One King for rebellion and sedition. All over the land, except of course for the Beautiful City of the King in the North, darkness fell as every citizen was led away in chains and entombed in towers, dungeons, caves, and a host of other foul places.

It was eternal night," she continued. One of the children sniffled. All three hung their heads. "None of the citizens were guiltless and none were spared the woes that followed. It was a land without joy or song of any kind."

Lydia looked down at her own wrists, chafed from years of chains. She rubbed them, still amazed at how they felt without her bonds. She knew Kal's story was true. She had lived it all of her life.

"And then," said Kal with a twinge of hope in her voice, "on the darkest of all nights, something happened. High in the North, at the King's city, there was a sound. A great host of trumpets sounded. They were not the high-pitched sounds of trumpets in revelry and celebration, but the deep sounds of war trumpets. The gates of the city swung open and out thundered a rider into the night. He was wearing the armor of war—shiny and bright and carrying a sword like no other. The horse, mightier than any other in these lands, bolted out, carrying its rider like a flash of lightning."

"Who was it?" a hopeful voice interrupted, trying to whisper.

"She's getting to that. Quiet now and listen," squeaked Lydia.

"And who do you think it was?" asked the King's Scout. "It was he. It was the King himself, dressed for battle and riding for war."

The children gasped and the young boy smiled at the thought. Excitedly they whispered, "The King. It was the King!"

"I knew it," said one.

"He rode out of the city on that darkest of all nights and headed straight for the Shadow Lands and the deeps. He crossed the once beautiful and peaceful countryside where he used to spend time with his citizens. He passed dark towers and dungeons. The cries of despair from his citizens spurred his horse to gallop faster. The goblin armies, who would never expect such an action, did not even know how to respond. Chaos reigned on that dark night.

"When the One King, the Only King, reached the dark fortress in the deeps, he thundered across the bridge and attacked without hesitation or thought for himself. The pretender king, dark and foul, unleashed all of his power and forces," continued the scout.

"Wh- ... what about the dragon?" asked Lydia nervously.

"Aye. Even Thanatos was unleashed. The battle lasted for days and the sounds of war were heard throughout the land. Finally, after days mind you, the sounds of battle subsided. Thanatos was never seen again, though people wonder where he is and what became of him.

"Then, something happened that astounded the inhabitants of the land and sent a shiver through the spines of the dark prince's forces," said Kal as she paused to slurp from her mug one more time.

"What? What happened?!" whispered the little ones excitedly. They could wait no longer.

"The King," continued Kal, just above a whisper, "rode out of the ruins of the dark fortress with something. *Someone*, to be exact."

"Who?" asked little Tem, his eyes fixed on the storyteller.

"One of us. A former slave and rebel, now set free. The King, through war and battle, had paid for and broken the dark prince's hold. No prison could keep out the warrior King.

"On that first night of hope, the war began. The war to set the citizens free and return the control of the kingdom lands to the One King, the True King. You see, the former slave was not sent back to the villages and farms or taken straight away to the Beautiful City. That night, the King brought the former slave weapons—special weapons."

"What kind of weapons?" inquired the boy curiously.

"Weapons made by the King and empowered by the King. The former slave became the first of a growing army, now forgiven and loyal. Armed with the King's power and on his orders, the war began that very night," said Kal triumphantly. Her smile was broad and bright and seemed to give as much warmth as the fire itself.

"And since that time, all over this land, the King's forces have made war against the enemy and his armies of villains. Though the darkness remains for now, the light is shining a little brighter all the time. It is spreading slowly and evenly in the hearts of those who are loyal to him. Even music has returned in some places where the King is loved."

The children were quiet for some time as they thought about the ruin of the lands and the King who would not leave his citizens to rot in dungeons. They thought about their own day of rescue. They considered the deeds of the King in silence while the wind howled in the background.

A question broke the silence.

"How were you rescued?" whispered Lydia.

Kal turned and looked at the knight standing just beyond the edge of the firelight. They exchanged a look of sadness and joy as volumes passed between them unsaid. The burly knight, covered in a fine dusting of snow and shifting a battle-axe from one side to the other, nodded slowly to her as if giving encouragement to answer the question. Finally, Kal turned and looked at the children.

"It is not a pretty story, but I will tell you. It is also a story of the King. And a knight. A scrawny knight, to be exact, who started his life as a slave. But you will soon see—that a slave he did not remain. Before I can tell you the story of my own rescue, I must tell you the story of his."

CHAPTER 1

The Slave

*"For He rescued us from the domain of darkness and
transferred us to the kingdom of His beloved Son, in
whom we have redemption, the forgiveness of sins."*
– Colossians 1:13-14

CRASH! The cell door exploded open as half a dozen goblin guards
rushed in and pummeled the prisoner. Startled awake by the terror
of sudden pain, raucous laughter, and dread of what might be next,
the slave found himself face to face with the menacing yellow eyes
of the goblin captain, Gruel. The captain, known by the nasty scar
across his face, loosed the prisoner from the great chain that had held
his head fast day and night. Several foul beasts beat him with clubs,
while two unchained his hands and feet.

"It's time, slave-filth! Time to pay for your crimes, once and
for all," bellowed Gruel. His vile guards roared with laughter and
cheering that sounded far more like metal grating on metal than
actual mirth.

"It's axe-day, worm!" cackled another.

The day the slave had been dreading had come. It was the day of
his execution. Found guilty of treason and sedition against the High
King, he had been remanded to the dungeon of the King's enemies

to await his last day. Apparently, his last day had come. The terror of what would be was only overshadowed by the guilt he felt over his crimes.

They dragged him across the slimy floor of the foulest place he had ever known. The fetid dungeon had been his home for longer than he cared to remember. Not a ray of sunshine broke through the darkness and dust in this place, leaving him hopeless. The air was always rank and he was always cold. Nobody fed condemned slaves well either, leaving his stomach as empty as the rest of him.

He tried to look away from where they were leading him, but he knew. The executioner's stump. Situated to be a constant reminder to him of his fate, the stump was in clear view of where he had been chained. His dreadful end always stared at him even if he did not want to look back.

Upon reaching the stump, the goblins lashed his head to the top of it with a strap. The guard jammed the slave's cheek onto the rough wood, forcing his head to the side so he could see a doorway that led to a small room. Standing in the shadows of that door was a hideous, sneering goblin named Leer. He was only slightly taller than most of the goblins, but nearly twice as cruel. The slave did not like any of them, but Leer was by far the wickedest. Without looking away from the slave, Leer scowled and reached for something behind the door. Pulling it out slowly, he brought it into the torchlight with a grin.

It was a great nasty axe with a jagged handle and large curved blade. There were rust stains on the blade. No. They were not rust stains at all; dried blood spotted the heavy iron.

Slowly, the yellow-eyed goblin began to walk toward the slave, dragging the great axe behind him. The giant blade made a sickening sound as it scraped the stone, growing ever louder and closer to the bound slave. The occasional spark flew as it nicked a rock on the floor.

This, the sound of his death approaching, was without a doubt the worst sound the slave had ever heard.

"Any last words, slave-filth?" asked Gruel as he motioned the other goblins to be silent.

"N...no. Only that I am guilty and I..." he started to say before being brutally kicked in the back and interrupted.

"No one cares, swine! Guilty or not, you have one thing to think about. In less than a few minutes, this axe is going to separate your worthless head from your wretched body. But don't worry, we plan to reunite your parts in the dungeons below as food for our pet. Right, boys?" They cackled with laughter. The blood lust was palpable.

"It's time," said the captain with a sneer. The executioner took his place where the slave could see him run a stone down the blade for a few strokes to sharpen it for the job. He placed one foot on the slave's back. It forced the air out of his lungs and caused him to heave out loud.

"Don't move, slave," Leer commanded with a snicker. "I wouldn't want to miss and only nick ya. Right?"

Then with all of his might, he drew back on the great axe and brought it down with full force. Time seemed to slow down for the slave. He was paralyzed from panic. This was the miserable end he had deserved but was terrified of reaching.

But instead of severing the neck of the slave, the blade slammed into the stump with a bone jarring *thwack*. The trembling slave felt his teeth jar into his skull.

He missed? No, the goblins were laughing too hard and celebrating too much. It was a trick. Just as roughly and painfully as the goblins had removed him from the cell, they dragged him back to his chains. Brutally, they bound him again, this time tighter than ever.

Not knowing whether he was relieved that he had not been executed or merely despondent that he was still a prisoner condemned, the slave sobbed, thoroughly broken. The goblins laughed still louder. One mocked him by reenacting the mock execution and adding a squeal.

It was humiliating.

He crawled as far away from the cell door as his chains would let him, leaned against the damp wall, and sobbed. He wanted to sleep, but the trauma of his near execution was too much. All he could do was shiver with dread and regret. The dungeon was darker now than it had ever been for the heartbroken slave.

Most of the time, the slave did not even know if it was day or night. He never saw the light of day or felt the warmth of the sun. He could not remember what green grass felt like on bare feet. He had long forgotten how a warm meal tasted in a comfortable house. He had forgotten what freedom was or if it even existed except in his mind. The slave was cold all of the time. The rags he wore were constantly damp. He was beyond miserable.

Chained in a dungeon in the bottom of a dark tower, the slave was a prisoner of the worst kind. His dark, wet cell faced the inside of the tower. Sometimes the water dripping down the wall was all he could hear. The only sign of life outside of the cell was the occasional guard who passed by hissing insults at the slave. From time to time, giant, snarling wolves led by the guards would walk by to check on the prisoner.

Hideous goblin guards with scaly hands and wicked grins guarded the tower night and day. They were the soldiers of a dark power and sworn enemies of the High King of the great City Beautiful. Some of them were greenish and some were pale, but all were terribly ugly. Strong and cruel, they loved to insult the slave through sharp-toothed grins. With ugly axes and crossbows and spears, they watched over the dark tower that was both his prison and his home.

The goblins reminded the slave at every opportunity that he was a prisoner under a sentence of death. They delighted in recounting to him the list of his crimes. "Traitor!" They would hiss. "Rebel!"

One night, the exceptionally cruel Leer sat outside his cell and recounted every time he was the executioner of a slave.

"Maybe today you'll join my list," he chortled as he finished reading and stood up.

Often they would keep him up all night reading through the extensive list of his crimes against the King. Not in a hundred lifetimes could the slave imagine a worse place.

He moved his arms slightly to relieve some pressure. Great, heavy chains moved with him, chafing against his wrists. He had been in these bonds for longer than he could remember. As soon as the chains moved, several of the wolves lifted their heads and growled. Any consideration of his situation brought more hopelessness. There was no escape. There was no reprieve. He was under a sentence of death. This prison cell was the best that would ever be for him— in these chains, and that was a terribly depressing thought.

In the past he resisted the guards when they hurled accusations. At times he would defend himself and give an excuse. Not anymore. The slave had come to realize they were right. He was guilty, and he was tired of fighting about it. Now he would just hang his head and listen to them spit their insults. But on this night, with the mock execution, he lay at the lowest point he had ever been. He had no hope, but he could not help wondering if there was any way it could be different for him.

He did not know if they were dreams, memories, or even rumors, but there was something. It was a distant glow in his mind, much like the beginning of a sunrise. *Things were not always this way. They would not always be this way.* Then the despair would chase the thoughts away and darkness would seep in from the dungeon to his mind and cover his thoughts like a fog.

As he drifted off to sleep, a low, rumbling thud sounded at the front gate of the dark tower. He wasn't even sure he had heard anything at first, but the wolves heard it too and began to growl. Then another *thud;* this one was a bit louder and caused dust to fall from the ceiling. The blow echoed through the tower like thunder off of a distant mountain. A goblin shrieked and blew on a horn, adding to the sound of the wolves, which were now snarling and howling. The slave sat up, and as he did, the great chains moved with him, though the wolves were preoccupied and did not even notice.

Goblins began to shriek, wail, and run back and forth grabbing their weapons. Some with crossbows ran up the stone staircases to the top. Others grabbed long jagged spears and ran for the gate. Several braced the gate with pieces of old iron and wood. Sounds of confusion, terror, and alarm filled the tower.

Leer let out a shriek, grabbed his axe, and ran toward the gate. The look of panic on his face surprised the prisoner.

The slave did not know what to think. What in the world could have such a fortress in distress and turmoil? Would the attacker be worse than his jailers? Who could it be? Questions swirled through his mind. He was afraid.

At that point the goblins on top of the tower began to shoot their crossbows. Arrows flew back at them. A flaming arrow hit a guard. He squealed and fell from his spot on the wall, shrieking loudly as he left a flaming trail in the dark tower. The guard landed in front of the slave with a terrifying crash.

It was clear a fierce battle was developing outside the walls. In the distance, the slave heard a trumpet sound he had never before heard.

The blows on the gate grew more frequent. Dull thuds became loud crashes. Several times he heard wood splintering. It seemed as if the gate would break at any moment. Captain Gruel was rushing with several more of his henchmen when he stopped by the cell door.

"Don't think for a minute this is good for you. You are a prisoner now and always will be. Do not trust any hopes you have—they are all false," he snarled.

But there was something in the goblin's voice. Was it doubt? When the slave realized the guard was concerned, the tiniest spark of hope flickered as it never had before. Something good was stirring outside of the tower if the goblin captain was afraid. Something the slave had never known.

At that moment the gate to the dark tower burst open, and a fierce battle began. The slave pressed his face against the bars but could only see the line of goblins fighting. Swords, axes, and spears were swung, thrown, and hurled, but still he could not see who was attacking. Then, one by one, the wolves at the front yelped and fell silent except for one that went running away howling with his hind-quarters ablaze. The goblins slowly retreated as their number dwindled. They appeared to be losing.

At that moment, the slave saw a flash of bright steel and a glint of silver armor. They were knights! But whose knights were they? The battle went on and on, and the goblins were driven back.

"For the King! Press forward men!" shouted a knight. A roar reverberated from the other knights in answer. At that moment the tiny spark of hope grew in the slave's heart—such a strange and foreign emotion.

Soon the battle lines were even with the cell door. It was a frightful scene to the slave. Every blow was powerful and loud. Sparks flew in all directions. Goblins shrieked. The knights pressed on.

Finally, in a panic, the goblin captain screamed down the staircase to a level below the dungeon, "Bring up Dragog!"

Moments later two goblins pulling chains appeared on the stairs, then quickly jumped to either side. Right behind them came a snarling lizard the size of a small horse. The lizard-like creature had rows of sharp fangs and sinister red eyes, and seemed to want to eat everyone and everything. It saw the knights and charged. One goblin was too slow to move out of the way and Dragog trampled him like an old wooden basket.

The beast was in a horrible rage, and the slave was terrified at what he saw. A female knight with blazing red hair shouted at the top of her lungs, "King's Knights! Shield line, center!"

The knights quickly formed a solid line with their shields to protect from the attack. They yelled in unison as they extended their shields to form a wall. As the creature lunged forward, a big bearded knight from the back of the line leapt forward with a giant axe. The shield line parted just enough to allow him through the gap. He brought the axe down on the creature's head with an incredible blow. The sound of the axe hitting the creature's skull echoed through the whole tower. Dragog shuddered and collapsed. Both sides paused to see the giant beast heave one last time and lie motionless, except for the occasional twitch. The red eyes, becoming lifeless, seemed to stare right at the slave.

"*Trespassers! Murderers!* On what grounds do you attack us?" shrieked Captain Gruel.

The redheaded knight moved forward and answered in an icy tone, "We are here in the name of the King and on his orders to speak with this prisoner. Lower your weapons and stay back, or the rest of you will meet the same fate as your pet."

The slave noticed the knight had emphasized the word "King" and the goblins cowered a little and looked at their leader.

"The prisoner is ours. His life is ours. He is filth, and he has nothing to say to you. Why would the King want to talk to this traitor anyway? You are at the wrong tower if you think he will ever be anything but ours," spat the goblin in a rage. The other goblins murmured quietly and nodded their heads in agreement.

"Nevertheless, we have our orders." While the other knights held their line and did not look away from the goblins, the knight turned to the slave. As she removed her helmet, red braids tumbled out. She was sweaty from fighting but seemed pleasant, which surprised the slave once again. Pleasantness was an entirely new experience. The knight knelt in front of the cell.

"Slave, look at me." He looked up at her serious face. "Why are you in this dungeon?"

"I have been accused of rebellion, sedition, and many acts of treachery. I have a sentence of death," the slave said slowly as he looked down again.

"Accused?" questioned the knight intensely. "Only accused?"

"No. Not just accused. I … I am guilty. I am guilty of it all. I am what they say I am. I betrayed a King who has only ever been good to me. I am where I deserve to be," he said sadly. The slave did not try to deny anything. He agreed with the goblins—the knights had made a mistake.

The goblins shrieked and hissed. Some even cackled and laughed. "You see? He is ours. By his own word he is our prisoner. Now, get out!"

The knight glared over her shoulder at the goblin, still clutching an extremely sharp sword. Her gaze alone caused several of the goblins to back down. She turned back to the slave.

"Yes. We know. The King has sent us to speak with you. He is aware of your great debt. He is aware of your sentence of death. But …" the knight's gaze softened a little, "He sends terms of peace and an offer of pardon."

"*NOOOOOO!*" howled the goblin guards. The big, bearded knight pulled the axe out of Dragog's skull, causing the whole beast to shudder. He held it menacingly toward the goblins as if he intended to charge. Immediately they grew quiet.

The slave could not believe the words he had just heard. How could this be?

"But I have nothing to offer. I cannot possibly meet any terms," the slave said quietly with great sadness. A sliver of hope emerged despite the recognition of his position. If there were any way at all this could be true, it would be unimaginably wonderful.

The knight smiled a little and said softly, "What if I told you that he has considered your great crimes against the throne and has had your debts paid in full by someone else—even the sentence of death? What would you say?"

"By someone else? That is not fair! Who would do such a thing for me? Surely you are mistaken. That doesn't seem likely or even possible!"

The slave could not believe what he was hearing. No one would take his place in this dungeon, in these chains, and take his sentence of death! No one! Was this a trick? He had been tricked so many times before.

"It's true, young friend. It is most certainly true," said a knight with black hair and a firm, solid smile. The slave could hardly take in what he was hearing.

"Like Sir Stephen has said, the King himself paid your debt, slave. And he offers you a full pardon," replied the knight with a beaming bright smile. It was the first real smile the slave could remember seeing. From out of a leather pouch, the red-haired knight pulled a piece of rolled up parchment tied with a dark red ribbon. She opened it for him to see.

It *was* a pardon! The King himself had signed it! His name was written at the top even though the document looked ancient. He scanned the writing over and over.

She continued, "So, what would you say to the King since the pardon is real and the offer is true?"

The slave stared in shock. He moved his trembling hands through the bars and touched the signature. "I would tell him I am sorry. I would cry for mercy and I would ask what I could do to earn this treasure!"

The knight snapped her hand back as if burned by fire.

"No. There is no *earning*. If you could do this thing by earning, you would not be here and neither would we," she said pointedly. Then her tone softened.

"The pardon is a gift already earned and offered by the only one who could. It is the proof of a debt paid. It must be received that way or not at all," she said seriously. "Do you understand?"

The slave nodded. He was beginning to see. "Yes! I think I understand," he said, then thought for a few moments as he read the pardon over and over. His own deeds loomed large in his mind, but this—this was an offer of pardon from the only one who could offer such.

"I am desperate for mercy and to be free of this dungeon. I am in such misery in this place, yet I know I am here because of my rebellion. You ask what I would say if the King were here? I would ask for his mercy and take his pardon. His name is signed and I truly trust him to keep His word to me."

"Truly? Then ask him yourself. He is here!"

At that moment, from the broken door of the tower, a cloaked figure moved across the debris on the dungeon floor. When he removed his cloak, everyone in the tower saw it was indeed the King! The knights immediately fell to their knees and bowed in reverence to their Sovereign. The goblins shrieked in terror and began to scurry into the cracks of the floor and passages in the walls. Some of the goblins in the tower jumped right over the walls. Others dove through windows. The captain of the guard jumped behind a stone column and hid his horrible face. The slave also hid his face in shame and fear and embarrassment.

The King walked over to the beheading stump and snatched the death sentence from the wall. Then he walked over to the cell door.

"Slave," he called.

"My King?" stammered the slave without looking up.

"My knights have delivered my terms and offer. What is your answer?" The voice, though deep and direct, also carried with it a warmth and hope like the slave had never known. Just listening to his question gave the slave such confidence that for the first time, he realized there was a greater power than the chains that held him or the bars that trapped him.

The King bent down so he could look into the slave's eyes. The slave had never ever seen anyone like the King. He was ashamed, but also desperate.

"My Lord, I am all that the charges say. I am a traitor and a treasonous criminal. I have been justly sentenced to death for my crimes. But she said you have paid that debt," said the slave, motioning to the redheaded knight. "She said you offer me a complete pardon as a gift. I do not see how this can be. I cannot understand why you would do this. But I am desperate. I am a slave. If you do not pardon me yourself, they will execute me."

The slave began to lift his head up slowly and look more fully at the King. With each passing second, hope grew inside him, warm and bright. *"The King would never sign a pardon he did not mean to honor,"* thought the slave hopefully. And in that moment, the idea of freedom did not seem like a far away dream, but a reality.

"My King, I want this pardon that you offer. I have nothing to offer in return. But I believe your words. Will you have mercy on me? Will you give me your pardon?"

The King stood up very straight and tall. With a blinding flash, he drew his sword and brought it down with full force on the cell door. The locks disintegrated in a shower of sparks, and the door flew in pieces to the back of the cell. The force of the blow destroyed even the chains holding the slave. The powerless goblins wailed and shrieked at the sight and sounds. The knights cheered.

Stepping into the cell, the King gently helped the slave up. Slowly the slave stood and took a step. No leg shackles held him in place. No chained collar kept him hunched over. He looked around in utter disbelief … *he was free!*

"Noooo!" shrieked Gruel. From behind a column in the cell, he screeched, "He is a slave! He is a prisoner! It is not fair to release him. He has committed crimes against the Throne!"

The King turned to the portly captain and answered, "Gruel. I might have known. I see no slave or criminal. I see only a citizen of my kingdom who is in a dungeon where he does not belong. You aren't suggesting I allow you to hold one of my citizens without cause, are you?"

Still hiding his face, the goblin hissed, "But his crimes! How is it just to release a criminal? The law—*your law*—says every crime must be addressed!"

The King looked at the slave-turned-citizen. He placed the list of charges and the sentence of death on the executioner's stump. He dipped a quill in a bottle of dark red ink and quickly scratched a line through the former slave's name at the top of each document. He then wrote his own name in its place. Then, next to each individual crime, he again wrote his name. When he came to the death warrant, he looked up at the former slave, who stood shivering outside of the cell. Then he dipped the quill again. In very bold letters he wrote his name, and under it the words, *"Sentence Paid in Full."*

The King turned a very hard and cold glare toward Captain Gruel. "True. All crimes must be paid for completely. This citizen's were paid. He will never be known by the name 'slave' again."

The King walked over to the now freed citizen and put his hand on his shoulder.

"Jonathan," he called the new citizen, "You are no longer a slave or guilty of these crimes. You are now a citizen of my kingdom with all of the rights and protections that brings. You are completely pardoned based on the fact that you have accepted my offer, and I have completely paid the debt for your crimes. Come, let's leave. This dungeon is no place for a citizen of mine."

With that pronouncement, the King wrapped a cloak bearing the seal of the kingdom around Jonathan. It was warm, but the idea of a robe carrying the King's seal warmed a part of Jonathan's soul that had never been warmed before. Even though he was tired and sore, he could not stop smiling. Several knights came over and helped him move, as he was hardly used to walking at all.

The former slave looked around at the dungeon that just a short time before was his only home. He looked at the stump that was his rightful future. He looked down at the pardon in his hand—his new future—and he followed the King out of the dungeon, never to return as a slave. He did not look back as he walked across the ruined doorway of the keep into the cold, clean night air.

Outside of the dungeon, a knight was waiting with horses—one for each knight and one for the new citizen. The knight with horses gave the citizen a powerful hug and helped him onto his horse. As soon as he was mounted, the knight gave him some cool, fresh water and a chunk of bread with cheese stuffed inside.

In the distance, the sun began to rise on a brand new day. The new citizen realized it was his first day of freedom. He took a deep breath of fresh air—air that for the first time did not smell like the awful, putrid dungeon.

The King turned to the redheaded knight who had led the rescue mission. Looking at the dark tower once before nodding to her, he said, "Lynd, burn it to the ground."

"At once, my King!" Followed by several other knights, she wheeled her horse around and charged back into the tower. Immediately a raucous commotion followed, with squeals and shrieks from the goblins inside. Within a few moments, flames began to shoot through every opening. Dark smoke billowed up into a brightening sky. Goblins and several other beasts poured out of the tower and scurried down the cliffs like rats.

As soon as the knights returned from the castle, the whole formation headed for the mountains in the distance. The new citizen turned to see the tower completely engulfed in flames. The former slave had awoken the previous day a prisoner condemned to death, but now he was in the company of new friends and a King he had previously only known as a wrathful judge.

Jonathan thought this had to be a dream. He could never have imagined his prison sentence would have ended in freedom and full pardon. He could not imagine his life getting any better. But it did.

CHAPTER 2

The Beginning

". . . so that He would be Just and Justifier . . . ."
– Romans 3:26b

Jonathan had to be dreaming. He was warm. He was comfortable. He was only a little hungry. Slowly he woke up and began to remember where he was—and it wasn't a dream! He was in a tent lying on a very comfortable cot. Sunlight streamed through a crack in the tent door. It was bright. Jonathan was amazed at how much he enjoyed being able to see, and not being in perpetual darkness. He had several very thick fur blankets on top of him and a number of exceptionally soft pillows under his head.

As he opened his eyes a little wider, he looked around the tent. He moved his hands and feet a little and remembered there were no longer chains to rattle and restrict his movement. Freedom was turning out to be a magnificent experience.

Reluctantly he crawled out of bed and dressed in the new clothes the King had provided him. They were a bit big; no, he was a bit small. In fact, he was not very muscular at all. In a word, Jonathan was quite scrawny. For a moment he wondered how he could be so hungry when he was so small. But he was.

He looked at the wooden chest in the corner of the tent. It was also a gift from the King, but he had not opened it yet. He had been too tired as they made camp in the early morning.

Jonathan could hear the knights outside the tent talking and laughing and banging the occasional pot. As the savory smells mingled with wood smoke reached his nostrils, his stomach growled a little. He thought about the contrast between the smell of the dungeon he was in yesterday and the smell of the food coming into his tent. This had to be too good to be true.

When he walked outside into the bright morning sun, all of the knights stopped what they were doing and began to greet him. There were hugs and handshakes. Everyone seemed to be trying to give him food or a drink. The entire encampment, almost a dozen knights, stopped what they were doing and came over.

"Come, sit down and eat," said Lynd, the redheaded knight who had led the attack the night before. "This is far better hot."

With a warm smile, she gave him a plate with bread, meat, and eggs. Jonathan sat on a long log by the fire and began to eat. He had never had anything like it. She then poured him a mug of delicious hot tea. As he ate, the knights resumed what they were doing.

Jonathan looked around at everyone and watched. Two had a leather-bound book and were in a serious but friendly discussion. Three, including Lynd, were standing by a wooden table studying a map. It looked like they were planning something important. They spoke in hushed tones—still, he was sure he heard "the Great East" several times. Whatever that meant, they took it very seriously.

Next to a tent, a couple of knights sharpened weapons and mended a few pieces of armor. One held up a helmet with a deep gash and joked about how close the strike had come to ruining the head of the other one. His companion joked how he could not spare many more blows to the head. Both laughed loudly as one put the helmet on backwards as if the "one-too-many" blow had already landed. Jonathan laughed out loud. One of the knights, a knight named Sir Stephen, saw him laugh, and winked.

Everyone seemed friendly. No, they were more than friendly. They were a family. Everyone looked after everyone else. "Did you eat?" "Do you need help?" "Do you need me to look at those boots and repair them?"

Jonathan could not help but be amazed at their love and care for each other. He had been more cared for since he emerged from his tent than in all the days of his life. These knights were different.

An older knight with a grey beard refilled his mug with hot tea and sat down next to Jonathan, who was enjoying the last bite of food from his plate.

"Hello, Jonathan. I am Sir Robert. And how are we this fine morning?" he asked.

"It's still morning? I guess just a few hours of sleep was all I needed," replied Jonathan.

"Ha! A few? You've been asleep for a day and a half!" laughed the older knight.

"Really? That long? Well, to be honest, I do feel like I could use a nap, too—after lunch, of course." Jonathan laughed. Sir Robert laughed, as well. Jonathan liked him already. He was happy, smiled a lot, yet seemed very experienced and wise.

"It is quite common to need sleep and rest for a while after leaving the dungeons. Feel free to sleep as much as you need. We are very happy to have you with us and as the King instructed, we will take good care of you. You can count on me for anything you might need. More tea?"

"Yes, please!" answered Jonathan as he held up his mug. "And thank you!"

Two knights had walked a few yards away from the camp and began to spar and train with their swords. The clink of the metal reminded Jonathan about the battle he witnessed the night before.

"Sir Robert, I have a few questions about last night. May I speak with you about it?"

"Of course. Ask me anything."

"Thank you." Jonathan took a sip of tea. It was a cool morning and the hot tea was a wonderful treat. He was not used to hot food and drink. The former slave felt ecstatic at being free, but he also could not help but wonder at his release. It seemed quite unfair. He struggled with his words for a minute, then blurted out several questions at once.

"Why me? Why did the King send you for me? Why did he offer a pardon? I have never heard of a king acting this way. Truly, I am guilty of all of the charges," he gushed.

As Jonathan began to ask questions, several of the other knights stopped what they were doing and gathered around to listen.

"No. You *were* guilty of all charges. They no longer apply to you," replied the older knight emphatically. He paused as if considering the weightiness of that truth. Then, with a far off look and broad smile, continued slowly, "*Were* guilty. Not anymore."

"I believe it. I do. But it is so hard to say it, I guess."

"Jonathan, the King *is* unlike any other. You have never heard of such a thing because there is no king like our King. He showed you great mercy last night as well as demonstrating great justice."

"Justice?" repeated Jonathan. "In what way did the King show justice? I really am ... sorry—I *was* guilty. But I am not in prison anymore. I am free, warm, fed, and among friends. How is that just?"

"True. It would seem as if justice was not served last night. You were convicted of crimes and condemned to prison and death. Yet, here you are, freed by the one you rebelled against and eating the food he provided. Where is the justice, you ask?" said Robert.

Now Jonathan was completely somber and focusing on Sir Robert. He was not as concerned that justice had been miscarried, but rather wanting to understand how he could really be free. He felt the pardon he still had in his pocket. Whether or not he had intended to, Jonathan had kept it close to him since he was released. It was precious to him and gave him great confidence.

Several knights nodded at Sir Robert's answer. One even joined in with a comment.

While polishing the blade of a sword, he looked at Jonathan and said, "Friend, in one sense, if justice were served last night, you would have received the axe. It would have been completely just and righteous for the King to have applied it himself. Yet in mercy, the King found another way to fully apply justice to your case." The other knights nodded in agreement. The air was thick with their passion about the King's mercy and impeccable character.

Sir Robert continued, "True. And mercy was there last night, for the King is as merciful as he is just, and he never exercises one at the expense of the other. The pardon was an act of mercy, but justice was served as well. Remember when the King took your sentence and list of crimes?"

"Yes. I thought for sure it would be the end," squeaked Jonathan, reliving the moment in his mind.

Jonathan recalled the nausea of that night with all of the trembling and horror of an execution. He remembered how embarrassed he was to have the King read through his list of offenses while signing his own name.

"He was not capricious in forgiving. No, he took your crimes as his own. Then he signed his own name to each and every one. He signed his name to your death warrant. He did not show you mercy at the expense of his justice, rather he fulfilled the demands of justice himself on your behalf. Then he was free to show you mercy and still maintain the law a righteous King must enforce. Before you even knew the King had an offer of pardon for you, he met the demands of justice on your account. He paid what you owed completely. Then, and only then, was he legally free to offer you pardon. And he sent us to deliver that offer."

Jonathan's head was swimming. He understood, he thought, but he had so many more questions.

"You see," the wise knight continued, "justice *was* served that night, and mercy *was* granted. From that, a pardon was offered on the basis of justice and through mercy."

Jonathan rubbed his chin as he thought about what he was hearing. Everyone seemed to be thinking about it as well, as all were silent for a few minutes. The only sound was the crackling of the fire and the wind blowing through the towering oak overhead.

Then the former slave had a frightening thought, and suddenly became sick to his stomach again with dread. He stood up abruptly and began to speak quickly in a panicked voice.

"But the King must know I can never repay Him! I have no wealth. I am not a knight like you; I couldn't fight for him and pay him back like you. What will he do if he finds out I am not profitable?"

"Pay him back?!" exclaimed a knight. "What do you mean pay him back?" Several of the knights began to join in the conversation now, all talking about what Jonathan had said. Some were talking very loudly with each other and more than one seemed to be offended.

"Is that not why you are knights? Do you not fight to pay him back for rescuing you as well?" asked Jonathan timidly. Now he was a little embarrassed. Had he misunderstood?

As Sir Robert the Wise began to speak, everyone quieted down to listen. With an intense gaze, he locked eyes with Jonathan and continued in a measured tone while emphasizing almost every word, "True, we have all been rescued by the King. True, we all owe a terrible debt. But we do not fight and serve to attempt *repayment*. It would be foolish to think we could. If we had a thousand lifetimes, we could not even come close to repaying."

"Furthermore, it would be an insult," interjected Sir Stephen. "Imagine walking through a forest with your only child by your side when you hear cries of help from a swift river. You quickly realize someone is in the rapids and in need of rescue. You have a rope, but you cannot throw it that far. Your child volunteers to swim the rope out to the person in danger and you allow it—no, you send him to rescue the person. He swims the rope out to the person, and you are able to pull him to shore, but in the process your child is lost—swept away by the river to his death. In that moment, when the one you rescued realizes your great loss, he flips you a coin for your trouble."

Jonathan was horrified at the thought of offering an item so cheap for a life so precious. The rawness of the idea shocked him.

"That would be wicked! That would be an insult of the worst kind."

Sir Stephen pointed his finger at Jonathan and said very solemnly, "And so it would be the same to our King if you attempted to repay so costly a gift as your pardon, as if you could earn it."

Sir Seamus, the knight who killed the giant lizard with his axe, spoke up. "Never forget this one thing: If you could have earned his mercy, you never would have been in a place where you needed his mercy."

Nobody spoke for a long time. Each former slave was thinking of his or her own debt to the King and the amazement of so great a gift of mercy. Jonathan realized they were all remembering their own rescues. After a long pause, he asked another question.

"Why then do you serve? Why then do you fight as knights?" asked Jonathan timidly, afraid of letting another misunderstanding slip.

"I fight out of gratitude. The dungeon I was in was far worse than any I have ever seen. I cannot ever forget the day my Captain and King rescued me. I am grateful beyond words, and I have taken up his cause to show my gratitude and love," said Sir Stephen as he ran his hand through his curly black hair.

"Indeed, it was dark and gruesome, brother," said Sir Reginald evenly as he put his hand on Stephen's shoulder. Stephen looked at Reginald and nodded slowly. "I will never forget the dark night and even darker prison when we delivered your pardon," said Reginald.

Though Stephen the Bold was normally jovial and mischievous, he answered with such passion and zeal that everyone around the fire knew he was serious. A brief pause, then, "It is an honor of the greatest order to carry the King's banner and bear the title of Knight and Ambassador."

Sir Robert spoke next, "I serve my King because there is no other King like him. He is the only wise, just, and merciful King. I fight to spread his fame and expand his kingdom because he is the only One worthy of such loyalty and service. There are many things on which a man can spend his days and minutes. I choose to spend mine in the service of the only One who truly deserves honor."

A knight with long, dark hair who was normally very quiet spoke next. "For me, it is simple. He is the King and I am his citizen. He said go, and I go. When he called me his knight, I determined I would serve him only. I will obey and go wherever he wants me," she said.

One by one the knights around the circle described why they served the King. Ten knights in all professed their loyalty and love for their Captain, and all ten stories were slightly different. One knight could not even speak what he was feeling and could only say softly while looking down, "He is the King. He is *my* King."

Jonathan was amazed at how passionately they spoke of their love for the King. He was beginning to understand more and more. He sat out by the fire for a long time, listening to his new friends discuss the nature of how things worked in the kingdom and recount the great deeds of their Captain and King.

Before long, it was time for lunch. Jonathan was amazed at how quickly time had passed while discussing the truths of his new life. And he was hungry again. Robert brought him a bowl of stew and sat down next to him to enjoy the meal.

"Sir Robert, can you tell me a little more about Sir Stephen?" asked Jonathan between mouthfuls of stew. "I think I have laughed more around him than in my entire life combined."

"Sir Stephen? Why yes, he has an incredible love of all things funny and witty," the wise knight replied with a chuckle, followed by a loud slurp of stew.

As if on cue, they both watched Stephen scoop out a healthy portion of stew then smoothly reverse the ends of the spoon and move on. When the next in line, Sir Seamus unfortunately, grabbed for the spoon, he picked up the broad end and realized his hand was now covered in his dinner.

"*STEPHEN!*" he boomed, holding up his hand. The entire camp burst into laughter, including Seamus.

"That is not the right end of that utensil, sir," said Stephen innocently. "You'll be more successful using the other end." More laughter. Stephen glanced at Jonathan sideways and grinned.

"He must be very beneficial to a company such as this," said Jonathan, still laughing.

"Indeed he is, Jonathan. But his value does not lie in his quick wit or a joke well played. Much more than his pleasant demeanor, his real quality rests in the truth that he dares great things for his King, much to the disregard of his personal welfare when the occasion calls for it," replied Sir Robert the Wise with a hint of admiration. Jonathan looked back at Stephen and thought about Robert's words.

After some time, Jonathan realized how tired he felt. He excused himself and walked back to his tent. While walking he continued to think about all that the knights had said. The more he thought about it, the more it made sense. He lay down in his bed but was unable to fall asleep. He kept thinking about the knights and their passion for the King. Their words echoed through his mind.

"*I wish I were like them. I wish I were strong enough to serve and fight. I wish I had something to offer back,*" he thought.

Jonathan began to drift off to sleep. It seemed as if his eyes had barely closed when a loud crash sounded just outside his tent. He spun out of bed, still dizzy from sleep, and began to run outside. It was early evening and the light was fading.

As soon as he stepped out of the tent door, Sir Stephen grabbed him by the collar and yanked him to the ground. As he fell, Jonathan saw the knight pull his shield over them both. Three loud *thwacks* sounded as he blocked flaming arrows launched from an unseen enemy.

"How was your nap, brother?" grunted Stephen.

"What's going on?" squeaked the horrified Jonathan.

"We are under attack, friend! Stay low for now! Things are about to become interesting," said Stephen with a grin.

Lying down, he surveyed the camp. Flaming arrows were landing everywhere. One tent was already in flames. The knights were armed and standing in a circle around—*him*. In all directions, everywhere he looked, there were knights with their backs to Jonathan, their shields and weapons facing the forest surrounding their hilltop camp. Jonathan crawled over to a log and peered down the hill. Just then a flaming jagged arrow slammed into the log an arm's length from his head.

"Stay down, Jonathan! They don't always aim well, but sometimes they get lucky," snorted Sir Stephen. He already had three arrows sticking in his shield, and one was still on fire.

Just then he heard a lone howl coming from the forest. The sound sent chills down his spine—he knew it was a wolf. A goblin's wolf. It immediately took him back to the days of his captivity when the wolves would howl at night. For the first time since his rescue, he was afraid.

It was not an ordinary fear. He began to tremble and shake. The thought of returning to a dungeon and chains was almost too much to bear. As fear coiled around his heart, Jonathan began to despair.

Just then a hand was on his shoulder. He wheeled in fright and found himself yelling in terror.

"Easy, Jonathan. It's me," reassured the kind face of Sir Robert. "I just wanted to check on you."

"Check on me?" asked Jonathan in a high-pitched voice. "What will we do? They're shooting at us, and they have wolves!"

"I can see that, of course. There is going to be an attack. Stay close. Do not run. We will prevail," reassured the knight. "But you must stay right here until it is over. Do you understand?"

Jonathan nodded and looked back at the wood line. The occasional arrow shot from a dark shape in the tree line landed in the camp, but no real enemy force had appeared yet. Maybe it was just a few goblins bent on harassing the knights.

Then the howls of the wolves were replaced with the rolling fury of goblin shrieks and war cries coming from the forest edge closest to the camp. As the goblins emerged from the woods, there were more than four times the number of knights. One big, ugly goblin with a scar on his face rode a giant wolf-like beast. He grinned menacingly when he saw Jonathan lying behind the log.

Jonathan's heart nearly failed. It was Captain Gruel! The slight citizen knew the captain had returned to take him prisoner again. The memory of warm meals and a soft bed and friends began to melt away, and in its place loomed the specter of misery and torment.

The goblins hoisted several dark banners and formed into two solid lines of twenty each. They were snarling and cursing. Jonathan did not want to keep looking, but he couldn't look away from their slobbering, sneering faces and sharp teeth. They banged their weapons on shields in unison as they began to march. The sound of their cadence filled the evening air and reverberated off of the forest.

"King's knights! Shield line! Center!" called Sir Robert. All of the knights moved as one to the center. They raised their shields, shouted in unison, and readied their lances.

Lynd stood in the rear next to Robert with her bow, nocking an arrow with an armored tip. She looked at Robert and grinned.

"I told you they would try this so soon. It looks like you are making dinner tonight," she laughed.

"Ha! Right you are. I'm not sure why I doubt you. You win this one. I hope you like my stew," Robert responded.

"I might have wagered differently had I known you were making your stew again," she quipped.

Jonathan could not believe they were laughing. He wondered at their easy joking manner. Did they not see the predicament they were in? He doubted they would even be around to eat that night, no matter who had mess duty.

The goblin line closed half the distance. Then the captain raised his hand and called a halt. However, riding on the back of a giant wolf, he continued forward until he was a few steps closer to the line of knights.

"Greetings, King's filth!" spat Gruel with mock respect and a mock bow.

"We are here for what belongs to us, namely, that worm you stole the other night. Send him over and we promise not to harm you … tonight, that is," said the goblin haughtily. "And before you say no, realize that we have you outnumbered four to one."

Jonathan's heart sank. He knew they could not hold back an enemy force of that number. He just knew he was finished.

"Maybe you should just give me back, Sir Robert," stammered the former slave forlornly. He would not even look up.

"Nonsense!" said Sir Robert sharply. His countenance had darkened at the thought. "You are a citizen of the King's City Beautiful. No force on earth can take you back there. Moreover, it would be a travesty of justice. You are free and have no place in the enemy's hands."

The former slave reached his hand down to the pardon in his pocket. As soon as he thought about it he was encouraged, even if only slightly.

"But how can you defeat such an enemy?" asked Jonathan, looking over his log at the goblin lines.

"It is the King who prevails, but that isn't the issue. It isn't winning or losing that bears on the decision. Only this: you are special to our Captain and King. He paid a price steeper than we can contemplate to rescue you from your former prison. As such, it is worth our very lives to protect you to our last breath. But take heart, it is the goblin captain who swiftly approaches his last breath, not us," answered Robert resolutely.

Their conversation was interrupted by the scarred goblin bellowing out another threat.

"We will not ask again, King's rats. He belongs to us. He is a prisoner and has yet to serve his sentence. His life doesn't concern you," snarled Gruel, barely able to control his anger.

Robert looked down at the slave-turned-citizen. Jonathan, still trembling with fear, looked at his new friend. Robert smiled at him confidently, then his expression darkened again as he turned to the enemy lines. He took one step up onto the log Jonathan was crouching behind so everyone could see and hear him.

Facing the goblin captain, Sir Robert's voice boomed sternly, "You can search this entire world from the deepest crevice in the darkest cave to the highest mountain top, and you will never find a scrap of legal charge laid against this citizen of the King's City Beautiful. All penalties were paid, and none other than the King himself has pardoned him. As such, he is beyond accusation, penalty, or sentence. You have no power or legal standing. At this point in time, you are falsely accusing a member of our family and interrupting an otherwise fine evening."

The goblin captain was enraged. "He belongs to us! *To me!* Is this your last answer?" screamed Gruel, barely able to stay in his saddle on the wolf.

Turning to Lynd he said, "Well, knight, would you like to send the goblin our last answer?"

"Absolutely. I was hoping you would ask," she answered. Jonathan admired her courage and the way she grinned broadly at the opportunity to deliver a message. But the message wasn't what Jonathan thought.

She tossed her red hair out of her way. In a flash, she drew her ivory-colored bow back to her right ear and released an armor-piercing tipped arrow with blue fletching. It flew with a shrill whine and landed with a bone-shattering crack. Through helmet and skull, it sunk almost to the fletching in the goblin captain's head. He did not even twitch—he just fell limp off the back of the wolf. The wolf turned to see what had happened to his rider when a knight's lance pinned him to the ground. The wolf kicked several times, then lay still.

Jonathan could not believe his eyes. The goblin captain, who had long tortured him and inflicted such misery, was gone. Dead. Again he was filled with hope. He let out a whoop.

The field was silent almost a full five seconds. Stunned, Jonathan wheeled around to look at Lynd, who was already loosing another arrow. This time the whine of the shaft was blocked by Sir Robert, who roared, "Charge!" with his sword held high above his head.

Jonathan turned around and saw the knights sprinting toward the cowed goblin lines. Three portly goblin axemen in the back of the formation had already fled. The death of the captain had taken the fight out of most of the enemy, though several still put up a brief and futile struggle.

Jonathan watched from the safety of the log in camp as the knights waded into the goblin lines. It did not take long for the lines to falter, then crumble. Minutes later, the field was littered with a dozen dead goblins. The remaining force had been routed into the trees.

Jonathan breathed in the moment of silence immediately following the battle and admired how fiercely and resolutely they fought for their King, and for … him. Yes, they were fighting to protect him! Why? Because he was important to the King. As he thought about the truth of his value to the King, Jonathan smiled.

As the knights turned back to the camp, they smiled broadly at one another and laughed as they checked each other for damage or wounds. They possessed a deep joy, even in the face of what seemed to Jonathan to be certain death—a joy that could not be squelched by fear of what may come. Jonathan realized he was with a real family that had an actual purpose. A seed of wistfulness began to grow in his heart. He began to wish deeply that he were strong enough and big enough to be a warrior and fight for his King like they did. He wished he were not so small and, well . . . unknightly.

The thoughts of his insignificance pursued him long into the night. Though he was grateful to have been saved from going back to the dungeon, he felt a longing to be one of them. It was a fitful night of less than perfect rest as he pondered his lack of stature and knightliness. Jonathan began to feel quite unfit for this band of knights. He lay on his back, staring up at the top of his tent, and shook his head in disgust.

"Quite unfit, indeed," he said to himself as he drifted off to sleep.

CHAPTER 3

Oath of Fealty

*"Therefore, take up the full armor of God, so that you will be able
to resist in the evil day, and having done everything to stand firm."*
– Ephesians 6:13

Early the next morning, they broke camp and began to move toward
a set of mountains in the distance. Robert rode with Jonathan, with
very few words between them. Everyone tried to move carefully and
quietly. Sir Seamus had explained they were moving toward the
frontier of a land called the Great East and it was heavily infested
with the enemy.

Shortly before evening, they found the perfect place to camp—a
small canyon that offered a great defensive position and shielded
the war party from the biting wind. Everyone worked together to
set up the tents and start a few fires. Sir Robert began to chop thick
slices of sweet carrot and onion to work on his famous stew, with
Jonathan's help.

Sir Reginald drew the first watch and stood guard at the entrance
to the canyon. Jonathan watched the sentinel pick the best place to
protect the group, then begin to scope the surrounding forest for
danger.

Sir Robert noticed Jonathan looking off and commented, "By

now you have noticed that we are ever on guard. You will learn that while we are here and not in the City Beautiful, we are at war. Every day and all over this land, the enemies of the King seek to do lasting damage to his people and kingdom. We have learned that the enemy will attack anytime, but he loves deception. Surprise attacks are his favorite type."

"Yes, I've noticed. The attack yesterday was frightening, to be honest. I was so afraid I was going back to my dungeon and execution, Sir Robert," said the former slave. "I was terrified."

Robert grunted. "That will never happen. You are free and no power of the enemy can undo what the King has done. Your home is the City Beautiful, and it will ever be your home. It is beautiful beyond description because it is where the King lives. It is as truly your home, too, as if you were already in residence. Not a dungeon tower. Never."

They stirred in pungent slices of onion and fragrant herbs as Robert continued teaching his new friend.

"In this life, the enemies of the King will always seek a way to take you away from the King's fellowship and service. He cannot ever rob you of your citizenship, but he can thwart your service to the King, young Jonathan. You may be sure he will try to do just that. He cannot change your citizenship, but he can ruin your journey there through deception that robs you of your purpose and intended life. That is the real danger to a citizen. The danger is so real it must be watched and guarded against at all times. There are worse fates than dying in battle, young friend. Languishing in a dungeon and missing the purpose of your life is far worse."

Jonathan gazed into the fire. He poked a log and watched the sparks and embers flow upward.

"I would love to do more than just watch. I would love to *take* a watch. I wish I could serve. I wish I could fight like you, Sir Robert," sighed Jonathan wistfully as he looked at Sir Reginald on guard. The sentinel was barely visible and hardly moved, except for slow turns of his head as he searched for signs of attack.

Sir Robert looked at Jonathan for a long time, then asked, "And why is it that you think you cannot?"

"Please don't make fun. You know why I cannot. Look at me! I am scrawny and small. Look at my arms and legs. Do I look like a soldier to you? Do I look like a knight? No. I am weak. I am not sure I could even lift one of your swords, much less wield it with authority and effectiveness. I only wish I could. I wish I could serve the King in the way he is worthy."

Sir Robert was quiet for a few moments, then began to speak.

"Jonathan. Yes, you are small. Yes, you are weak. Do you think the King made us knights because of our strength and skill in battle?"

"Of course. Look at you. That night in the dungeon. Then at our camp yesterday. You were laughing! You attacked and conquered with incredible speed and skill. The goblins were terrified of you. I was too, a little. Who could ever be terrified of me?" They both laughed a little.

"Jonathan, you have much to learn, and we might as well begin now. I have some very shocking things to say to you. Are you ready to hear them?"

"I believe so," answered Jonathan timidly.

"What if I were to tell you that you have been selected and commissioned to become a knight for the King and join us on our missions and quests?"

Jonathan snorted, then laughed. "Really? I wouldn't believe you. I couldn't believe you. Are we to attack a small garden? Perhaps liberate a few cabbages?"

Jonathan was a little irritated, or maybe embarrassed—he was not sure. He was so far below the station of a knight, and it stung a little that Sir Robert would be dangling it in front of him. He wanted to serve the King so much. But he was so slight of stature, and he knew it.

Several other knights gathered around, including Lynd. They were quiet and serious, except for Sir Seamus who was laughing at the thought of liberating cabbages.

"You haven't looked in the chest the King left for you, have you? If you did, then you would surely know that what we are saying is true," said Lynd.

"No ma'am, I have not. Just tell me the truth. Are you joking about serving? How is that possible, seeing as I am so scrawny and untrained?" asked Jonathan quietly.

"No. No, there is no joke and no mistake. We are simply relaying to you the wishes of the King. It is his offer and command for you to join us—to join *him*—in the fight against the enemy. The King has invited all of those he rescues to join him. The tasks and positions are different, but the call to follow him is the same. This includes you. What do you say?" asked Lynd with the same intensity she had when she discussed the King's terms of pardon.

"But how? How would I serve? I am so . . . so . . . so *unknightly!*" squeaked Jonathan.

Sir Robert took a long, thoughtful sip of tea. He locked his eyes on Jonathan. "Forget about your estimation of your own ability and worth for a moment. Imagine for a moment that skill was not an issue and strength was not a hindrance. If the King commanded you to serve, what would your answer be?"

Jonathan did not have to think long at all. Before he realized what he was doing, he had stood up. All of the knights were watching him. "Without question, my answer would be yes. I would do whatever he asked."

"Why?" asked the burly Sir Seamus pointedly while stroking his red beard. Only later would Jonathan understand why this question was so important. "Why, exactly, would you choose to serve him?" he asked, putting great emphasis on the word, 'exactly.'

Jonathan stood as tall as he could. "He is the King. And he rescued me. And I am grateful. I am pitifully weak; I know that.

And I don't know anything about war or soldiering, but anything he wants me to do, I will do," answered Jonathan slowly but confidently. Sir Seamus' face broke into a very warm smile. Finally Jonathan had arrived at a right answer, it seemed.

"Then your first lesson is this, my friend: It does not matter how stout you are. The King does not choose his knights based on their strength, sword arms, or supposed worthiness. He chooses the weak and, as you say, 'scrawny,' then provides them with everything necessary to be victorious in the most shadowy of places against the foulest of enemies. It is the King's strength and the King's armor that secures victory. Remember that, and you will never know defeat. Forget it, and you will never see victory," said Sir Robert.

All of the knights nodded heartily at the real secret of their numerous victories.

Sir Robert continued to address Jonathan. "Truly, you wish to obey and answer the King's command to join him in his great cause?" All of the knights were looking at the former slave. Even Sir Reginald had moved a little closer so he could hear, yet remain watchful.

Jonathan felt the nervousness in his stomach again—but it wasn't fear this time. He was thinking about his King and the depth of the dungeon that was his fate just a few days ago. He remembered the torment and misery. He remembered the night they faked his execution, and shuddered. Then, he remembered the moment his King drew his sword and shattered his chains forever. What he wouldn't do to tell him or show him how deeply he loved and appreciated him!

"I do. I will do anything for the King. Anything," answered Jonathan resolutely.

Sir Robert pulled a piece of parchment from his leather satchel. It was very old and worn and bore the King's seal on the top right corner. He very carefully handed it to Jonathan and said, "This is the oath of fealty to the King for a knight. The King desires and calls all of his citizens to join him in his cause. He provides the source of victory. If this is what you are committing to, then kneel and swear your allegiance to your King in our presence."

Jonathan read it over several times and thought about the words. It seemed like an impossible commitment, but it also expressed exactly how his heart felt about the King and his offer to join him.

Jonathan kneeled by the fire and began to read the words aloud softly at first. Then as he read, they grew louder and bolder. All of the other knights except Sir Robert also kneeled. Several others were mouthing the words from memory. Sir Reginald still stood guard but had removed his helmet and was also repeating the words. Sir Robert had drawn his sword and stood in front of Jonathan as he spoke the oath of fealty:

"I, Jonathan, former slave to the enemy and justly condemned to death, do hereby acknowledge I have been pardoned and set free based solely on the mercy and justice of the King. As a free citizen of the Kingdom, I pledge and swear my allegiance to the One and only wise King. I give myself over to his service. I will bear arms and fight wherever and whenever and against all enemies of the King. I will fulfill my duties as knight through any difficulty, against any foe and in the face of any danger. I will carry out my orders all of my days, from this day until my last day. I will rely on the King for the strength necessary to keep this oath. I will keep no glory for myself or own any victory as a result of my skill. Long Live the King."

Sir Robert then raised the sword and tapped Jonathan, the former slave, on each shoulder, then on his head. "Rise, Sir Jonathan, knight of the only rightful King. Endeavor to trust him only for your power and victory. Be brave in the face of danger and endure hardship for your true Captain."

Sir Jonathan slowly rose to his feet. He still felt very small, but he now felt that his purpose was very great. He knew he could never fulfill his oath, but he was determined to give his all and trust his Captain.

"Now you will learn the reason you are alive. This path will be dangerous and difficult, but in the end, you will never regret your decision to follow your Captain," said Sir Robert with a smile. "You are now one of the King's knights. Welcome to the Light Mounted Rangers, His Majesty's 5th Cavalry Regiment."

Sir Robert took out a patch with the Regimental seal under the King's Coat of Arms. He attached it to Sir Jonathan's cloak. The new knight ran his fingers over it repeatedly.

Then, Sir Robert the Wise gave Sir Jonathan a gift that would become one of his most treasured possessions—the weathered parchment with the Oath of Fealty. The young knight knew it was an ancient treasure. In the future he would reread it many times on the darkest of nights and remember that day.

"It's time to look in the chest he left you," said Lynd. "Come with us."

Sir Jonathan returned to his tent with a few of the knights and hurriedly broke the royal seal on the chest. He opened the lid and could not believe his eyes. The first thing he saw and removed was a shield with the royal coat of arms. It was bright and shiny. He ran his fingers over the designs and smiled to himself. He set it to one side and picked up the next piece of armor—a helmet. It fit perfectly and was light, but seemed exceptionally strong. When the faceplate was lowered, he could see out of a cross in the front. The cross design allowed him to see and breathe, but the openings were small enough to offer complete protection. Next, Jonathan removed a leather and chain mail chest piece. It had pieces of strong plate armor woven in certain places, but leather in others to make it flexible. The King's crest was on the centerpiece, over the heart. Jonathan also found boots, pants, gloves, and a thick wool cape.

"There's more, Sir Jonathan. Pull out the leather satchel in the bottom. There is an object of extreme importance inside."

Sir Jonathan removed the satchel and reached inside. He pulled out a leather-bound book with the King's seal on the front cover.

"What is this?"

"This is the Kingsbook. It is extremely important. You said you do not possess the knowledge or skill to fulfill your oath. You are correct. So, the King has given you an ancient book to guide you in your training, to instruct you in your duties, and light your path when you do not know what to do. Of all of the gifts you received today, this is the most important. You must learn this book, Sir Knight. It is your very life. Disregard it to your own peril, Jonathan," said Robert.

"I will learn it and follow it, Sir Robert."

"Many knights have made this book their passion, and they have become skilled, proficient knights in no time at all. But I have also known many knights who have only lightly read or applied this book and even after years, they continue to struggle with the basic tasks and duties," warned Lynd.

Jonathan listened to Lynd and set his heart to be one of the knights who read and trusted and followed the Kingsbook relentlessly. He felt nearly overwhelmed with the seriousness and excitement of it all.

Next, Sir Jonathan looked into the chest and saw a sword hilt with the Royal Coat of Arms on it. He grabbed it and pulled it toward him. As he did, he noticed a ringing sound he would never forget—a sound that would become all too familiar. The sword was long and sharp and required two hands to wield it properly. It was unbelievably beautiful and flawless.

He turned to Sir Robert but was unable to speak. Robert had a knowing look on his face as if remembering the first time he drew his own sword.

The handle felt formed for the young knight's hand. It was perfectly balanced. Sir Jonathan found various other items in the chest, and a lance in the corner of the tent.

After a quick survey, Sir Jonathan recognized that he had everything needed for life and battle as a soldier. As he ran his fingers over his armor and weapons, he realized something and turned to

Sir Robert. He looked at him for several moments before the words came.

"When the King freed me the other night, he had this chest with him. How did he know I would take the oath and serve as a knight?"

"Sir Jonathan, the King has a chest with the weapons of war for every citizen. He forged them himself, and he has a role for every one he rescues. The roles are different and the places of service are different, but all are called and expected to serve. It is not a condition of citizenship—for that has already been settled that dark night in the dungeon. Instead, it is an expected privilege, a gift, and a sacred duty."

After a few moments of pondering Robert's words, Jonathan asked, "Do all citizens serve the King as they have been commanded?"

Sir Robert continued, "It is possible for a citizen to waste the life the King purchased, but it is neither a pleasant path nor a common one. Many citizens, at different points and in different ways, of course, have chosen to follow their King into battle. Each one finds their path is different from the next citizen. You have chosen to begin your life as a rescued slave following the path he has called you to walk. You will not regret it in the end, but the path is long and hard. Your first lessons begin immediately. You are a target of the enemy. Never be without your armor and weapons. The enemy is watching—even tonight. Your friends were not the only ones who witnessed your oath of fealty. You declared your loyalty to your King; that is a declaration of war to them."

Sir Jonathan nodded and unsheathed the sword again. The blade was amazing, though he realized it was not a decoration but a weapon of war. He believed Sir Robert and vowed silently to keep it nearby at all times. First he had received his freedom, now he had been given a purpose. He smiled when he thought about his new position.

The knights sat silently in the tent as Jonathan continued to examine his new life. The wind whistled through the firs around the camp. The heavy canvas tent flap whipped with the wind as the only other sound. It was quiet, but the knowledge of what lay before the knight made the atmosphere anything but peaceful.

Some distance away from the camp, scaly hands shielded fiendish eyes from the sun as the dark creature observed the young citizen kneel, then rise a knight. It cursed under its breath and muttered about the message he now had to relay to its shadowy captain. It was as its master had feared. The filthy scout had seen all it needed to see and turned to sneak away. As it slinked away, it dislodged a small rock that rolled down the canyon wall.

Sir Reginald heard the rock tumbling down, loosing other rocks in its path. One came crashing through the underbrush. His hand on his sword and his eyes to the forest, he caught a few glimpses of greenish skin moving fluidly through the trees. Just a patch here or there. He looked over at the camp and his eyes met Sir Stephen's. Stephen had already drawn his sword. Lynd crouched with an arrow ready. Her bow was at half draw as she strained to find a clear shot. She scanned the ridge and trees for the ghoulish scout.

They doubled the guard that night.

In the days and weeks that followed, Jonathan began to spend long hours with the Kingsbook. He trained with his new gifts and new friends. He learned from their words and examples and made many mistakes. He learned from the mistakes more than almost anything else. Training with the new weapons was both exciting and slightly embarrassing. A wayward arrow nearly ruined dinner one afternoon when it struck a pole holding the pot. Though Jonathan's aim became increasingly better, Lynd kidded him about almost saving them from Reginald's cooking.

The knights began to talk more of their mission to the Great East. Now that Sir Jonathan was one of them, they began to fill him in on the orders the King had given them. The land sounded both interesting and dangerous.

"What is the Great East exactly, Sir Robert?" asked the young knight one evening after a hard day of training. Except for the sentry, they all sat around the fire enjoying good company and good food. It was a favorite time of Jonathan's to ask questions.

"It is a land, like the rest of the kingdoms, that belongs to the One King, but is held in the grip of the enemy. The enemy is exceptionally strong there. And though we, the armies of the Great King, have orders to take it back and have been given all of the King's power to do so, we have been remiss in our duties to fully obey. As such, there are countless numbers of slaves for whom the King has provided pardon but are still in chains," answered Robert the Wise. Jonathan could tell the weight of an unfulfilled mission hung heavily on him. He slowly looked around the fire-lit faces and saw the same determination on them, as well.

"Can you imagine, young Jonathan, what it would be like to be imprisoned and awaiting the axe, but there is a pardon for you undelivered?" asked Stephen rhetorically. "A pardon only sets one free if it arrives before the day of execution."

Sir Seamus grunted a sad agreement, then continued the thought in his friendly deep voice. "The King has offered us the opportunity to go. He has given us the privilege of carrying his banner into the Great East to help reclaim it for him. And we *are* going," continued Sir Seamus. "Even though now we have had such a poor showing, it seems we are more like rebels behind the lines than the armies of the rightful King."

"Why is it so difficult?" asked Sir Jonathan.

"The enemy loves doing damage to the kingdom and the citizens of the kingdom. He delights to ruin and enslave. This area is important to him. It was the first he captured and he covets it above all else. Our forces have always paid a heavy price when we are engaging this territory," answered Sir Robert. "We always lose friends. And this will be no different. It will be fearsome. Does this concern you?"

"It does concern me, to be honest. I am afraid, but I am with you.

It will be a privilege to carry his banner," said Sir Jonathan before he realized he was saying it.

"Well, well. It would appear we have a knight among us," grinned Sir Stephen. "Sir Jonathan the Slight, King's knight. We will see your pretty armor dented soon enough, I believe." And with that, he slapped the young knight on the back with a laugh and went to relieve the sentry.

All of the knights were grinning and laughing. Sir Jonathan laughed too. He thought about his title, "Sir Jonathan the Slight." He felt such a sense of purpose and adventure. He did not know what the Great East held, but he was determined to follow the King.

Not long after that, Sir Jonathan was preparing for bed when he heard Sir Robert's voice outside.

"Sir Jonathan? I have a gift."

"Come right in, especially if you have a gift," laughed the young knight.

"Here," he said as he handed him an oil lamp. "Use this."

Sir Jonathan looked at the smallish lamp and was a little puzzled. "A lamp?"

"Yes. You have been spending a lot of time with the Kingsbook, but we will be putting it to use soon. Maybe some extra reading at night might be profitable?" said Sir Robert with a smile.

"Yes. Yes, of course. Thank you." Sir Jonathan took the hint and began to study long into the nights. It was obvious the perilous times the knights had spoken of were approaching.

CHAPTER 4

The First Lesson

". . . be on the alert. Your adversary . . . prowls around
like a roaring lion, seeking someone to devour."
– 1 Peter 5:8

One morning, Sir Jonathan the Slight awoke early. As the young knight shook off the drowsiness, his first thoughts were of his freedom from slavery and his purpose. With a sleepy smile at the thought, he yawned and rolled out of bed. As he looked over at his armor stacked neatly in the corner of his tent, his smile widened. It was *his* armor. His sword was in the corner leaning against the lance and axe. He was overwhelmed with the thought of the significance of it all.

He had been training and sweating with the other knights for some time now, but still he felt rather small. But when Stephen called him Sir Jonathan the Slight, he liked the nickname. Although small, he did not feel helpless. In fact, he felt confident. Too confident.

He slipped out of the tent and stretched. As he looked around he realized he must have awoken before the rest of the camp, except for Sir Seamus who had drawn the morning watch. Sir Seamus was standing with his shield and lance and watching the sun come up over the mountains in the distance. His Kingsbook was open on a rock beside him.

The young knight picked up a long stick and stirred the fire after placing a few logs on the coals. *We will need water for tea soon,* he thought as he looked in a nearly empty bucket.

I know there is a creek nearby, he thought to himself. *I'll get a start on this task and show them I am not just about oaths, but actions as well.*

Sir Jonathan picked up two buckets and quietly slipped down a trail toward the sound of a babbling brook. As he walked along, he began to whistle. He was just so happy. It felt wonderful to be free, and to have a purpose with the one who had set him free. Could things be any better? The birds seemed to join in.

The path began to descend into the beginnings of a thick forest, and the sounds of the creek grew louder. He must be getting close. He smiled at the thought of helping out and beginning to prove his worth to his fellow knights. *Fellow knights!* What a thought!

Sir Jonathan's whistling and thinking about the others had kept him from noticing that the woods were becoming much darker. The path had steepened. The birds had ceased to sing along. The wind was beginning to blow a little in the treetops. The bright, sunny morning rapidly turned into an overcast, gloomy day without warning.

The path rounded a rocky corner, and immediately Sir Jonathan found himself standing in a very small clearing with a rough creek bubbling through the center. He found it! But Sir Jonathan was not as happy as he thought he would be. There was a slight chill in the air, and something did not feel right, though he could not quite say what. A thick mist was forming around the clearing.

I'll fill up my buckets and get out of here as fast as I can, he thought. He closed the distance to the brook and filled his first bucket. As he pulled the unwieldy container out of the water, he noticed something out of the corner of his eye. With a start, he dropped his bucket and whirled around. In the clearing moving toward him was a cloaked figure leading a mule. Sir Jonathan was terrified at how quickly and noiselessly it had appeared so close to him.

"Whoa! I mean you no harm. I did not mean to frighten you. I did not see you until just now," rasped an older sounding man from beneath the cloak. "What is your business in these woods anyway, young man?"

Jonathan eyed the man carefully before answering. He seemed old and his movements were slow. He moved almost wearily. The mule he led mirrored his master's movements, burdened down with packages and sacks. But something was different. It was as if Jonathan could not quite focus on the two figures—as if the mist of the forest also shrouded the man and his beast. It was unnerving. The pit in the young knight's stomach ached.

"I … I … I am only after water. How did you sneak up on me like that? What is your business on this path?" asked Sir Jonathan nervously. His heart was still racing. The older man seemed harmless enough, but something was off. Jonathan wished he had that bright shiny sword with him now.

The older traveler pulled his hood down, revealing a worn, weathered face. His lips formed a smile as he said, "I am traveling this path to a very nice town a few leagues from here. I am a merchant and I pass through this forest between towns quite often. I sell everything and anything the people in the surrounding area request. Today I have a load of spices and baked goods. Care to sample any? I won't charge you for a taste."

"Um, no thank you, sir," Sir Jonathan stammered. "I am only filling these buckets, and I'll be on my way."

"Well, now, what is your rush? I have only just met you. There are no houses in this forest. Where did you come from? Where are you carrying the water?" asked the traveler in a slow, friendly voice. Jonathan noticed he looked him over carefully. The young knight felt uneasy but was not sure why. He felt as if he was being studied or sized up.

"I am a knight in the King's service, and I am gathering water for my companions and fellow knights," said Jonathan proudly, though he sounded more confident than he felt.

"A knight? Well, well. You do not look like a knight. You are quite small. I mean no offense, of course. And you have no weapons or armor that I can see," answered the traveler as he looked Sir Jonathan over, then glanced quickly around the clearing.

Embarrassed at the truth of the stranger's observations, Jonathan stammered a reply, "True. I left my armor in my tent since I only went to get water." He gave a quick nod of his head, and continued, "I know I am scrawny. I am new at this. At being a knight, that is." Sir Jonathan could feel his face getting red and hot. Maybe he was fooling himself. He was no knight.

"A new knight? Recently freed? Well, well. I see. Why are you going to war so soon after being released? Shouldn't you consider resting for a while in a comfortable town while you recover your strength and learn how to fight? You must be exhausted and still weakened from your horrible and unjust ordeal," answered the traveler in a fatherly voice as he slowly moved closer.

"I am a little tired, that is true. But I joined the knighthood at the invitation of the King. I am happy to serve him," Jonathan answered but was becoming more and more nervous. His stomach turned over and over again inside him with a sickening uncertainty.

"The King invited you? He isn't, I mean, he isn't here at your camp up the hill, is he?" Now the traveler seemed nervous, but just for a moment as he glanced around.

"Oh no. He is not. I wish he were, though. I would love to talk to him again," replied Jonathan wistfully.

"Ha! Of course! Wouldn't everyone like a minute of the King's time? But he is certainly too busy for all of us," chortled the traveler. He rubbed his weathered chin and smiled crookedly. "I have an idea. Why don't you come with me to the next town? It is only right down the path. It is the perfect place to rest. You can eat with me at the inn—my treat, of course. Then we can refill your buckets with fresh, cool water, and my mule can carry them back to your camp up the hill. What do you say?"

Sir Jonathan replied, "It does sound tempting, but I am afraid my friends would be worried about me. Besides, I am now under orders. I would need to speak with Sir Robert. I am supposed to train today."

"Oh, they won't mind. They aren't even awake yet. Come with me to the next town. You won't be sorry. It will be a nice place to rest and relax and enjoy some well-deserved comforts," said the traveler convincingly.

Sir Jonathan did feel hungry, and he was a little tired. Surely the others would not want him to struggle too much with the buckets. Someone to help with carrying the load would be great. His friends wouldn't begrudge him that, would they? As Jonathan struggled to think through the offer, he did not notice the traveler edging closer.

"What do you say, knight?"

Sir Jonathan looked up at the traveler's smiling face and noticed that cold eyes accompanied the smile. He began to search inside for the source of the growing doubt. He wished Sir Robert were with him. He would know what to do. At the thought of Sir Robert and what he might say, Jonathan realized he must refuse the invitation. Something was not right.

"I am sorry, sir. I cannot go with you. I need to return to my camp. They will want their water for tea," answered Jonathan. He knew the excuse sounded weak, but he wanted to leave immediately.

"But they are still asleep in their tents up the hill. You have time," soothed the traveler as he inched even closer.

"Well, that may be… WAIT! How do you know the camp is up the hill or what they are doing? How do you know so much if you are a merchant on a path to town?" asked Sir Jonathan with growing concern. "I decline your offer, with thanks and respect, but I will not be going with you."

Jonathan turned to leave without his other bucket. He did not care; he felt great alarm and wanted to put as much distance as possible between him and the stranger.

Like a flash of lightning, the traveler's hand shot out and grabbed Sir Jonathan's wrist in an iron grip. In horror, Sir Jonathan looked down and saw the old, wrinkled fingers of the traveler transform into their true form—the powerful, bony claw of a skeleton-like creature. The hideous creature was tall and covered in rotting, leathery flesh. The mule transformed into a giant red-eyed wolf. Its fangs dripped and lips snarled as it nuzzled up to its master. The fogginess had lifted and both could be seen clearly for what they were.

The skeleton creature breathed out an awful, "It is no longer an offer, Sir Knight. It is a command. You are now mine and will go where I say. I have just the place for you in my dungeon." The creature's voice had morphed from that of a weary old man into a slithery, hissing tone full of malice and hate.

Sir Jonathan tried with all of his might to wrestle free from the grip of the creature, but it only laughed. The iron tight bond reminded Jonathan of the chains of his former life.

"Let me go, you wretched beast! I am not going anywhere with you! I am a knight!" shouted Sir Jonathan at the top of his lungs. "Help! Sir Robert!"

"Silence, prisoner! I have you now! These are my woods and all those in it belong to me." As he spoke, he poked Jonathan's chest with a bony finger. He brought his rotting smile closer—just inches from the young knight's trembling face. "You'll be a nice addition to the dungeon. Stop resisting or I'll chain you up like the others!" hissed the grotesque beast.

Sir Jonathan feigned submission for a moment then hurled the bucket at the face of the creature. It loosened its grip for just a second, and the knight pulled free. He rolled backward and scrambled to get up. Jonathan heard the creature roar and could feel the vibrations from his feet as they hit the ground behind him, giving chase. The giant wolf also growled in pursuit. Jonathan knew he was doomed.

He felt a searing pain in his left foot as the beast bit, then jerked him to the ground. Jonathan fell hard. His head was spinning.

"No!" yelled Sir Jonathan as he rolled over and looked at his attackers. The wolf had him pinned to the ground by his foot. Every squirm to break free brought more and more pain. Jonathan could see the skeleton creature approaching. He was no longer a hunched over old man, but stood at least eight feet tall—maybe even nine. He was holding a giant hammer in each hand and grinning malevolently as he strode toward the wounded knight.

The creature stood over the knight and announced, "You had a chance to live in my dungeon as a slave. Now, you will die alone in these woods as food for my hammer and then for my wolf. Be sure to greet your king for me, worm."

The creature raised the hammer high into the air. Sir Jonathan closed his eyes as he saw it begin to fall. He did not know what felt worse—the impending fall of the hammer or the fact he had failed miserably as a knight.

Just then, there was a loud crack and a thud. The beast-wolf yelped in pain.

The hammer never fell.

Jonathan opened his eyes and saw a long lance protruding from the wolf, and three arrows with blue fletching in the arm of the creature. The creature's giant hammer dropped harmlessly to the ground as Jonathan quickly rolled away. Almost instantly, the silence of the clearing was shattered with the sound of a battle horn and the shouts of knights charging the creature and the wolf.

Sir Jonathan got to his hands and knees and scurried toward the sound of the horn and his friends. But the wolf, though wounded, was not ready to give up his meal. He attempted to charge the knight. Sir Jonathan looked up to see Lynd shooting arrows as fast as she could. He felt them split the air as they flew over his head. Each arrow made a vicious whine followed by a violent thud as it struck the wolf.

Two knights had run right past the dying wolf. With shields and swords, they engaged the giant skeleton creature. It was a frightful scene. There were shouts and loud clanks as the knights attacked and defended. The knights circled from different directions, lunging and feinting in counter attack. They struck and stabbed the creature. Seeing that the wolf was dying, Lynd turned her bow on the creature to add to the assault.

The sound, sights, and smell of the battle were absolutely horrifying to Sir Jonathan. Should he run or help? He was so confused and overwhelmed. Just then, he felt a very strong hand on his shoulder. The grip was so strong he was afraid it might be another wolf. Then he looked up into the stern but kind face of Sir Robert.

"On your feet, Sir Jonathan! Take this!" It was his shield. Immediately he felt reprimanded for not having it with him.

Sir Jonathan grabbed the shield and ran back toward the path through the woods. Again he felt a strong hand on his shoulder that wheeled him around. "Stand your ground, *knight!*" The emphasis on the word knight sounded like a rebuke. "Hold your shield forward!" barked Sir Robert in a tone Sir Jonathan had not heard before. He was scared of the skeleton creature to be sure, but Sir Robert had his full attention.

The creature was wheeling and swinging and lashing out at the knights, who had him encircled. His pet was dead. Several arrows protruded from his cloak. Every now and then a blow would land, and he would shriek in pain and anger. He gave one last look at Sir Jonathan and bellowed, "I will see you again, worm. Count on it!"

After spitting out that final curse, he hurled his remaining hammer at Sir Jonathan with all of his evil might. Then with lightning speed, while the hammer was still in flight, he bounded into the darkest part of the woods.

Sir Jonathan saw the hammer flying and ducked behind his shield. There was an earsplitting bang, and everything went black for the young knight.

Jonathan woke up some time later with a terrible headache. He sat up shakily as Sir Seamus forced water into his mouth. "Easy, lad. Drink slowly and sit up even more slowly. You have quite a lump."

Sir Jonathan remembered where he was and anxiously looked around the clearing. "Is it gone? Is it dead?"

"Ha! It appears we have one of each," laughed Lynd, who was trying to pull her lance out of the wolf's carcass. Already buzzards were circling and waiting for the knights to move away from their claimed breakfast. Two other knights with bows at the ready stood a few feet away, scanning the forest intently.

"What happened? Who was that?" asked Sir Jonathan between sips.

"Little brother, it was a foul beast that lives in woods and forests like these to attack and kidnap knights and citizens like yourself. We call them Shifters. They can change their appearances and lay elaborate traps. You were being watched from the moment you entered this forest. You are fortunate you are not now in his dungeon . . . or worse," answered Sir Robert as he helped the young knight up.

"Thank you so much, friends. I am sorry I put you in danger. I was only trying to help with the work," confessed Sir Jonathan.

"Your desire to help was noble. But you have already forgotten some of what you have been taught. Nevertheless, it would seem you have another chance to learn it, and now even better motivation," said Sir Stephen with a smile as he playfully slapped Sir Jonathan's reddening cheeks. "Remind me to tell you how I learned this lesson sometime," he whispered with a grin as he walked passed.

The knights formed a loose formation, handed Sir Jonathan the buckets, and moved back toward camp in silence. A few times, Jonathan tried to ask a question, but was shushed. The forest was gloomy and the young knight now saw it differently. As he looked around, he saw it as enemy held territory and a scary place to be all alone. How had he missed the signs a few hours ago? Jonathan felt embarrassed but also a little wiser. At least a little more educated. He looked around at his friends. They were under no illusions.

The knights still had weapons drawn and were clearly expecting a counter attack.

But it never came.

As they approached the camp, several knights came out and seemed to be genuinely glad to see the young knight in one piece. One knight, who was normally quiet, grabbed Jonathan in a bear hug. Two knights each took a bucket and walked with Jonathan, asking if he was hurt. One examined the injured knight's wound and said he had just the thing to help.

Breakfast was already started, and with the arrival of the water the tea was put on. Everyone moved about, preparing to sit down and eat around the fire. Most of the camp acted as if nothing had even happened. It was not very long before the first prank was played and the old familiar laughter started up again.

But not Sir Jonathan. He was shaken up by everything that had happened that morning. In fact, at one point his thoughts drifted toward the hazards of the path he had chosen. Was this really for him? Were all of the enemies that powerful? He used his shield the best he could, but still was rendered unconscious. He had so many questions. He kept himself busy most of the day as he reflected on the events. Finally, toward evening, he was sitting by the fire thinking when Sir Robert came and sat down. Jonathan hardly noticed him.

"Sir Jonathan! Are you there?" inquired Sir Robert.

"Oh, yes. I am just thinking."

"About what happened out there?" asked the wise knight.

Sir Jonathan nodded as he kept looking into the fire. It crackled and glowed. Nothing helped Jonathan think like a roaring fire.

"Well," answered Sir Robert, "you have just received the benefit of an accelerated lesson in warfare. You forgot a very simple lesson and nearly paid for it with your freedom or head. Would you like to know where you went wrong?"

"Yes. I guess I need to know all I can." Jonathan paused, then turned to his friend. "What did I miss?"

Sir Robert sipped his tea as he opened the Kingsbook and handed it to Sir Jonathan. He waited for him to read the page he had selected, then leaned forward intently. His eyes locked on Sir Jonathan's and he paused until he was sure he had the young knight's full attention. Then he said passionately and firmly, "You forgot one of the most important lessons of your new life. It must never be forgotten again. It is this: *you are at war.*"

Robert let it sink in. He drank a long, noisy sip of tea and sat quietly with the sullen knight. Then he continued. "It will never be otherwise until you are safely within the gates of the City Beautiful. Because of this fact, this constant war, you must never be more than an arm's length from your weapons. They were provided for your protection and success, but the King's weapons will never be of much use when they are in your tent and you are far away. Had your weapons been with you, this morning would have been different. It is possible the Shifter would have only tried to deceive and not fully attack—but even if he had, you would have had the opportunity to defend.

"There are no lazy days in the sun. There are no aimless jaunts through the meadow. The life you are in is one of danger, duty, and warfare. If you forget you are a soldier in battle, you will be the only one, for the enemy ever has his eye on you and will leave no course of attack unexplored. Keep your weapons sharp and close. Keep your mind ready for action. Understood?"

Sir Jonathan nodded slowly. He remembered the icy grip of the creature and sharp fangs of his pet. He remembered the feelings of helplessness and the shock that came with the surprise attack. He was at war, and he would never forget it now. He wondered if all of his lessons would be learned so violently.

"I guess this is what happened to the others that foul beast mentioned. Perhaps that is why they are in his dungeon," Sir Jonathan wondered out loud as he took another sip of his tea.

Sir Robert's eyes lost their warm glow and turned to ice.

"Others? Did you say 'others'? Tell me everything, Sir Jonathan. Every detail."

CHAPTER 5

First Battle

*"But in all these things we overwhelmingly
conquer through Him who loved us."*
– Romans 8:37

Sir Robert and the other knights listened intently as Sir Jonathan recounted the creature's words. There was no other way to interpret them. It sounded as if the creature had other citizens in his dungeon.

"But what if it is a deception? The Shifter was very clever. I had no idea he was evil until he had me in his grip!" exclaimed Sir Jonathan.

"You had no idea? No sense of warning at all?" asked Sir Stephen. He raised one eyebrow and looked at Jonathan with a hint of a grin.

"Well, I did sense something was wrong. I just could not put words to it," shrugged the young knight meekly.

"And how about now? Can you put words to it now?" smirked Sir Stephen. Jonathan nodded, then laughed with Stephen.

"In time you will learn to listen and take heed when your heart warns you of danger. When there is a doubt, draw your sword. It is far better to be ready for battle and no fight come, than to be ambushed with your sword in its scabbard and your weapons stowed. But in answer to your other question, yes. This could be a trap, but that is not for us to decide. We will be cautious, but if there is a chance of citizens being held, we must act," said Sir Robert. Then he looked over at Sir Seamus who was poring over a map of the area. "Sir Seamus?"

Sir Seamus looked up from the map and nodded slowly. "Yes, it is very possible he has a lair in this area or that one," said the burly knight while circling both areas with a piece of charcoal. "These areas lay in the center of the forest. It is called Felwood. There are few paths and the terrain is very inhospitable. It will be perfect for an ambush, which means it is also perfect for hiding a dungeon. The direction he ran leads me to think we should scout this area first. Thoughts?" He looked around at the others, waiting for any input.

The knights shook their heads. It sounded simple enough.

"I have a question," said the newest member of their group.

"Okay. What is it?"

"Well, as a citizen, the King said I was free. If these are citizens, how then are they in a dungeon again? Are they no longer free?"

"A good question," began Sir Robert. "It would appear so to an observer, but the truth is that before they became citizens, they were held for crimes they committed. It was just. They were condemned. But now that they are free citizens, all the enemy can do is deceive and capture. Their bondage is based on a lie. Before they were citizens, their bondage was based on truth—they were, in fact, criminals. Their chains are real and duly earned. But now, as citizens, it is a different matter altogether. Many times we rescue citizens to find their cages are not even locked. If they were to accept the truth of their position as free citizens they could just walk out, were it not for the guards. We fight to free them from that deception and return them to life as a citizen and service to the King."

"Any more questions?" asked Sir Seamus, scanning the group. "Okay, then. Everyone prepare for battle. We move out in half an hour." Sir Seamus would lead the operation.

Sir Jonathan wondered how long they would be gone and how he would pass the time in the camp. He just sat on the log as the other knights began to move with purpose. Sir Reginald and Sir Thomas joked back and forth about avoiding the "one-too-many" blow to the head again. The young knight snickered at their antics.

"Sir Jonathan." It was Sir Seamus.

"Yes sir?" Sir Jonathan looked up.

"Let's go. Suit up. You will need your shield and sword for today, but not your lance this time. And bring your axe, but not your bow. We will move quietly, so wrap in cloth anything that clinks. Make haste, we leave soon," ordered Sir Seamus in a fatherly but firm tone.

Sir Jonathan felt sick to his stomach. He was sure they did not want him along. It was a nagging fear that had begun to grow ever since he learned there would be a rescue mission. He wanted to rescue the citizens, but he could not forget the feeling of the creature's grip on his arm, the bite from the beast-wolf, or the hammer blow that knocked him unconscious. He did not feel ready for this type of work at all. Surely there would be more training before he would go to battle. Sir Jonathan was terrified.

"Sir Robert? May I speak with you?" asked the young knight timidly.

"Of course you can," replied the older knight as he fastened leather buckles on his chest armor. "Just one moment." Sir Robert finished adjusting his armor with a wince. He then followed the knight into his tent.

All of Sir Jonathan's armor and weapons lay spread out on the cot. It was an impressive arrangement. All of the seals and finishes were bright and unscarred. No dings, tears, or rips marred the appearances like Sir Jonathan had noticed on some of the other knights' gear. He worked up the courage to ask his questions.

"Sir Robert, I do not regret the decision to swear fealty to the King. But I am questioning my ability to go with you today."

Jonathan looked down at his trembling hands. He voice was squeaky and unsure. Robert stopped what he was doing and turned to face his young friend. He sat down and motioned for Jonathan to do the same.

"After the incident in Felwood yesterday, I feel completely inadequate for this task. I ran. And then I was knocked unconscious. All I succeeded in doing was risking the lives of my friends," stammered Sir Jonathan, refusing to look up.

"You are right to question your abilities, Sir Jonathan. In fact, it would be more accurate to say that you have no abilities," chuckled Sir Robert.

The young knight's face flushed red. He could not remember ever being more embarrassed. In fact, he even felt a little angry.

"There is no need to poke fun," he defended.

Sir Robert's smile faded. "I am not poking fun. I am saving your life. You have no ability, Sir Jonathan. You are not a mighty warrior. You must understand this or you have no hope of surviving the conflicts that are coming. Do we agree?"

Confused and irritated, Sir Jonathan answered, "I do understand and I agree. That is my point! So why then am I here? Why then was I told to suit up for battle? How does this save my life?"

"None of us are the mighty warriors we seem to be. Soldiering for our King is not our profession; it is our calling. None of the strength in battle you witnessed yesterday was from our own strength or skill," replied Sir Robert patiently.

"But I saw you all defeat the scariest creature I have ever seen! You all fought so well. You looked like real knights," cried Sir Jonathan. "Not like me."

"Of course. But the reason is the next lesson. One you must learn *today* because you will most certainly need it today. But first, let's review. What lesson did you learn yesterday, Sir Knight?"

Robert spoke slowly and chose his words carefully. The air in the tent was thick with the importance of the lesson the older knight offered. He realized young Jonathan was on the edge of learning a critical truth, and it was one of his favorites to teach.

Without even needing to think, Jonathan recited, "I am in a war from this day until the last day. I must always have my weapons at hand. If I forget I am at war, I will be the only one, because my enemy will not forget." Jonathan had reviewed that truth over and over since the encounter. It would not be something he would ever forget now.

"Excellent! You see, you are learning. You are becoming a knight!" exclaimed Sir Robert with a hard slap on Sir Jonathan's shoulder.

"But what good are my weapons if when I use them I am knocked unconscious by the first blow of the first battle? You have to admit, I was not very effective yesterday," said Sir Jonathan ashamedly as he held his sword and looked it over skeptically.

"No. No, you were not. Tell me, when you held your shield up, what were you trying to do? What were you thinking?" asked Sir Robert.

"Well, I saw the creature begin to throw his hammer at me, so I held the shield up with all my strength to block the attack. Then I was out cold. I thought I could block the blow better than that," replied the smaller knight. "I tried my best," he said dejectedly.

"Hmm. Well, I see the problem. Your enemies in this war are beyond you and your strength. But they are not beyond the strength of your King. There are powerful enemies out there, beyond the next turn . . . ."

The young knight expected Robert to continue, but his voice had trailed off. Jonathan glanced up into the face of Robert, but the eyes of the older knight were looking as if into a far off place.

As Robert began to teach, his memory reached back to his early days of serving the King and how he had learned this all-important lesson. He lost track of time and even forgot for a moment that his young apprentice was in the tent. He was lost in the memories of learning lessons, battles already fought, and far away friends.

If Jonathan could have seen what his teacher was remembering, the lesson would have been completed—but it also would have been terrifying. Robert ran his hand over his shield and looked down at the punctures on the sides of the dented piece of armor. As he did, he remembered the roar of the beast, the smell of its rancid breath, and the sound of its fangs trying to crush him. To bite and chew and tear him to pieces. But the jaws of the beast could not. The shield had stopped them cold.

Robert remembered the battle from so long ago that had shaped him as a servant and as a warrior. He also remembered how his mentor and friend explained the power of the King's weapons wielded in the King's strength.

"Robby, my boy," he had said to Sir Robert so long ago, "use the King's weapons in the King's power and you can be as safe in a nest of dragons as in your own tent." Robert could still hear his mentor's thick, roguish brogue as he spoke. For a moment, he missed his friend dearly yet at the same time was warmed by the memories of long ago.

Jonathan, who was known to speak quickly, knew Robert was thinking important thoughts so for once he waited quietly. After a few moments, Robert's eyes narrowed and he spoke. Barely above a whisper, the older knight relayed the story, handing Jonathan his shield to show him the scars of the fight. The young knight ran his hands over the jagged holes in the shield as he thought about the encounter his friend had survived. He listened intently to every word. He could scarcely believe such awful creatures existed or that his friend had actually fought them.

When Robert finished, he picked up Jonathan's shield and passed it to the young knight. With great solemnness, he emphasized every word: "Your King made these weapons, Jonathan." He let the words hang thickly in the air as he maintained intense eye contact.

Jonathan examined his armor and weapons again with a new perspective as Robert continued.

"He forged them himself. He alone has the power to wage this kind of warfare. When you fight the King's battles, you must fight with the King's armor and weapons, and—most importantly—you must fight in the King's strength. When you think your victories are the result of your own strength, you are on the verge of defeat. Had I trusted myself against that foul beast so long ago, you surely would have a different teacher right now." He quietly stroked his long grey beard, then added with a far away look, "I would not have survived."

"When you recognize and trust in the King and his strength and power, then you will have victory. In fact, when you recognize this truth and trust him for strength, then your weapons will have no equal on the battlefield. No enemy will stand; not even when you are greatly outnumbered. Do you understand this?"

"I think so. But if I understand correctly, then these are not ordinary weapons. A normal sword would cut as deep as the arm swinging it can, but not mine?" asked Sir Jonathan as he picked up his sword and studied it carefully. "But how does it...*work*? How do the weapons know what I am thinking? Or trusting, or whatever?"

"I cannot explain it fully, but these weapons were forged and created by the King. The qualities they have are beyond us. They are powerful beyond the one swinging them, but only when it is the *King's* power. And the enemy knows this. Fight in the King's power and they are terrified. Fight in your own power and they will prevail. Then, unexpectedly Sir Robert announced, "Up now, it's time to go. Quickly!"

Sir Jonathan finished arming himself. He was still very nervous but not terrified like earlier. Instead of fearing defeat a kernel of hope had sprouted and begun to take root in the deep places of his heart. He smiled and determined to fight in the King's strength.

Once the unit was assembled, Sir Seamus strode over to Sir Jonathan and placed a reassuring hand on his shoulder. With a smile, he said, "Steady, son. Things could get interesting today. I remember my first battle. You will never forget this day."

Sir Jonathan nodded, trying to be confident. When he did, his face plate slammed shut with a clank. He chuckled softly, and the sound echoed from the helmet. Stephen snickered with him and nodded quickly also, clanking his own shut. Laughter filled the camp once again at Stephen's antics.

The group formed and began moving down the mountain toward the woods. Now the forest looked and felt different to the young knight. He was not on a search for water; he was in a war party hunting an evil creature and trying to free the citizens of the King. The forest was foreboding, but the knight was excited to be involved in a rescue operation.

They approached the pathway into the woods that now looked more like an open mouth waiting to swallow them than an entrance to a forest. The tall trees blocked the sun, casting long shadows across the path and the young knight's heart.

Sir Seamus took the lead as they moved deeper down the trail in noiseless vigilance. Each knight watched the trail and surrounding forest. Every twenty paces or so, the entire formation stopped and listened before moving on again. The first few times the group stopped, Jonathan bumped into the person in front of him with a muffled clatter. The others seemed to understand, but still his cheeks warmed as he purposed to be more alert. Soon he learned to stop with them before scanning the dark forest to his side. Turning, he noticed Sir Reginald, braced for another collision. Reginald smiled reassuringly as Jonathan adjusted to his position.

On they went, with no sign of the creature.

As the knights approached the clearing, Sir Seamus halted the formation with a raised hand. He turned to look at Sir Reginald and Sir Thomas, then motioned them to scout either side of the trail. They exchanged hand signals without a word as the two knights moved into the forest on either side of the path. Everyone waited and watched a very long ten minutes, but the clearing remained silent.

Only after watching and waiting carefully did Sir Seamus motion the column forward. The two knights on the flanks rejoined the column and they all moved into the clearing. Jonathan's heart began to beat faster as they approached the scene of the previous day's battle. His eyes fell on several large, ugly vultures picking at the wolf's bones. The rib cage, clean and white, was clearly visible.

"A fitting end," thought Sir Jonathan. He kicked it when he walked by, causing a cloud of flies to buzz angrily and Sir Stephen to snicker.

The knights moved toward the Shifter's last direction, reentering the canopy of trees on the other side of the clearing. The woods were dark and wet. Thick undergrowth seemed to claw at the knights, slowing the procession. Sir Reginald whistled a bird-like signal and motioned to a crudely formed trail. As the knights gathered around, Sir Reginald held up a finger with a sticky midnight fluid on it.

"It bled well as it passed this way," he whispered.

Without a word, Sir Seamus nodded and motioned for them to follow. One by one they fell in line, with Sir Jonathan in the middle. His heart beat steadily faster, pounding in his ears. He felt guilty hoping that they would find no sign at all.

Before this hope was fully formed, the night of his own rescue grew larger in his mind. The smell of the dungeon, the ache of his every bone, and further still, the ache of his desperate existence flooded his heart once more.

Remembering the horrors of his previous life changed his perspective.

If the creature had captives, they must be in terrible shape. Unsure of the help he might offer, he slowly became determined to try. He unconsciously ran his fingers over the pardon in his pocket and the oath of fealty next to it. With a firmer resolve than he had yet experienced, he put his hand on his sword and remembered why he was there. Each of his steps, though quiet, held much more purpose.

The trail led down a small hill that gave way to a low, wet forest. Eventually the woods turned into a formidable bog. Murky water covered several parts of the trail. Even the trees appeared unusually heavy—laden with moss, they sagged low over the swamp. Thorns, thistles, and sharp rocks protruded everywhere. An ugly black snake, which seemed to glare at Jonathan for a moment, slinked off a low hanging branch into the water and disappeared without a sound. Even in the heat, it chilled Jonathan that the ugly snake had looked right at him. Nothing in this swamp was friendly.

Sir Seamus stopped abruptly with hand raised. The knights halted. Their eyes roved the surrounding mire for any sign of an ambush.

Slowly and quietly, they drew weapons.

Sir Jonathan, his mouth dry and heart pounding, followed them and pulled out his sword as quietly as he could. Its small metal clank caused Sir Stephen to turn and give him a grin. Jonathan could not smile; his last meal threatened reappearance at any moment. Knight or no, danger hung in the air amongst them. It was a new and unpleasant feeling for Jonathan. Unpleasant indeed.

As the knights moved up, Sir Jonathan saw why they stopped. Two massive wooden doors framed by a roughhewn stone archway covered the entrance to another rocky hill. The dungeon appeared to be mostly underground. Strange writing ran along the sides of the wall. The handles to the doors were skulls. Whether or not they were real skulls Sir Jonathan could not tell, and he had no interest in finding out.

"What does the writing say?" he whispered to Sir Robert.

"*Hope Has Fled,*" answered the older knight. "Well," he began, "its return is imminent. We are going through that door, Sir Jonathan. Stay close. We will most definitely encounter strong resistance. I am counting on you to stay on my right side. Trust the King's strength and kill anything that gets close to us. Look at me. Who are you?" asked Sir Robert.

"Jonathan," he whispered timidly.

"No. You are Sir Jonathan the Slight, knight in the Light Mounted Rangers, of the King's own 5th Cavalry. Beyond that door are the sworn enemies of your King and high Captain."

"Yes sir. I am Sir Jonathan, King's knight," he answered, sounding more confident than he truly felt.

The older knight smiled broadly. Instantly, Jonathan felt more confident. "Good. Now be ready. Here we go."

Sir Reginald and Sir Stephen stood on either side of the door, axes poised to swing on the lock. Sir Seamus readied his lance; it had a very sharp, twisted point on it. Standing right next to Seamus was Lynd. She nocked an arrow and pulled her bow to full draw. Jonathan tightened the grip on his sword and drew his shield closer. He moved the shield just under his chin the way he saw the other knights and the way they had trained him. His mouth was dry. With a tiny clink he reached up and pulled his faceplate down. His stomach was in knots.

Jonathan was terrified of what might happen next, but he also grew angrier with the Shifter for putting citizens in such an awful place.

Sir Seamus nodded to all.

The axes came down one right after the other. There was a shower of sparks and the doors flew open. They heard a muffled shriek inside and a goblin's greenish face came into view. One of Lynd's arrows struck the goblin in the head and the beast crumpled to the ground without another sound. A wide staircase descended into the bowels of the dungeon. The knights moved quickly, with Sir Seamus in the lead.

The air was foul and damp. A bat fluttered across the tunnel as they snuck forward. Spiders' webs hung thickly along the walls. The whole vault smelled rotten.

Torches lit the bottom chamber of the dungeon. As they crept downward, it was clear that the guards were not yet aware of their presence. The Shifter was not in sight. Cell doors lined the perimeter of the circular chamber. A door at the far end led to another staircase and down further into the hill.

Sir Seamus motioned to the knights to form a line abreast. In the shadows they formed quickly and noiselessly. Sir Jonathan had never been more excited or scared in all of his life. His heart pounded. He felt a little sick in the pit of his stomach, too. The smells of the dungeon and sounds of the goblins laughing and eating around a table in the middle brought back horrible memories of his former life. The more he watched and listened, the angrier he became. He was ready for the command when it came.

"*Forward!*" thundered Sir Seamus. As the knights rushed in, the goblins shrieked with rage and terror. Immediately three goblins fell, mortally wounded. Howls, shouts, and clanging metal filled the dungeon.

One large goblin saw Sir Jonathan and charged. The young knight saw him coming and raised his shield with all of his might. The goblin crashed into him, and they hit the ground and rolled. The goblin ended up on top and furiously swung a hideous-looking mace against his shield. Sir Jonathan heard a scream and realized it was his own voice. This was not what he envisioned. Each blow from the mace brought the shield lower and closer to Sir Jonathan's head. The goblin sensed this, and laughed has he continued to attack.

I cannot do this, thought Sir Jonathan. *I am not knightly at all.*

The goblin snickered at his soon-to-be prey and swung his mace even harder. A sharp spike on the mace nearly punctured the shield.

Across the dungeon, Sir Stephen saw Jonathan's desperate situation and moved to help, but was stopped by Sir Robert's arm. Stephen looked at Robert, who said, "Let him trust. Let him trust and fight."

It was all Stephen could do to not intervene. He moved closer but left Jonathan to fight on his own.

I am not strong enough, thought Jonathan again.

And, then, from deep down inside his heart, a quiet voice agreed and added, *but your King is.* Jonathan remembered the way the King had split his cage and shattered his chains. And in that awful dungeon, in that awful predicament, Jonathan was encouraged ever so slightly at the thought of his King and the strength he had. *The King is ever victorious,* the voice deep down inside whispered quietly but surely.

And then it struck him: *Of course I cannot prevail. Only the King can!"*

At that moment, something curious happened—the shield became very light, even with the goblin on top of it. Unbelievably light! Jonathan shoved the shield upward and the goblin flew with it, as if yanked back by an unseen hand. Quickly Jonathan jumped to his feet with a renewed trust in the King and the armor he had given him. Sir Jonathan picked up the sword he had dropped, and it too, felt light, quick, and . . . powerful. *Very powerful.* As the goblin scurried to stand, Sir Jonathan the Slight, trusting the King's weapons, sliced downward with his sword and split the goblin's helmet, and everything in it, from top to bottom. Jonathan's jaw dropped in amazement but he found no time to think about it.

An incredible roar reverberated through the dungeon as a creature, the Shifter, angry and foul, bounded up the stairs in a rage. He had a hammer in one hand and a pike in the other. He was furious and shouting curses at the invaders. Seeing all of his goblins slaughtered in his own lair did not help his mood in the least. As soon as he saw the knights, he focused on Sir Jonathan and shrieked, "*WORM!* I told you I would see you again. Now I will finish what I started." And with that, he hurled his hammer with all of his might at Sir Jonathan.

Sir Jonathan raised his shield, this time with a renewed confidence that the enemy was no match for the King's weapons.

Jonathan looked at the Shifter and was not afraid.

The hammer slammed into the shield with a thunderous crash, but the shield held. The hammer fell to the ground, broken. In shock the creature hesitated.

The hesitation was all that was needed. Sir Seamus charged forward and rammed his lance with all of his might into the throat of the creature. The other knights also attacked with speed and ferocity. Even Sir Jonathan charged forward, this time with his sword raised high.

Jonathan heard a scream. It was his own voice again, only now it was a war whoop. Blow after blow from the knights chopped the creature down. It stumbled and fell, and never again regained his footing. The Shifter swung his arm in a dying flail, and Jonathan jumped over to avoid being hit. As he cleared the arm, he landed next to the creature's head and brought his sword straight down with a loud clang. A few moments later, everything was silent and still. The creature was dead.

"Search every cell. Find the King's citizens!" commanded Sir Seamus. Sir Thomas and Sir Reginald began to open cells and found several citizens in chains.

Sir Jonathan the Slight, still gulping air, ran to a cell door. He kicked it with all of his might, but it wasn't locked so it flew open with such great force that it slammed shut again. If the memory of the battle were not so fresh, he would have laughed. With a torch in one hand and a sword in the other, he entered the cell.

He had been in a cell before, he thought. But this time he was not a captive but on the King's business. The thought encouraged him greatly.

He searched the cell in the torch light and saw what might have been a person laying under filthy rags. He ran over and crouched over the body. Was he dead?

"Hello? Are you okay?" asked the knight. He shook him to see if was even alive.

The body turned over and began to flail his arms and shriek, "I am a citizen of the King, turn loose! Let me go!"

"Easy brother, I too am a citizen of the City Beautiful. I am here on the King's business to get you out! Come with me," answered Jonathan.

"Who are you?" asked the dazed prisoner.

"I am Sir Jonathan of the 5th Mounted," said the knight. Inside Jonathan smiled at the truth of his new identity.

"Bjorn. I am a new knight, from the King's 2nd Regiment, Heavy Horse," he answered and threw his arms around Jonathan. "Thank you, sir."

"Come with me, brother. This is no place for a soldier of the City," said Jonathan.

Bjorn, with help from Jonathan, rose to his feet and hobbled out of the cell.

In all they rescued eight citizens. Most of them could barely walk. Some needed full assistance.

"Sir Robert!" exclaimed Jonathan when he saw his friend. "The doors were not even locked!"

"No. Of course they are not. They are citizens and therefore cannot be locked in the enemy's dungeons. They have been deceived into thinking they are prisoners with neither hope nor alternative. The enemy cannot condemn whom the King has declared free, he can only deceive into a false imprisonment of lies," answered the wise knight. His face was contorted as if he had eaten something bitter.

The knights searched the dungeon thoroughly, then set it on fire. All of the citizens were helped outside of the walls and given food and water. Sir Jonathan helped a young girl outside, then sat down on a mossy log. He looked at his shield and saw a significant dent right in the center, as well as several long scratches. The shield had held. A smile broadened his face in spite of the very recent danger.

"Sir Jonathan," said Sir Robert.

"Yes sir?" he answered.

"Well done. It seems you listened and fought well. You are ready for your next task."

"Task? What do you mean?"

Sir Robert smiled. "Rest for a while as we finish preparing the citizens to travel. I'll come get you in a few minutes. You will certainly need your rest for what comes next."

CHAPTER 6

First Quest

". . . for the weapons of our warfare are not of flesh,
but divinely powerful . . . ."
– 2 Corinthians 10:4

Sir Jonathan opened the Kingsbook and began to read. He searched for information on the weapons of the King and how to use them properly. Glad the fight went as well as it did, he was still shaken from having been knocked over and nearly clubbed to death. Jonathan wanted to know more about the enemy's deceptions as well. He had trained and studied, but real combat was not like he had imagined. He still had a headache. One side of his ribs was rather bruised. He was deep into the Kingsbook when Sir Robert called to him.

"Sir Jonathan, we have a task for you. These citizens are in no condition to fight or be turned loose. The King has a refuge town not far from here, on the other side of the forest. They will be safe there and can take time to recover. We want you to provide escort and see them safely there," charged Sir Robert.

Sir Jonathan looked at the eight citizens they had rescued. Most of them were in very bad shape. Some could not even stand, much less walk. A few looked like they might be knights, but to Jonathan they all looked pitiful.

"Of course. I am happy to serve. They look as though they need help. But you are not coming with me?" asked Sir Jonathan, somewhat confused.

"No. Sir Reginald found a trap door in the back of the dungeon that opened to a staircase. There might be more here than meets the eye. If we run into trouble, we will need every knight available; however, we must get these citizens to safety."

"Of course. But—well . . . what if I run into trouble?" asked the knight nervously.

"You just might," laughed Sir Seamus. "But after what you did to the goblin in the dungeon and his master, we think you will manage."

Even Sir Jonathan smiled at the thought. He looked down at the dent in his shield and the blackish stain on his tunic. Goblins were filthy creatures, but somehow not as formidable now. He found himself hoping he ran into a few on the way.

"May I see the map?" asked the young knight.

"Of course. Follow this road through the swamp. It will come out of the forest between two hills. Not long after that you will come to the gates of the city. See to it they are housed and fed and left in the care of the council there. You should meet an old friend of mine at the gates and he will see to your needs. The whole journey should take a little over a day. Try to exit the forest before making camp for the night, though. You will not want to be in this foul place after dark. Any questions?" asked Sir Robert.

"No. Well, maybe one. What if you and the others find trouble? What if the trap door hides enemies and a battle follows?" asked Sir Jonathan.

Sir Thomas and Sir Reginald laughed together. "We sure hope it does! A dozen goblins and their master were not quite enough to make this hike worth it."

Sir Robert looked at Sir Jonathan carefully. "Are you afraid we might find more trouble than we can handle, or that we might find trouble without you?"

"I know you can beat the enemy. I just want to . . . to be involved in the important work. That's all," stammered Sir Jonathan without making eye contact with Sir Robert.

The other two knights stopped smiling, exchanged glances, and walked away from the young apprentice and his mentor. Words needed to be spoken.

"Sir Knight," began Sir Robert a bit sternly, "every task and assignment given to His Majesty's knights is important. Do not think escort duty is any less important than cleaning out a nest of dragons. It isn't the epic battle against impossible odds that makes a servant of the King a knight of great worth. It is the daily discipline of rising to march in the direction his Captain orders that makes a knight dependable and effective. In fact, no knight that has ever been fit to fight in the most significant of battles became so without a steady faithfulness in the smallest of tasks. You must see in these citizens what your King sees, then you will understand that your task is critically important. Their worth to the King makes this quest worth your life if need be. Do you understand?"

"I do, Sir Robert. And I apologize," confessed the knight.

Sir Robert put his hand on his young apprentice's shoulder and smiled.

"Never mind that. Turn your thoughts to the task at hand and your charges. They are weak and scared. Be strong and take good care of them. After you have completed your mission we will meet you here," said Sir Robert warmly as he pointed to a place on the map. It was considerably closer to several areas contested by the enemy and regarded as fairly dangerous.

"The map says this is the beginning to the Great East. It is strongly enemy held, is it not?" asked the young knight.

"Yes. It is time you learn what our orders truly are. For a very long time the King has desired to liberate the citizens in these lands, but the enemy has been strong and determined. At times, unfortunately, the soldiers of the King have been defeated. Some have not obeyed the command to take his terms and pardon to the people there. The cost is great," said Sir Robert.

"However, our Captain is not willing to let his citizens languish in the enemy's dungeons any longer. He has asked for volunteers and our unit—*your* unit—the Mounted Light Rangers has answered. We intend to carry out the King's command," he continued.

"That sounds dangerous. I don't know if I can help, but I'm all in. What are our instructions?" inquired Jonathan.

"The King has ordered us to scout the enemy strength on this mountain and in the valleys on either side. Hurry back. The job is going to be tough and we will need everyone," said the older knight.

"Yes, sir!" he answered.

Sir Jonathan the Slight nodded and began to think about what he had just learned. As he walked over to the citizens, he saw his friend Stephen hitching a horse.

Sir Stephen had liberated a cart that seemed perfect for eight people. After the knights helped the citizens into the wagon, Stephen made them as comfortable as possible. Sir Reginald reached inside the bag he had been carrying all day and began to distribute loaves of bread, a wheel of cheese, and several skins of water to the freed captives. He worked with such compassion that Sir Jonathan thought maybe he knew several of them. He was amazed at how this important knight, this warrior, was so warm and kind to them.

Another one of the knights, Sir Thomas, had returned to the camp with a horse for Sir Jonathan and another to pull the cart. The knight's horse had his lance, his bow and quiver, and several other saddlebags. Jonathan was impressed by how thorough his friends were at not only rescuing captives but also taking care of them afterward. Everything was ready.

Sir Jonathan walked over to the cart and checked on everyone. Some were already asleep. One muttered to himself over and over. He seemed to be very upset that he had been tricked and captured.

"Are you taking us out of this horrible place, Sir Knight?" asked a woman with a kind but dirty face.

"Yes, ma'am. I am your escort to a city where you can rest and recover," answered the knight. He could see the relief in her eyes.

"Oh, thank you so much, Sir. We are so grateful. May I ask your name, Sir? My name is Rose," she gushed.

"I am Sir Jonathan. Sir Jonathan the Slight at your service." He felt the need to encourage her further. "You will be safe and warm in a day's time. We are leaving shortly." He smiled at her and she seemed perfectly content at the thought of leaving soon.

The smoke of the ruins rose through the thick canopy of the swamp. Sir Stephen and Sir Reginald stood by the trap door discussing what could be on the other side. Sir Jonathan looked over at Sir Seamus and Sir Robert, who were whispering and looking at him. He nodded and saluted.

"Godspeed, Sir Jonathan. Long live the King," said Sir Seamus stoutly.

"Follow what you have learned in the Kingsbook, Sir Jonathan. Do not leave the trail and do not drop your guard. The foul master of these woods has been killed, but there are always more. Be on your guard at all times," warned Sir Robert. "And . . . ."

"Enough, enough!" laughed Sir Seamus. "Let him begin. He'll be fine."

"I will. Long live the King," saluted Sir Jonathan. And with that, he turned and headed toward the trail marked on his map. One of the prisoners, Bjorn, was strong enough to drive the cart. He followed the young knight down the trail with the wagon full of citizens.

It was not long before the trail turned this way and that, then they were out of sight of the others. The forest was thick and thorny. Jonathan wondered whether the woods were dark and dangerous and therefore attracted the enemy, or did having the enemy in them make them so?

Suddenly the knight began to feel anxious. He scanned the

woods for any hint of an ambush. Nonchalantly, he moved his hand to the hilt of his sword. He turned to look at the wagon and saw that most of his charges were asleep. Bjorn looked at him and smiled. He seemed to feel completely safe and relieved to be out of the dungeon.

How could they be so calm? Do they not know where they are? wondered the knight. It began to irritate him just a little. They were in great danger in this evil forest. He slowed his horse to walk next to Bjorn.

"Bjorn, this is a bad place you have found yourself in, yet you look rather calm," stated Sir Jonathan flatly.

"Yes. Yes, it is an evil place and it has been a rotten time. I was captured not far from here when I let my guard down and listened to a stranger tell lies about our King. But I am not afraid now," answered Bjorn with a smile.

"And why is that, friend?" countered Sir Jonathan. He was not going to show it, but his irritation grew. Perhaps it was this kind of carelessness that caused all eight of them to be captured?

"Why should I be afraid? I am with a King's knight. I saw how your friends destroyed that dungeon. I don't remember all of it, but I did see some of it. You split the goblin sergeant's head in two with one blow! Then you charged that filthy creature without any fear—at least none that I could see. You are smaller than the average knight, this is true, but I saw you in battle. I wouldn't want to be on the other end of your attack. Seeing you fight reminded me of who I am."

He had not thought of it that way. Yes, he was in the thick of it, to be sure. And it was true: he had won a battle. He smiled at the thought of his first successful encounter with the enemy.

A malicious idea twisted its way around Jonathan's thoughts like a thorny vine. *If these eight citizens had decided to fight instead of allow themselves to be deceived, this would not have happened. Why could they not have stood like I did?* Sir Jonathan began to think about how fortunate they were to have a knight escort them out of the forest. How long would he have to play nurse to these wayward children?

"May I ask you a question?" ventured Bjorn. "From your actions in the dungeon I would guess that you have been fighting for some time. How many engagements have you fought in?"

Bjorn's inquiry jerked Sir Jonathan back to reality. He was not an experienced knight. He was brand new to this war and to the office of soldier.

Jonathan stopped thinking about how much of a knight he was; instead, he was reminded of his first attempt at being a soldier. It embarrassed him. And protected him.

Sir Jonathan stammered, "Um, well, only two. And that was the first successful one."

"What do you mean?" squeaked a little voice from the wagon. Sir Jonathan wheeled around. He had an audience. Several of the citizens were awake now and listening to their conversation. He guessed the squeak had come from a young girl.

"To be honest, yesterday was my first run in with the enemy since being freed from the dungeons." He paused. "And it did not go well," replied Sir Jonathan truthfully. "See?" He showed them the lump on his head and explained the story.

"That's how he tricked me, too!" exclaimed squeaky. "My name is Margritte. Thank you for rescuing us, Sir."

"How did you get away from that monster and his wolf?" asked Bjorn.

Sir Jonathan explained the battle and how he failed. He was quite embarrassed, but mostly at his thoughts of their weaknesses. He realized as he recounted the story there was only one difference between their fates and his—he had friends with him that day who were vigilant when he was foolish. If it were not for them, he would have met them in the dungeon as a fellow prisoner instead of a rescuer.

And *that* was an embarrassing thought.

After telling the story, he felt even worse for thinking he was so much better than his new friends. He was thankful he had not been alone yesterday—very thankful, indeed.

"We are grateful you are with us now, Sir Jonathan," came Margritte's high-pitched voice. "Thank you for saving us like your friends saved you." She smiled at him the way only a little child could.

Thinking of how he was helping them the way his friends helped him made Jonathan feel a little better. Margritte had encouraged him when he really needed it.

He reached into his saddlebag and tossed the little girl an apple and a smile. She kept the apple and returned the smile. Still feeling embarrassed, Jonathan pretended to scan the woods for possible enemies so he did not have to look at his passengers.

For several hours they plodded along through the thickening forest. Everyone in the wagon had fallen silent; some were asleep. The only sounds were the horses' hooves on the trail, the occasional humming of young Margritte, and the birds in the trees.

As they moved along, Sir Jonathan tried to concentrate but kept thinking about his lesson in humility. Had Sir Robert given him this task to illustrate his needs as well? Did he need that lesson all the more urgently after his first victory? Jonathan was thinking about these things when the woods fell silent. Not even a bird chirped. The noisy insects were either gone or quietly hiding from an unseen danger.

A warning bell sounded in his head. Unlike before, this time he listened to the alarm. Slowly he gripped his shield and raised it ever so slightly. His other hand moved over to his sword, which was slung across the horse's back. He glanced over at Bjorn, who returned his look of concern. Bjorn was beaten and tired, but he was also a knight. He had noticed, too. Though his body was exhausted, his mind was sharp.

Inside, Sir Jonathan began to think about all that could lie ahead. He knew he was not up to the task.

I can't do this. I shouldn't be here, he thought. He remembered the conversation he had just had and his own thoughts about his new friends. *They will soon find out what a fraud I am.* Jonathan looked down at his weapons and recalled his conversation with Sir Robert. *It is the King who wins the battles, Jonathan,* he remembered.

If the King doesn't empower these weapons, I won't survive and neither will they. They are important to the King. Make me strong, please.

In that instant, without thinking, he raised his shield to his head. A split second later he heard a loud *thwack* as a jagged arrow impacted the shield and fell to the ground. Sir Jonathan was drawing his sword before the arrow hit the forest floor.

"Get down!" he yelled at his new friends in the wagon.

The knight was alarmed and knew his charges were helpless in their weakened state. Sir Jonathan turned his horse to the source of the arrow and saw three hulking goblin archers and one goblin axeman. Without hesitating, he charged the four.

"*For the King!*" he thundered as he charged.

Twice more he blocked arrows that were launched his way. The goblin with the axe was heaving his weapon backward to wind up for a blow when the knight's sword separated his head and body. Another goblin was frantically trying to nock an arrow when he met the same end. The other two archers squealed and slithered down a hole in the ground, pulling a boulder on top of the opening for cover. It all happened so fast!

Sir Jonathan looked around. As quickly as it had begun, it was over. One arrowhead remained lodged in his shield. His shield was splattered with muck. His horse pawed and snorted. Apparently she did not like the smell of goblins, either. Winded from the excitement, the knight surveyed the area. He tried to slow his breathing but could not seem to get enough air. He circled the area with sword in hand, waiting for another attack. But no attack came.

Sir Jonathan returned to the wagon and tried to smile as he said, "Well, that was fun. Let's get going." He knew it was not how he felt at all—it was terrifying. He just didn't know what to say.

The sword clinked as his shaking hands returned it to its scabbard. And with that, Jonathan steered his horse down the trail, hoping to catch his breath soon. Bjorn was white as a sheet, but continued after the knight.

"A random goblin patrol, Jonathan?" asked Bjorn.

"No. They must have been scouts guarding the entrance to the forest. I can see the end of this awful road," said Sir Jonathan the Slight, pointing at the thinning trees.

The trail made one last curve before entering a field with hills and grassland. There were clumps of trees and the occasional stream, but they were out of the swamp and forest. Everyone seemed visibly relieved, especially the knight. The sun was going down in the distance and he was glad to be out of the forest before dark.

"Let's camp over there on the other side of the stream," said Jonathan, pointing in the distance.

The party moved across the field and crossed the stream. The citizens who were able went about setting up a makeshift camp while Sir Jonathan rode a large circle around the immediate area to look for any signs of the enemy. He was glad they were not in the woods, but he was still wary of an attack.

When he was satisfied they were relatively safe, he galloped over to the wagon and dismounted. He pulled one of his saddlebags off and felt a weight inside. Wondering what it could be, he reached in and pulled out a sizable lump of dried meat and a bag of flat bread loaves. Sir Thomas had also left a note: "If you find yourself in need of this food, it is likely you have survived the pickets that are normally at the entrance of a forest such as this. Enjoy your mission!"

Sir Jonathan should have been angry that he was not warned,

but all he could do was laugh. He took the joke as a welcome from the knights and began to heat up the meat over the fire that roared in the middle of the camp. The night was turning cold and the sky was becoming overcast. Jonathan asked Bjorn to pile a significant amount of wood near the fire. Bjorn seemed happy to help and never went too far from the knight's side.

After making sure everyone had eaten and was comfortable, Sir Jonathan moved a short distance away to a group of rocks resting on a small hill. He sat on top of them and leaned back against a big boulder. He could not see behind him very well, but he had a great view of the camp and surrounding area. It seemed like the best place to stand guard. Except for the slight hill on which he was keeping watch, the valley was relatively flat. As he thought about the need for a guard, he realized his entire perspective had changed to that of a soldier.

He ran his hand over his pardon oath and smiled. He picked up his shield and wondered at how differently it had looked that morning. As his fingers fell into the deep scratch of the shield, he realized it was easier to remember the events of the day now that the headache had subsided.

Sleep would be more than welcome but the watch was chief amongst his concerns. They were some distance from the woods, but by no means did Jonathan consider them to be safe. He looked around and wished for more moonlight. A light wind picked up, and Jonathan quickly removed a dark wool cloak from his bag and wrapped it around himself tightly. He was thankful for all of the King's gifts, but the cloak was especially welcome on a night like this one. He looked down at the royal coat of arms on the outside and warmed at the thought of serving his King. As he looked at the cloak, he noticed something happening. It began to change colors to reflect the boulders he was on. In just a few seconds he was not just warm, he was camouflaged as well! The King's gifts were full of surprises.

Soft snoring caught his attention and he looked back at the camp.

They were all asleep around the fire. They were warm and fed and free.

Free. What a wonderful word, mused Jonathan.

They were safe. He smiled as he examined how similar their situations had been to his own just a day ago with the creature in the clearing. The similarities caused a laugh in spite of himself. He had been foolish. He had needed help and rescue and watching. Now, on the King's business, he was helping, rescuing, and watching.

As he considered his own great needs and how he was being used by the King to meet the needs of others, he gradually felt his heart soften to his new charges. Yes, as Sir Robert had mentioned, they are important to the King and that makes them important to him.

Jonathan had the Kingsbook open, but he did not want to light a torch for fear of making his position more vulnerable. Instead he just leaned back against the rock and looked over the camp and the valley back toward Felwood. One thing was certain—this life was to be very exciting.

Later in the night, as the knight fought drowsiness, the sky began to clear a little. Slivers of moonlight peeked between the clouds. Gradually Jonathan was able to see more of the field around the camp. And what he saw made his blood turn cold.

CHAPTER 7

City of Rest

*"Since we have gifts that differ according to the grace given
to us, each of us is to exercise them accordingly . . . ."*
– Romans 12:6

From all directions, dark masses crept silently through the grass toward the camp of sleeping citizens. Jonathan made a quick scan and counted six figures in total. His heart pounded so fast and hard he wondered if it would alert the enemy. It was time to act, but the young knight did not know what to do next. The extreme danger the King's citizens were in caused him to be torn between seething anger and extreme terror.

He was still sitting motionless thinking how to defend his friends when a wretched stench assaulted his nostrils. It smelled like a combination of a hideous beast and the fetid slime of a swamp. The putrid odor made the knight want to wretch. Then, in the corner of his eye, Jonathan spotted movement. The owner of the horrid smell was quite foul and dark and incredibly close.

A hairy foot moved noiselessly over the rock by Jonathan's head. Either the knight's dark wool cloak had hidden him, or the beast was too focused on ill deeds to notice his presence.

Regardless, it was a fatal mistake for an enemy of the King.

As its head came close to the knight, Sir Jonathan the Slight, with lightning speed, grabbed its snout at the same time while thrusting his dagger up through the creature's throat. It kicked twice but was unable to make another sound. The knight sunk the blade up to the hilt until the beast quit struggling. Gently Jonathan lowered the creature to the rock he was on as it writhed a few more times.

The enemy was a large wolf-like creature with jagged fangs, but looked as though it could stand upright like a man. It appeared powerful and gruesome in a black tunic with a sinister insignia of a skull and crossed red daggers. It carried a jagged axe in one hand. Jonathan breathed a sigh of relief that it was a weapon it would never use again.

The other creatures nearing the camp stopped and looked at the rock outcropping for a few moments, but did not seem to notice anything wrong. Jonathan crouched motionless behind the wolf creature. After a pause that seemed to drag on forever, the enemies returned to stalking the camp.

Without a doubt, Sir Jonathan knew it was an enemy assault, and he only had a few moments to thwart the attack on his friends.

Quickly he grabbed his bow and was thankful it was retrieved with his horse. He fumbled for an arrow and nocked it on the taut bowstring. Jonathan pulled back carefully and aimed for the beast closest to him. He slowly let out a breath and loosed the arrow. It flew straight and true, into the ear of the nearest creature. The beast dropped without a sound other than the crack of the arrowhead finding bone. Again the assailants stopped and looked around at each other and in the direction of the now dead wolf. This time they did not continue their advance very quickly.

Only four left. I think I can handle that many, thought Sir Jonathan. Slowly he began to creep through the tall grass toward the assailants. Even though he had the familiar butterflies in his stomach, he realized something important. The enemy was stalking the camp, but he was the hunter now.

They will not take one of my King's citizens while I live, he said to himself. *These weapons are not mine but his.*

He nocked another arrow and waited for the right time. Gradually, the wolves began to ease forward again. This time Sir Jonathan aimed for the farthest beast on the opposite side. His aim was lethal but it hit a little off. Instead of the head it hit the back. The wolf dropped, mortally wounded but not yet dead. It let out a howl, a snarl, and a curse. The other wolf-beasts stood up immediately and began to search for the attacker.

Sir Jonathan was already running forward with his lance and sword. The first beast to see him growled and turned to him, but just a second too late. The knight had already hurled his lance with all of his might, trusting the King's craftsmanship. It was the first time he had used this weapon in battle. The smell of the enemy reminded the knight he was not in training. This was war.

Sir Jonathan's lance hit in the center of the beast's chest, turning its growl to a high-pitched yelp. It dropped to the ground, howling in pain, snarling and pawing at the dirt. The other two turned to attack Sir Jonathan.

By this time the sounds of the growing battle had stirred the citizens. Margritte screamed shrilly and Bjorn quickly threw wood and hay onto the fire. The light from the fire lit the sky so everyone could see Sir Jonathan fighting the wolves. One enemy beast stood on its two hind feet and swung a flail with all its might. Sparks showered off of Sir Jonathan's sword as he blocked the attacks. The other creature circled behind the knight, hoping to attack without being hit with the broadsword Sir Jonathan brandished.

Just as the wolf in the back pounced toward Sir Jonathan, Bjorn shouted a warning. The knight sidestepped and swung his sword backward, catching the beast in midair. It let out a gasping screech as it hit the ground hard. It tried to scurry sideways, but Jonathan was already coming down with a second—and final—blow. The beast never moved again.

The enemy with the flail started to advance, then thought better of it when Jonathan turned and charged. It bounded off into the night, cursing and snarling as it fled. When it had run far enough out of the light to be safe, it let out a low howl in the direction of Felwood—an eerie, moaning howl that sent shivers through the spines of the King's citizens.

A few seconds of silence passed after the howl died away. Then deep in the dark forest, several low howls answered the escaping enemy.

"Is everyone okay?" asked Sir Jonathan, still breathing hard from the sudden battle. His ears rang and his heart pounded. He suddenly felt overwhelmingly exhausted and thirsty. He leaned on his sword, trying to hide the trembling in his hands and knees.

"We are fine," answered Bjorn. "Those were Greys. They guarded the dungeon the King rescued me from when I first became a citizen. I wish we could have killed that last one. I really hate them."

"I have never seen them before, and I would be fine if I never saw them again," said Sir Jonathan as he exhaled. His breathing was returning to normal as he asked a second time, "Is everyone okay?"

Bjorn looked around and counted. He quickly looked back at Sir Jonathan, his face contorted in alarm. "We're missing one! There are only seven!"

Sir Jonathan ran to the center of the camp and began to count for himself. How could the beasts have grabbed one? He only counted seven. His heart raced. He felt nauseated. He could not lose one. He just could not. He drew his sword and intended to chase down the last Grey. He would make him talk.

Then he saw a lump move under a blanket beneath the wagon. He moved closer and picked up the blanket with his sword, revealing a little girl curled up in a ball. Margritte's dirty face looked up as she whimpered, "Are they gone?"

"Yes, and we thought you were, too!" gasped Sir Jonathan as he scooped her up and placed her next to the fire. Another citizen gave her a hug and sat next to her.

Slowly the panicked knight began to calm down. He shuddered at the thought of losing one. He could not imagine anything worse than losing little Margritte to those filthy creatures.

Sir Jonathan mounted up. "Stay close to the fire. Bjorn, take this," he said, passing his axe. "Keep watch and prepare to move out. I am going to scout around to make sure there are no more."

Bjorn looked at the axe in his hand for a moment as if recognizing a long lost friend. He blinked a few times, as if trying to return to reality. He was holding an axe, forged in the City Beautiful and made for battle. The last time he was armed was the day he was captured. He realized, to some degree, he was returning to duty; to serving the King. Bjorn nodded to Jonathan and turned to scan the darkness surrounding the camp.

Sir Jonathan wheeled the horse and began to ride a circuit around the camp. The fields were still. In the distance, the sky slowly crept from black to dark grey. The sun would be coming up soon. Sir Jonathan looked off where they had come from and studied the tree line. It was still dark, but he could barely make out some shapes.

Was that movement? Was that a light? He saw a few dim lights from torches among the edge of the forest. It looked like the enemy was gathering for another attack. There would certainly be more on the next assault. It was time to get the King's citizens to the city. There was no telling when the next attack would come or how strong it would be.

"Bjorn, load them into the wagon. We have to move," said Sir Jonathan, trying not to sound alarmed. Bjorn, however, knew what Jonathan was thinking and moved with purpose.

In the distance a low howl echoed through the forest. It was answered by several more throughout the woods. Bjorn looked at Jonathan and nodded in silent agreement. Things were about to get worse.

Jonathan put the rest of the wood on the fire to make it seem like they were still there. He also threw the leftover meat on the coals as well. Enemy or not, a wolf will smell meat. Then the wagon moved out with the knight in the lead. The first rays of the sun peeked between trees in the distance, but it was still rather dark. Sir Jonathan hoped his ruse would put enough room between them so he could slip away with his charges. He had to succeed. They were counting on him. He did not feel like the same soldier that ran days before.

They rounded a hill and descended down a small grade. The road straightened and after some time they crossed a little bridge with woods on each side. The natural restriction looked like a good place for an ambush. Sir Jonathan stiffened and readied his lance as they went through. He was prepared for an attack, but none came. On the other side of the bridge, the road led upward and the trees around the bridge gave way to tall grass. The sky was becoming lighter and the countryside was passing from grey to dawn.

They had gone just a little farther when they heard a dreadful commotion in the distance. The Greys were ravaging the camp. Their deception had worked! The sound of the attack was chilling, and caused the horses to quicken their pace. One citizen moved to the back of the wagon and stared behind them into the distance.

As they rounded the next hill, they saw the city. What a welcome sight! The first things Sir Jonathan noticed were the banners and walls. It meant safety. They were close, and he allowed himself to smile.

A citizen called out, "They are coming after us, Sir Jonathan! I see them chasing us—at least a dozen or more!"

Sir Jonathan replied, "Bjorn, take the wagon to the gates. I'll follow when you're clear."

"Yes, sir!" answered Bjorn, grabbing the axe in one hand and the reins in the other. "Everyone, hold on and get down!"

Bjorn cracked the reins and the horse began to gallop. The

wagon, not made for high speed travel, began to croak and creak as it strained. Little muffled screeches squeaked out with every bump.

Sir Jonathan wheeled his horse and galloped toward the bridge. He would not be able to see an attack coming from the side, but the bridge created a funnel. They would have to come through him.

The morning sky burned orange and lit the countryside with a warming haze. Jonathan could see at least twenty dark shapes coming down the hill. He held his shield in his left hand and readied his lance with his right. He was sure he could hold them long enough to allow the wagon to reach the gates. Even though he was nauseous again, he smiled at the thought of being successful in his quest, even if his own outcome was in doubt.

The beasts were now in a full charge. Sir Jonathan lowered his face- plate on his helmet and decided to charge down the bridge at the advancing enemy. He was sure he could take out at least five and break up their formation. He really did not know what his plan would be after the charge.

Just then he heard hooves thundering behind him. He turned to see an amazing and welcome sight. At least a dozen knights roared up behind him. One carried the King's crest on a bright yellow banner. All of them looked genuinely eager to fight. Jonathan noticed their shields were dinged and banged up. One bore three large gashes down the length of it, as if from a giant claw. That knight's helmet also had a severe dent, and the knight himself had a patch over one eye. The squadron of soldiers looked ready for anything.

"Hail in the name of the One King, Sir Knight, and good morning!" boomed the voice of a large knight who was obviously in charge. "Your friends said you are Sir Jonathan the Slight and you are being pursued. I am Captain Tanganye. May we join you?"

The captain was riding a monstrous horse that looked even bigger beside the small knight.

Without waiting for an answer, he turned to the other knights,

"Men, form a line abreast on Sir Jonathan." He smiled and took his place next to the young knight's horse. "Shield and lance! Prepare to charge on Jonathan's order!" bellowed the captain.

At Tanganye's order the knights lined up and brought their lances down. Jonathan was speechless. Their assistance brought on the wave of courage he needed at that moment. He turned back to the bridge and looked for the enemy.

Where were they? The charging dark shapes had melted into the tall grass moving in the wind. Not one Grey could be seen.

The knights waited but the attacking enemy never reappeared, much less attempted to cross the bridge.

"It appears there will be no battle before breakfast, young friend. Pity. My men were hoping for a good fight to begin the day." With that, the entire formation of soldiers laughed.

"I don't feel like I have earned my breakfast now. I think I shall only eat six eggs instead of the usual," chirped an exceedingly skinny knight. The rest of the company of knights roared in laughter.

A knight farther up the hill whistled to signal Sir Tanganye.

"Your friends have arrived. Shall we join them? The enemy does not mind attacking a wagon, but a squadron of knights seems to make them reconsider. They are smelly, but they are not foolish."

The knights fell into formation and rode for the city. Sir Jonathan enjoyed being surrounded by other knights and listening to the thunder of hooves. Entering the city gates was quite a relief—and amazing. He had not yet seen one of the King's cities.

The first detail Jonathan noticed was that it was a fortress. Rough-hewn stone walls surrounded the city. Archers and soldiers alike manned the towers and looked vigilantly in all directions. They were ready for battle, it seemed. Inside the walls were dozens of buildings. And there was laughter everywhere. Jonathan's first thought was, *I wonder if the City Beautiful is like this?* He could not help smiling and enjoying both safety and the realization that he was surrounded by those who loved his King.

As Jonathan dismounted and removed his helmet, Sir Tanganye approached and extended his hands.

He grabbed Jonathan's shoulders and said, "Welcome to the King's city of refuge. I am the Captain of the Guard, a member of the council and assigned by the King to protect this city in his name. It is a pleasure to have you here, Sir Jonathan. I have already begun to prepare accommodations for you for as long as you care to stay. May I inquire as to what unit you are attached to and your mission?"

"Yes sir, certainly. I am one of the King's new knights assigned to the Mounted Light Rangers, of the King's 5th Cavalry. I am serving under Sir Robert the Wise. These citizens were being held in a dungeon in Felwood. We raided the dungeon, defeated the keeper of the dungeon, and rescued these citizens. My orders were to see them safely here and deliver them to your care."

"And so you have, Sir Jonathan," replied Sir Tanganye. "I know your captain, Sir Robert. He delivered the King's terms to me many years ago when I was chained in a dungeon and sentenced to death. It was a long time ago, but I will never forget the sight of him jumping into that swarm of vile enemies for me. You are welcome here, my friend. But I have heard the 5th is moving toward the Great East. Is that true?"

"Yes sir. As soon as I rejoin them we will be on the move," answered Jonathan. He could see concern in Sir Tanganye's eyes as if he knew something the young knight did not yet know. He quickly changed the subject.

"May I show you to a warm meal and a safe bed for the night?" asked his new friend.

"Of course. Thank you very much, but first I need to check on my charges. Several are in need of medical care and I am sure all of them are hungry."

Sir Tanganye smiled and put his arm around him. "They are already being looked after. Our physician is tending to one and the other seven are eating a warm meal in a warm inn. Your quarters are upstairs in the same place, so you can check on them on your way to your room."

Sir Jonathan agreed and they began to walk toward the inn. The city was welcoming and friendly. It seemed like a wonderful place. Citizens were everywhere and Jonathan heard laughter and pleasant conversation. He felt a great joy at being around others like him.

"You are assigned here? As Captain of the Guard?" asked the knight.

"Yes. I have been here for almost twelve years as Captain and as a city guard for seven before that."

"You served with Sir Robert before then?" asked Jonathan as they walked toward the inn. So many people smiled and waved. One came by and without a word gave him a large cup of cool water. It was sweet to the taste and refreshed him from head to toe.

"He trained me in my duties here. He is one of my dearest friends and most trusted advisors. You are fortunate to have him training you. Here we are," said the Captain as he opened the door of the inn.

The inn was warm and cozy, with great fireplaces on every wall. Something savory was cooking in large kettles over the fires and the smell of freshly baked bread flooded the room. Tables covered the floor and citizens ate, laughed, and talked together. Jonathan had never seen anything more inviting in all of his life. He had never even imagined a place like this existed, short of the Great City itself.

Sir Jonathan looked around and saw his new friends eating and drinking together. Bjorn was listening to Margritte tell a story and was laughing between bites. Sir Jonathan felt a great sense of relief. They were safe.

"See? Mission accomplished!" laughed Sir Tanganye. "Please, sit!"

Sir Jonathan sat on a bench and a very kind citizen placed a plate in front of him. It had a piping hot meat pie with a roll on the side. Sir Tanganye sat across from him with a plate also stacked with food. Jonathan suddenly remembered how hungry he felt.

The two began to eat in silence. Within just a few minutes Sir Jonathan's plate was clean, and fatigue began to set in. Jonathan's head was spinning with questions, but his eyes were heavy.

"Your things are in your room. Second floor, second door. Please rest as long as you need. Something tells me you did not sleep much last night?" assumed his new friend with a grin.

"Not even a quick doze. I am ready to pass out right here. I am deeply grateful."

"The service of the King is adventurous but at times not as comfortable as one would like," said Tanganye thoughtfully. "I would not think of you as rude if you went to bed now. I will watch your charges."

"Good night, sir," said the knight. Sir Jonathan grabbed another roll and began to munch on it as he went upstairs. He opened his door just as a young girl wearing the insignia of a knight of the city was turning his covers back.

"Welcome to the city and our inn. Please rest well. When you are hungry, come downstairs. If you need anything, let me know. You are most welcome here for as long as you care to be here." She smiled, curtsied, and left the room.

Sir Jonathan started to loosen his boots but gave up, toppled onto the bed, and fell fast asleep.

Jonathan awoke to a noise and the smell of food cooking downstairs. He stood up and saw it was growing dark outside. Apparently he had slept all day!

He looked around his room and realized someone had washed his clothes and cleaned his muddy boots. He had slept right through somebody coming into his room. He was glad to be in a city and not sleeping in the cold forest.

Sir Jonathan walked downstairs and sat at an empty table. As soon as he arrived, the same knight who helped him in the room came with a plate of food and a mug of hot apple cider.

"Sleep well?" she asked.

"Yes, thank you. Are you the one I should thank for washing my clothes?"

"Yes. You may thank me. Many of the others have thanked me already for washing your clothes, as well," she teased.

They both laughed. As he took a bite of stewed beef and vegetables, an older knight with shiny armor sat down across from him. Sir Jonathan noticed immediately that the knight was very well dressed. Apparently the innkeepers could work wonders on clothes, armor, and boots because this knight was spotless and ready for a parade.

"Greetings, young man. I am Sir George. I saw you come in last night. I would have introduced myself then, but I was giving some last minute instructions to a group of younger knights heading to the front. They are part of a heavy horse squadron for reconnaissance and information gathering. They are headed to the Great East, I believe. Extremely hazardous duty. As I have extensive knowledge in these matters, I offered my services to instruct."

Sir Jonathan was chewing and was about to ask a question, but Sir George continued.

"To be honest, I am quite skilled and knowledgeable in many different forms of warfare and tactics. Military maneuvers and strategies are my specialty. I hear you are rather new to the Light Mounted Rangers. Rumor has it your unit is also headed to the Great East. You do know it is said a terrible dragon guards the entrances to those lands? It is no easy thing to fight a dragon, Jonathan. I would be happy to give any advice and counsel you might need," said Sir George confidently. He flashed a toothy smile as he looked down a rather long, crooked nose.

Sir Jonathan started to thank him but was cut off by Sir George again, "I heard you tangled with Greys. Nasty creatures! But there are worse things out there. Some evils in these areas have never even been identified. Did you know that?"

Sir Jonathan shook his head. He decided not to attempt another question and kept eating. As it turned out, he would not have had an opportunity to ask. Sir George went on, "Well, it's a good thing. You are much too new to succeed against evil such as that. I, on the other hand, know much about them. I'll give you all of their weaknesses and strategies for victory."

Sir Jonathan continued to eat and listen as Sir George spoke for what seemed like hours about all manner of beasts and evils. He told stories of fights and battles and encounters that were unbelievably frightening.

How had this knight survived? He must be a great warrior, thought the young knight. Finally George paused to take a drink.

"Sir George, tell me, how did you survive such battles?"

"Well, it has not been easy," replied the knight with a far off look in his eye.

"We just battled in Felwood. The dungeon was awful but it does not sound as bad as your experiences," said Sir Jonathan. "We also found a trap door. The rest of my group assaulted the hidden entrance when I left to escort the freed prisoners here."

"Humph," grunted Sir George. "They certainly would have wanted me to help assault the rest of the dungeon instead of escort duty. My skills are in the dangerous work without a doubt." He leaned in for emphasis. He was so close, Jonathan was afraid his long nose would get in the way if he were to try and drink his cider. "It is not easy, but I do the important work, and with time, you will be doing the important things as well. The escort could have waited. It makes me wonder if your captain had any other motives in sending you away," mused the older knight.

Sir Jonathan frowned. He was thinking about Sir Robert's words regarding service and how each task has its own importance. Was his friend wrong? Sir Robert was a mighty warrior for sure, but Sir George seemed to have fought dragons and much more powerful creatures. Sir Jonathan was a bit confused.

As Sir George continued speaking with the young knight, Sir Tanganye interrupted them. "I am sorry to interrupt your dinner conversation, but I was wondering if I could have a word with Sir Jonathan?"

"Of course, sir," replied Sir Jonathan, jumping up from his chair. "Please forgive me, sir. I would like to hear more when I return. Will you be here or are you leaving soon? I would hate to miss the end of our conversation," said Sir Jonathan to Sir George.

Sir George shifted his eye toward the captain, then away and over the room. "Oh, I will be here. I am happy to pass along what experiences I have had to those who need training," replied Sir George.

The captain of the guard escorted the young knight to the city wall. They climbed up a ladder and passed by some guards to the embattlements and a lookout tower. In the tower, Sir Tanganye pointed to the forest in the distance. A column of black smoke rose from deep in the forest.

"It would appear Sir Robert and your rangers have found the trap door and whatever it led to, and set it on fire as well," said the captain.

Sir Jonathan smiled. It made him feel good to see evidence of his friends hard at work. Then he recalled Sir George's words and his eyes fell a little.

"Sir Tanganye, may I ask you a question?" he inquired meekly.

"Of course, friend," came the quick response. "I was rather hoping you would, after overhearing some of your dinner conversation."

"Do you ever—well . . . desire to be out there facing the enemy and doing the important work? Does it ever bother you to remain here? You have been in this city a long time. Do you wish to be somewhere else?" asked the young knight.

"It sounds like you have been speaking with Sir George. Tell me, what is important work? No, don't answer. Let me ask another question. Who gives the orders, the servant or the master?"

"The master, of course," replied Sir Jonathan. He had the same feeling in his stomach as when Sir Robert was teaching him a hard lesson after asking a hasty question.

"Right you are. Listen carefully, young friend. It is the duty of the knight to tell the King, 'I will serve,' and it is the province of the King to decide where and when those battles are fought. Some of us are messengers, some rangers, some innkeepers, and some guards in a city of refuge. All positions are honorable and important if done in service to the King. In fact, it is a disservice to the King and a dishonor for a knight to desire a post outside of the King's placing for the reason of wanting an 'important' job. Does this make sense?"

"Yes sir," answered the knight quickly. Then he paused, mulled over the words, and continued, "It does. And may I say you sound a lot like Sir Robert?"

"You have honored me, Sir Jonathan," laughed the big knight as he slapped Sir Jonathan on the back.

A friendly lookout archer chimed in, "The King doesn't ask where we want to serve. He chooses and we serve, and we all find we are the better for it. He knows where we should be, and that is where he puts us. And I would not want to be anywhere else. One day he will send a messenger for me to call me to the City Beautiful and he is going to find me where he put me. I'll be standing watch on this wall with my sword and my bow. Even if there were not honors and rewards without number for faithful service, it will be honor and reward aplenty to be found where the One King has ordered me to be." The archer turned to scan the wood line. As he did, Jonathan saw a very large and genuine smile on his face. No doubt he was thinking about the day he would see the King.

Sir Jonathan looked out over the wall toward Felwood and the smudge of smoke as he thought about their words. He remembered reading something like that in the Kingsbook.

"Thank you both. I understand more and more each day, it seems," said Sir Jonathan.

"And that is the way it should be," encouraged Sir Tanganye. Then he looked in Sir Jonathan's eyes and became very serious. "But that will also depend on who you listen to. Age does not equal wisdom necessarily, nor should youth be despised as foolishness. Truth is truth and error is error, regardless of from whom they come. Choose your counselors carefully. Do not lend your ear to anyone who only *talks* of battle. Think about these things." The captain leaned in and made sure he had Jonathan's full attention. "If you will permit me, I have an assignment for you. One Robert gave me so long ago. Ask yourself this question, 'Where should I be today?' Then tomorrow, let's discuss the answer."

They shook hands and Sir Jonathan started back to the inn. He felt like he should head toward the rendezvous, but it was getting dark again and light snow flurries had begun to fall. He decided to spend another night in the city. A winter storm was coming. He thought about the approaching campaign and the words of Sir Tanganye as he stepped back into the inn.

CHAPTER 8

Of Posts and Positions

"Now, little children, abide in Him, so that when
He appears, we may have confidence and not shrink
away from Him in shame at His coming."
– 1 John 2:28

As Sir Jonathan the Slight pondered the good captain's question, he grabbed a mug of hot cider and sat down next to the fire. He gazed at the coals and thought about Sir Tanganye's words as well as Sir George's as the dull roar of friends talking and laughing filled the inviting space. The wood crackled and popped. The warmth was exactly what Jonathan needed.

"Well, hello, friend." Jonathan looked up to see Sir George standing next to him. "I was hoping I would find you. It seems it is possible you might need a little more training and counsel, and I thought I would offer my services. It is important work being a trainer of knights and soldiers!"

"Yes, I imagine so," said Jonathan.

The pristine appearance of the older knight struck Sir Jonathan again. Sir Robert had nasty battle marks in his armor. Sir Tanganye had the look of someone who spent night after night on the wall, regardless of weather. Even his boots looked old and used. The claw marks on his shield combined with the eye patch gave strength and force to his words.

But not Sir George. Every inch of his armor seemed to shine. His boots looked new, and every button was bright. In that moment, Jonathan realized an important truth.

"Sir George, may I ask you a few questions?" queried Sir Jonathan.

"Of course, young friend," came the reply. "Many people do."

"Are you assigned to the city?"

"Um . . . well, no. I am not, but I serve here. I live here," answered Sir George as he looked around the inn.

"Oh. Well, where are you assigned? I am just curious. You must have seen lots of battles already with your experience," continued Sir Jonathan.

Sir George looked through a snow-covered window for a few moments before responding. He cleared his throat before answering.

"Hmmm . . . well, I was assigned to a Long Range Mounted Regiment stationed in a city of rest far from here. Our orders have been to go to the lands in the Great East to spy out the enemy's activity and look for citizens. But that land is far away. There are very few cities of refuge there. My talents and experiences are of much more use here," justified the older knight. "Who is there to teach and train so far away?"

"Oh. Where did you see action, exactly? What knights were you with? Were you able to see any citizens rescued?" questioned the young knight. He was genuinely curious, but at the same time, things did not seem right.

"Well, I have read a lot about war and have talked to others, but I really haven't—well, I, um . . . I haven't been outside of the city much, to be honest," stammered Sir George as he looked down. "And I do not hold a regular position inside the city walls because I am too valuable a resource to be tied down. But I know so much. I have studied so much. You can trust me." As he spoke, he examined his uniform inch by inch, flicking an imaginary speck of dust from his tunic.

"But you aren't dwelling where you have been assigned? Do you go out on patrol every now and then?" asked Sir Jonathan. He was desperately looking for a way to not discount the words of his new friend.

"Well, I give advice and counsel wherever I can. And I have plans to join my assigned unit soon. I just feel so needed here. There are times where I believe the City Guard is not prepared for certain attacks from particular enemies. I try to trust my leadership, but I seem to know more at times and, out of concern, of course, I feel the need to help out in my own way. I have knowledge about these enemies so I feel somewhat useful. Also, to be honest, it has been a very cold fall. That means a frigid winter. I believe I will wait until spring to join my unit," reasoned Sir George while fidgeting with a shiny button on his tunic.

"And what about last year or the year before that? I don't want to sound rude at all, but have you ever been on a campaign with your assigned forces?" asked Sir Jonathan directly.

"Are you questioning me? I am very important and knowledgeable in many things regarding this war. I am needed in different places. I have been where *I* believed I was needed most. I will be joining my company soon. Perhaps I will join them when the snow melts. But I do not need a new knight questioning my service," retorted Sir George.

"I meant no offense. Truly, I did not. I am very new; that is all. You have given me a great deal of strategy and advice, and I was just curious where you had gained this advice. It does not sound like you have gained it in the field, though."

Sir George was opening his mouth to reply when the door to the inn opened. The wind was picking up and it whistled through the hall, causing some of the low hanging candles to flicker.

Just then, two knights walked in the back of the inn. They were different. Their armor was shiny and had purple trim. The plumes on their helmets were also purple. One carried a leather satchel and both were heavily armed. They greeted the citizens and knights warmly as they passed. One of them threw a piece of fruit to Bjorn, who was sitting at a table by the door reading the Kingsbook. Bjorn smiled and caught the fruit.

They walked up to the fireplace from behind Sir George, who was just starting to craft another defense.

"Sir George?" asked one of the knights.

"Why, yes it is. What can I do for you, sir?" replied the older knight with a smile as he turned around.

"Sir, we are Kingsguard from the City Beautiful. We have orders to escort you there. You have been called home and are finished with your service here. It is a permanent transfer on the King's orders. We are ready to depart immediately, sir," said the knight warmly with a genuine smile. "The King is anxious to welcome you home as a valued and loved citizen."

"Oh. Really? Is it already time to go to the King's City? I still had things to do, actually," replied the knight nervously.

"Yes, well we are sure you do, but our orders are specific. It is time to go."

"But I really need to join my company. I haven't really been to the front in a while. I should be with them. Do I have time to go there at least for a while?" pleaded Sir George.

"We are afraid not. We thought you would be there as well, but you were not with your company. Someone said we would find you here and so we have. Unfortunately, there is not time to finish any tasks left undone. It is time to go. When the King calls, there is time only to answer. He is anxious and happy to see you. Shall we be off?" asked the Kingsguard.

Jonathan saw real happiness in Sir George's face. Every citizen was excited about being called to the King's City Beautiful. It was a place like no other. It was home. A home free from all battle and hardships. It was where the King lived and ruled. Though his face shone with joy of being called home, sincere regret also flickered in his eyes. Sir George was visibly excited to go but also hesitant. Sir Jonathan grappled with what he witnessed. His thoughts were interrupted by one of the Kingsguard.

"Sir Jonathan the Slight, you fought the Greys well. You brought your charges safely here and managed to survive. May you fare well in the battles ahead and trust the King's wisdom at all times."

"Yes, he is absolutely right," said the other Kingsguard to Jonathan. "It seems your charges are recuperating well. But not all who came into this city in need of rest still need to rest. Some may be ready to rejoin the ranks they were called to serve."

The knight looked over at Bjorn as he spoke and gave Sir Jonathan a powerful and encouraging handshake. "There are many in the Great East who need the King's pardon, but the enemy is difficult and strong. Every sword will be useful," he continued. "You are going into dangerous lands, but you are not going alone. Long live the King."

"Long live the King," answered the knight.

And with that the three were off and headed for the City Beautiful, leaving the young knight alone with his thoughts.

That night, Sir Jonathan slept fitfully. He would awaken with a start but could not remember why he was breathing so fast or why he felt so alarmed. Then, in the early hours of dawn, he began to slowly wake from sleeping. In the fog of returning to consciousness he remembered his horrible dreams. He dreamed that several times during the night he was awakened with the Kingsguard coming to get him, but he was old and grey and still in the inn. He had not left to serve. He had lived out his life like Sir George; he was always talking but never doing. And in his old age he realized he had wasted so many days talking that there were no longer days for doing. In one nightmare he had seen Sir Robert and his friends surrounded by hordes of goblins and fighting a hopeless battle. *"Where is Jonathan?"*

he could hear them shouting as their lines were overrun with the enemy.

He sat up like a bolt of lightning. He ripped the blankets off and his feet hit the cold floor. He dressed quickly and prepared his things for immediate travel. Jonathan determined he would be found where he was assigned.

But first, he had to see someone.

Sir Jonathan ran down the stairs and toward the door of the inn. The innkeeper who was delivering plates to tables tossed him a hot roll as he ran past her. He smiled and took a bite.

Sir Jonathan wrapped his cloak around him to fight away the cold. He ran down the main street of the city to the headquarters of the captain. He walked in quietly. Sir Tanganye was discussing increasing patrols in the area of Felwood with three Sergeants at Arms. He was also giving instructions on increasing the training regimen with all citizens willing. When they were finished, he dismissed them and turned to face Jonathan.

"Good morning, my young friend. How did you sleep?" asked the captain.

"Truthfully, not well at all," answered the young knight.

"Good. I was hoping you would not," laughed the Captain.

"Really? Why?" asked Sir Jonathan.

"Did you think about my question?"

"Yes. Yes, I did think about it. And I had dreams about not being in the right place. I did not rest well at all in your restful city," laughed Sir Jonathan.

"This is a city of refuge. You are always welcome. But you are under orders and they take you far from here. It would not be good to be comfortable in a place you were not posted," said Sir Tanganye with a warm, fatherly look.

"That is my question. You. You *live* here. You are always here. Sir George lived here. He has just been recalled to the City Beautiful. Both of you *live* here. Yet when he left, he was happy, but also showed loss and regret. But you seem content. I am not content. I am restless. In fact, I am leaving as soon as my questions are answered. We are all in the same place, but it seems we all feel differently. What am I missing?" gasped Sir Jonathan desperately. His questions were gushing out like grain from a ripped sack.

"Slow down. Listen carefully. You were called and put under orders to serve with the mounted rangers for now. It is the place you are to serve. If you were to stay here, you would be losing something very valuable that you can never replace."

"Time," offered Sir Jonathan. "I would be losing days."

"Exactly!" exclaimed Sir Tanganye. "Minutes, hours, and days you can never recover would be slipping away. Sir George became comfortable in a place he was not posted. *He substituted talk of battle for battle.* He traded the reputation of a dragon killer for actually facing any enemy in the King's name. His regret was that he wore the title of knight without ever hearing the frightful sound of steel crashing in conflict or the thunder of horses' hooves in a desperate battle to save those precious to our Captain and King," said Sir Tanganye passionately.

"Sir, have you ever felt restless?" asked Sir Jonathan cautiously. He regretted the fact he always seemed to ask awkward questions at awkward times.

"Absolutely! I did feel restless in the past," came the answer with a bright smile.

"Why not now? What changed?" asked the young knight.

"I used to hear the stories of the knights who came here for rest. These knights had fought dragons, ghouls, and a host of other terrors and evils. I wanted to be with them. I wanted to be in the 'valuable' jobs. Then an older and more patient knight showed me what it meant to be in the sworn service of our King. He said, *'It isn't the epic battle against impossible odds that makes a servant of the King a knight of great worth. It is the daily discipline of rising to march in the direction his Captain orders that makes a knight a mighty man of valor. In fact, no knight that has ever been fit to fight in the most epic of battles became so without steady faithfulness in the smallest of tasks."*

"Sir Robert!" exclaimed the young knight. "I heard those words not three days ago."

"You would do well to listen and take them to heart, then. I am content here because this is my post. This is where the King has assigned me for now. I would be settling for lesser things if I were to raid a dragon's lair and make off with its head. From the innkeeper to the messenger to the dragon slayer, all are part of the King's army and dependent on each other for the prosecution of this war. None are more 'important' than the other, though some are more visible than others. Embrace the role you have been given and pursue it passionately. Pursue it today, Sir Jonathan. Do not tarry," said Sir Tanganye in a fatherly tone.

"I am already packed. I'll be leaving within the hour. And I will not be going alone, either," replied Sir Jonathan.

"Good. Remember, the location doesn't matter one bit so long as you are where you are assigned by the King. Faithful service to the King is always defined by doing the 'whats' and the 'wheres' the King desires. The difference is I *serve* here and Sir George *passed his time* here."

"Thank you, Captain. Though my time here was short, it was incredibly valuable, thanks to your counsel. I am grateful." With that Jonathan attempted to shake the burly captain's hand, but was instead caught in a bear-like hug.

"It is always a pleasure to meet a servant of the King and a friend of Robert's!" he thundered.

Sir Jonathan returned to the inn. The sun was just coming up, but the sky was grey and there was a chill in the air. He felt a few snowflakes on his face. He knew it was only the beginning of a storm.

Jonathan walked into the inn and looked around the tables. There was Bjorn. He walked over and sat down across from him.

Bjorn was almost finished with a plate of eggs. The innkeeper came over with a steaming hot plate of eggs, meat, and bread.

"Eat," she said.

"Thank you, but I don't have time. I have to go."

"Which is precisely why you should eat," the knight countered as she poured his tea.

Sir Jonathan laughed and took a bite.

"Leaving? Where are you going?" asked Bjorn.

"I am off to rejoin my unit," replied Sir Jonathan between bites. The eggs were really warm and slightly runny in the center, just the way he liked them. The crispy brown meat filled an emptiness in his stomach he had only just realized. *"The knight serving the plates of food may be the wisest in the entire citadel,"* he thought.

"Before I leave, however, I have a question for you, Bjorn," he said between bites.

"Sure. What is your question, Sir Jonathan?"

"When you were captured, what were you doing? Who were you with?"

"I was just starting my training to be a knight. I was with another knight and we were riding on the edge of the forest. The enemy ambushed us and we got separated. I rode through the woods for some time before I realized I was hopelessly lost. I came upon an old man who said he could help me. Before I knew it, I was a prisoner," recounted Bjorn.

"And now, what will you do, Bjorn?" asked Sir Jonathan intently.

"I am not sure. I am not sure what I should do," answered Bjorn. "I do not even know where my other knights are. I might be the only one left, for all I know. This town is safe and a great place to rest. Perhaps I should stay. Besides, I am not worthy to be a knight. I was so easily deceived so early in my service. Instead of being profitable, I became a liability. I am not sure I measure up."

"I do know how you feel. We have made some of the same mistakes. And the truth is, neither one of us is worthy of this task.

Look at me. I am smaller than any knight I have met. And you—well, you and I were both deceived in the very beginning of our training. Regardless, you were called to be a knight and you swore to serve your King, yes?" asked the young knight.

"Yes, I did," answered Bjorn a little more resolutely, even a little defensively.

"And do you intend to keep this vow?" pressed Sir Jonathan.

"I . . . I do. I will keep my vow," said Sir Bjorn with growing conviction.

"Then on your feet and fill your boots. Grab your things. It is time to keep your vow. Join my squadron and me until you find yours," said Sir Jonathan the Slight.

"I am afraid. I am afraid I will be deceived again—that I will fail. I am not adequate for the life of a knight," said Bjorn despondently.

"No. You are not adequate. None of us are. But the King is mighty. His weapons are powerful. I would rather be found on the battlefield at the end of my days than somewhere I was not ordered to be. So I am leaving and I want you to go with me. The only question is, *Will you serve your King?* Or will you let your fear get in the way of a life well lived?"

Bjorn frowned for a few moments as he thought about what Jonathan had said. Then he looked up and grinned at his new friend. Jonathan had his answer.

"I'll get my things." And with that the youngest knight rose from the table and bounded up the stairs.

CHAPTER 9

Darkwood

"But he does not know that the dead are there . . . ."
– Proverbs 9:18a

Captain Tanganye saw them to the gates. He was encouraging, yet cautious. He knew of the dangers ahead. One of the Captain's Sergeant at Arms was concerned and offered a few words of encouragement and warning.

"The King is strong enough to meet any challenge. His weapons will not fail you so long as you remember He is the one who powers them, friends. However, be ever vigilant. The trail you are taking is very dangerous."

Tanganye nodded in agreement, then put his arm around Jonathan and continued, "You are sure Sir Robert wants you to meet him in that valley?" Jonathan nodded. "There is only one road there, and it has been reported to be quite hazardous. You will have to go through a forest we call 'Darkwood.' It is known for its horrors. There is an evil in the woods that we have not located or even fully identified. It has been poorly scouted. We know only that it draws in everyone alike. Some we do not hear from again. Use extreme care. The Kingsbook says to stay on the road in these kinds of forests. Not everything is as it seems—unless it is trying to end you, then it is exactly what it seems," Captain Tanganye finished as they all chuckled a little.

"The enemy surely knows of the knights answering the King's command to invade the Great East. The enemy prizes that realm. He will double and triple his attempts to keep you from going, you can be sure of that. He hates the King and his soldiers. When you decided to follow the King to the Eastern realm, you changed from a target to a hated foe. But take heart—your King is mightier than the enemy and his dragon guarding that realm," said Sir Tanganye. "And you know where you are going?"

"Yes sir. Sir Robert pointed out the place. We have orders to scout the areas around two hills on the other side just at the foothills of a mountain range. That will be our start into the Great East. It should be interesting," replied Sir Jonathan. He was trying to hide the fact that at some times he wished he were assigned to the city wall.

Sir Tanganye smiled, "I understand. Keep to the road and keep to your guard, young knights. Remember, all you have ever needed to know is in the Kingsbook, and all you have ever needed in the way of weaponry the King has provided. Trust him, my friends. Your life depends on it."

"We will, Captain," said Sir Jonathan.

Sir Tanganye turned to Bjorn. He was sitting on his horse ready to depart. He did not look like the same Bjorn that arrived a few days ago. His cheeks had color and he was wearing the armor and uniform of a knight.

"What is your name?" asked the captain of Bjorn with a very serious tone.

"Bjorn," came the meek reply.

"No. You are Sir Bjorn, a King's Knight and soldier of the City Beautiful. Do not forget that fact. When you ride out of this city for battle, leave any doubt behind," answered Sir Tanganye with conviction.

"I will. I am Sir Bjorn," he corrected himself with confidence.

"Remember this: Make haste. Do not delay and stop to smell flowers or see the sights. A pardon is only good news if it reaches the dungeon before the executioner," encouraged a Sergeant at Arms.

"Brothers, stay on the road. If you venture off for any reason, you may not be heard from again. Please tell Sir Robert the Royal High Ambassador that his friend and pupil is holding his post for the King. Fare well, friends. Long live the King!" called the Captain.

His troops on the wall thundered, *"Long Live the King!"*

Half of a dozen knights rode out on either side of the two rangers. The Sergeant at Arms rode next to Sir Jonathan and they traded stories on how the King had rescued them both from slavery. The city guard rode with them for almost half of the day. By this time, they were past the rolling hills and farms of the area and the terrain was becoming more rough and rocky. When they approached the rocky crags, a thick fog began to cover the countryside.

"Sir Jonathan, the forest begins just ahead, but the fog obscures it. Unfortunately, we must return to the city now to get there before dark. The enemy is aware of our push into his territory and has increased attacks on the refuge city. We will be needed for the increased watches and training. We wish you well," said the Sergeant at Arms as he reached out to shake the knight's hand. "Oh, and the Captain sent this for you. It is a letter for Sir Robert and a sack of food for you both. Godspeed."

"Thank you for your kindness. We'll see you again, my friend," replied Sir Jonathan.

The squadron of knights turned and left Sir Jonathan and Sir Bjorn alone. They looked around at the foggy landscape. It was quiet and desolate. Bjorn started to say something about how different it felt to be alone again instead of surrounded by laughing citizens and friends, but he knew Jonathan was thinking the same thing.

Jonathan felt isolated, but he did not feel alone. He was also excited to be on the move again. He breathed deeply. It was cold, but Jonathan did not feel cold yet. He was too excited.

The two knights continued on. As they approached the forest, they could smell it before they could see it. It smelled wet with decay. After a few more minutes of travel, the shapes of massive trees appeared through the fog. The tree trunks looked like great columns, and the trees were so tall that their tops were obscured by the fog. Even though it was just after noon, the woods were ominously dark and dusky.

"How long will we be in the forest, Jonathan?"

"About two days, I believe. At least, that is what the map seems to say. If we keep moving, we may be out sooner. How is your armor?" he said, changing the subject.

"The clothes fit fine. The armor does as well. Though I am not sure I have much confidence in my ability to use it," said Bjorn gloomily.

"Sir Robert has made it clear to me on several occasions how important it is to read the Kingsbook for instruction and trust the King's weapons. *It isn't the arm wielding the sword that makes a cut lethal, but the trust in the one who forged the weapon.'* We are not the reason we have success. He is. So, in part, your lack of confidence in your ability is a great thing. But if you don't temper that with great confidence in the King, then you have no hope of surviving battle, much less being victorious," said Sir Jonathan.

As he spoke, he heard the words of the Kingsbook coming out of his mouth and the instructions of his teacher, Sir Robert, as well. As he taught, he was also reminded of the truths himself. He looked over at Bjorn and smiled encouragingly.

"I think I understand. I cannot win; but the King cannot lose," rephrased Sir Bjorn.

"Precisely, Bjorn. The steady trust in the power of your King makes the battle a sure thing," affirmed Sir Jonathan. He smiled when he remembered how he had learned that the hard way. "Besides, if Captain Tanganye was right about these woods, I will need you to watch my back."

They continued on deeper into the forest. The shadows grew and it was harder to tell how long before all light would be gone. The normal sounds of a forest were replaced with sounds the knights did not recognize. Shrill screeches, howls, and hoots echoed through the woods. Occasionally some creature lost its battle with another creature and the sound of the meal-to-be was unnerving. More than once, Sir Jonathan wondered why he had not looked for a better road around this place.

At one point a large creature moved or slithered off to their right. It was massive. The knights dismounted and hid behind a huge moss-covered boulder. The creature was snorting and growling and shuffling along. The knights were terrified. They saw glimpses of scaly skin but could not make out what it was—and that was fine with Jonathan.

Around a bend in the trail, there was a small clearing surrounded by giant tree roots. The fog was closing and darkness was falling.

"Let's camp here tonight, Sir Bjorn. What do you say?"

"Sounds good to me. I'll get a fire going."

Sir Jonathan tied up the horses and pulled out some of the food Sir Tanganye had sent for them. Soon the fire was going and casting shadows on the giant roots that formed the walls of their shelter for the night. The forest was foreboding, but there was something about a camp that Jonathan always liked. A few low branches gave the feeling of being in a small cabin. At one point a very large bat with an upturned nose landed on the branch. It looked at them with large yellowish eyes for a few moments, then flew off.

"I prefer the inn," said Bjorn flatly.

They both snickered at the comment.

The knights ate in silence. Then Bjorn yawned.

"I'll take first watch," "Let's change watch every two hours to stay fresh, okay?"

Bjorn agreed and fell fast asleep. The woods were gloomy in the daytime, but at night they were absolutely awful. Sometimes the night was so dark and thick Jonathan thought it was hard to breathe. He also preferred the inn. All through the night they took turns standing watch over each other and waited for an attack that never came.

The next morning, Bjorn and Jonathan both had the same story. They had heard sounds of something or someone coming close to the camp, but never within range of the fire's light. At one point, Sir Bjorn had thrown a rock near the sound and heard it run a little way. As they compared tales, it was obvious they were being watched.

"We will have to be extra careful today. Whatever watched us last night will undoubtedly want to ambush us today. Stay sharp," warned Sir Jonathan.

"I will, but I am a bit nervous."

"Me too. I knew this forest was bad, I just didn't realize it was this bad," confessed Sir Jonathan. The woods were ominous and foreboding, as though they teemed with death and dread.

They quickly scarfed down bread and cheese, then broke camp. The knights moved out on horseback in single file. Sir Bjorn watched Sir Jonathan move his shield to a ready position and did the same. They did not talk. They steadily watched and continued forward.

The woods seemed to resist the daybreak for a long time. It was gloomy and filled with shadows. The branches hung low and obscured visibility. The forest was rancid with wetness and decay.

Both knights were sure something was watching, but they could not see it. Then, something unexpected happened. They came to a fork in the path.

"Sir Jonathan, is that supposed to be there? I don't remember one on the map," whispered Bjorn.

The young knight did not answer for a few moments. He stared at the map and at the trail. The horses pawed nervously at the ground. Finally, he spoke.

"No. I don't see it on here. We have to make a decision, though.

The one on the right looks like a better path. Of course, that means it is a trap. Let's take the one on the left."

"Agreed," said Sir Bjorn.

They started to ease down the path on the left. The forest gradually grew darker and darker. The trees turned from green to dark green to black. Even the bushes were black. On and on they rode for hours through the morbid forest. The dry air pressed upon their lungs.

"I think I prefer the ambush," said Sir Bjorn, moving a blackish branch out of his way as he rode underneath.

Then the vegetation cleared slightly and the woods became very still. Something inside Sir Jonathan's head screamed in alarm. He gripped his shield and reminded himself that the King's weaponry was more than sufficient.

Just then he heard a click and a series of swooshes. He raised his shield before his brain registered the threat hurtling at him. A crossbow bolt crashed into his shield with a crack. Drawing his sword, he quickly dismounted to take cover. As he leaped over a fallen log, he looked back for Sir Bjorn. His friend was moving too slow. Then he slumped over in his saddle and fell to the ground.

He is hit! thought Sir Jonathan. His heart raced. He looked around for the attackers but could not see anything. He looked at his shield. The black crossbow bolt had lodged in his shield and a green ooze was dripping down. The bolts were poisoned!

Jonathan vaulted back over the log and dashed into the open to reach Bjorn. His friend was not moving, but seemed to be asleep. He grabbed the fallen knight's leather harness and dragged Sir Bjorn to some thick bushes while holding his shield high above them both. Another bolt slammed into his shield and ricocheted into the underbrush.

Once obscured by the thick bushes, he began to look for Bjorn's wound. Seeing a rip in his friend's shirt, Jonathan noticed that a bolt had scratched Bjorn's arm. Apparently that was enough for the poison to take effect. Sir Bjorn was alive, but unconscious.

Jonathan could not see very well in the bushes; he hoped he could not be seen, either. He tried to force some water into Sir Bjorn's mouth. It was difficult, but he did get a few drops down before gulping a few mouthfuls himself. Jonathan then poured water over Bjorn's wound and tried to force the poison back out.

He waited silently, but no further attack came. Bjorn slept soundly.

Sir Jonathan grabbed his sword, raised his shield, and crept out of the bushes. The horses were gone; they had run off in the attack. Jonathan could not blame them. The woods were silent and the fog was creeping back. The forest was rapidly becoming high on the list of Jonathan's least favorite places.

Sir Jonathan agonized over what to do. He could not carry his friend, nor did he want to leave him. If they were both there at nightfall they would surely be overrun and killed. He had to find the horses. *Perhaps they ran down the road*, he thought. The fog seeping into the forest clouded his mind as well. He was unsure of what to do.

Jonathan fought to suppress the panic rising in his heart. The indecision and worry for his friend was as thick as the dreadful forest around them. He did not know what was worse: the coming attack or not knowing what to do. Something had to be done. But what? What would Sir Robert do? What would the King have him do?

He decided to cover any signs of dragging the knight into the bushes. He grabbed a nearby branch and swept over the drag marks, then scrawled a note for Bjorn in the dirt explaining where he was heading. Jonathan concealed his friend as best as he could and slipped quietly down the trail. He was hoping to run into his horses or maybe even someone friendly.

He did neither.

For almost an hour the young knight moved cautiously along the path. Once he raised his shield just in time to block another poisoned bolt. He was being followed; no, he was being stalked. The woods were still as black as ash. It was positively the worst forest he

114

had ever been in. His only consolation was knowing that if the enemy was stalking him, it was not hunting Bjorn.

Then, standing by itself on the side of the road was a patch of green grass. It was so green it almost looked like it had been painted there. It so startled Jonathan that he stood there with his mouth agape for several minutes.

The knight walked up to the oasis of green. He removed his mailed glove and ran his fingers through the grass. He smiled at the thought of something alive in this wretched place. It was cool and refreshing to the touch.

He lifted his eyes and saw that the grass actually formed a very inviting path leading off the trail. It was the only color in the forest and the only life he could see.

I shouldn't leave the road, but this path wasn't on the map. Neither was this trail or the ambush. Perhaps someone is down there who could help me with Sir Bjorn, reasoned the knight.

Ignoring the alarm in his mind and the strict instructions he had received, he stepped off the road onto the grass.

Almost immediately, he saw more grass and even some fruit trees. And the smell—it smelled like fresh flowers in spring even though he knew it was autumn. It was such a contrast of conditions to Jonathan. After only a few steps, he stood in a clearing. The grass was green, bearing lush trees and fragrant flowers all over the yard. The noise of a healthy forest had returned. Birds were chirping and bees were buzzing on the flowers. The sky even looked blue. For a moment, the young knight forgot that he was a soldier and at war.

In the back of the clearing stood a magnificent house. It had great columns around the perimeter and a courtyard in front. Fountains babbled all around the grounds lining the courtyard. How had he missed this paradise from the road?

Then he noticed her.

Lying on a couch eating a piece of fruit and reading a book was the most beautiful woman he had ever laid eyes on. She did not seem to notice him as she took another bite and turned the page. He was unable to look away and began to walk toward her. She set her fruit down and was taking a drink from a golden chalice when she looked up at him and smiled warmly. She had the most beautiful smile and the most enchanting eyes. He could not stop himself from smiling back. He sheathed his sword, removed his helmet, and stepped forward.

"Hello, there. I am very sorry to intrude but I think I have lost my way. I am looking for help and a pair of horses," he stammered while looking at her.

"No intrusion at all," she replied as she put down her book. "What is your name?"

"I am Sir Jonathan. What is your name?"

She smiled even more brightly and sat up straight, "You are a knight? A King's knight? Are you really? I have never met a knight before! I have heard of your kind, but I have never seen one. Your bravery and skills in battle are legendary. I am so pleased to make your acquaintance. Please, sit down and join me? You must be starving."

Sir Jonathan blushed. He could feel his cheeks getting hot and wished he could put his helmet back on. Awkwardly he walked over to a couch facing his hostess and sat down. She poured him a glass—she just happened to have another—and handed it to him. The longer he was there, the more relaxed he felt.

"May I get you something to eat? Would you be interested in refreshing yourself while I hear all about you and your travels? Set your armor over there and relax. I'll be right back with some food," she said sweetly as she stood up. Had she waited for an answer, she would have seen all Jonathan could do was nod an awkward "yes."

As he set down his shield, a small voice in the back of his mind whispered to him. It was almost as if he had forgotten something. But he felt so relaxed. He did not really care to think about alarms and warnings right now. He could smell the sweet aroma of the trees and the flowers and it calmed his mind. He really wanted to relax, not be on guard. Surely somewhere and sometime he could rest and not look over his soldier. Surely.

Sir Jonathan stood up to pace. He could not get the beauty of this place or his stunning hostess out of his mind. He walked a few steps and looked around. He began to have that nagging feeling of forgetting something again. He leaned over and smelled a flower. The feeling disappeared. He felt so relaxed.

As he turned back to the couches and table, something caught the sunlight and his eye. He bent over and picked it up. He was just rubbing the dirt off of the item when his hostess returned with a tray of food.

"You haven't touched your drink. You must be very thirsty. Was it not good?" she asked with a mock pout.

"Oh, no it is very fine. I am just, well—this place is so beautiful. I have never seen anything like it," he said while looking around at all of the beauty surrounding them.

"Oh, there is no place like this, I assure you," she cooed smoothly.

He was still rubbing the item he had found.

"Of course. It is beautiful here. You should stay a while. Please, have a seat and enjoy your food and drink," she said with a bright, beautiful smile. She motioned to the couch she was sitting on. "I have never met a knight before and I simply must know everything about you. Please, have a drink and tell me where you are from."

Sir Jonathan thought about how enchanting everything was and how pleasant his hostess was as well. He smiled. He never would have imagined this.

It's almost too good to be true, he thought. Again, he felt as though he was forgetting something but could not place it. His brain felt foggy. Maybe a rest was exactly what he needed.

She smiled at him as if she could read his mind. He smiled back and shyly looked down at his hands. He could finally see the item he was holding. Nervously he turned it over and over in his hand. It was a button. No, it was a crest. It was a King's crest from a knight's sword.

The fog in his mind began to clear a little.

A knight's sword? But she said he was the first knight she had met . . .

The alarm bell rang louder and louder. He remembered Sir Tanganye's warning, *"Not everything is as it seems unless it is trying to end you . . . ."* He looked up and saw the woman twirling her long hair and smiling at him. He did not smile back. Her smile faded just a little, almost imperceptibly.

"I think you should rest here a while. Set your armor over there—it must be heavy. Have some food. It would be rude not to eat with your hostess," she said persuasively.

She was still smiling, but he could tell there was a slight edge to her voice. Why was she so concerned with him setting his weapons down and eating and drinking with her?

As she leaned over to pour more drink into the goblets, her foot caught the cloth draped over the couch. It moved the corner up a little, revealing a black crossbow and a quiver of jagged crossbow bolts. The bolt tips were dripping with greenish ooze. *Poison.* Jonathan's head began to clear.

She had been the unseen enemy attacking them in the forest!

She moved her foot and quickly glanced up at the knight. She read the look in his eyes and they both knew the pleasantries were over. Her charming gaze changed ever so slightly, but it was more than enough for Jonathan to recognize the look of the enemy and the beginning of a fight.

Sir Jonathan lunged for his shield and held it up just in time to block a viciously strong blow.

How could she be so strong? he thought. Then he glanced at her over the top of his shield. The beautiful face transformed in front of his eyes. The skin seemed to melt, revealing a decayed, partially covered skeleton. The hair had turned from a beautiful brown to a ghoulish white. Her eyes were red and hateful. This was no woman. Her arms and legs were no longer dainty and ladylike. They were bony like a skeleton's, but covered in partially rotted flesh. And she was big. When "she" stood to swing another blow, Sir Jonathan realized it was at least ten feet tall.

It screeched and swung an axe with incredible force. Sir Jonathan blocked it with his shield but the blow made him dizzy, and his head hurt. He tried to get to his feet, but the ghoul was moving very fast. He blocked another blow, but this time he almost lost his shield. He could not get it back in front of him in time. He knew the next strike, already falling, would be the last blow.

Just then the creature wailed. Sir Jonathan looked at it. An arrow was sticking out of one eye. It was desperately trying to remove the arrow with one hand while swinging wildly at the young knight with the other. Sir Jonathan ducked a blow that would have removed his head for sure. He rolled a few times to get out of the way, stood, and darted for the edge of the forest.

The creature had removed the arrow and was looking for Jonathan. The terrified knight almost reached the edge but his vision was becoming blurry. He could not seem to find the forest and turned back to the creature several times. He could also hear arrows whine by and the occasional thwack of a hit. Finally, a voice called out.

"Sir Jonathan! Run to my voice! *Move!*" It was Sir Bjorn.

The young knight stumbled toward the sound of the voice and finally stepped clumsily out of the garden onto the road. As soon as he was clear of the garden, his vision cleared and his senses returned. He was gasping for air. He turned toward the garden and was shocked at what he saw.

There were no green trees. They were all black. The ghoulish creature walked through them with a jagged axe. The beautiful house was not a house at all. It was a rocky outcropping covering a pit. Both of the knights could see bones and even pieces of armor surrounding the pit. The smell of decay and death was so pungent, Sir Jonathan gagged. Bjorn also wretched. It was a house of horrors for sure. How many had that filthy creature slain?

As they were looking at it, before their very eyes, it transformed back into the lie that had almost cost the knight his life. The pit took on the form of the house, and the trees went from ash and ruin to beauty and tranquility. The ghoul itself passed behind thick bushes and emerged in the form of the woman again. "She" walked daintily across the garden as if she were tending to her plants. She was humming and nearly dancing as she skipped along.

"She is beautiful," said Sir Bjorn with a smile. "Do you think we should warn her about the creature?"

"*BJORN!* Look at me. Not her, look at me." Bjorn turned to face him. "*She* is the creature. *She* is the evil," gasped Sir Jonathan.

"Are you sure? She's beautiful, and that ghoul wasn't. Maybe we should go down and warn her?" asked Bjorn again as he tried to turn his head toward her.

"No! Listen to me. She is the creature. She tried to kill me. Remember that fight we just had? What happened? What did you see?" asked Sir Jonathan as he turned Bjorn's face back to him. He began to lead him down the road away from her lair.

"Well, I woke up and found your note. I followed you down the road and found the horses along the way. When I came to the clearing I saw that creature trying to split your head open so I shot arrows at it to cover you. I did not rush in because of our instructions to stay on the road," recounted Sir Bjorn.

They walked for a few minutes, both deep in thought.

"Why did you leave the road, Jonathan?" asked Bjorn.

"I . . . I made a mistake. I was deceived. That thing almost got me. Don't even look at it, Bjorn. Stay on the road and let's get out of here."

They kept as far to the other side of the road as possible. It had been a close call and neither really wanted to talk about it yet. They led their horses beside them so they would not even be tempted to look over at her again.

"It was so incredibly well camouflaged, Jonathan. Incredibly and terribly well," whispered Bjorn.

"Yes it was, brother. But never forget what you saw and heard and smelled. It was death and decay to the core," answered Jonathan, still trembling at the thought.

As they put more distance between them and the enemy, they heard the "lady" begin to sing. It was enchanting. If it had not just tried to kill them, they would be sorely tempted to return. Sir Jonathan could not get the sight of the bones and the discarded armor out of his mind. How many of his brothers in arms had been deceived? How many had enjoyed the pleasures of that place until they realized too late what it really was, and ended up dead?

CHAPTER 10

Rangers

*"For the word of the cross is foolishness to those who are perishing,
but to us who are being saved it is the power of God."*
– 1 Corinthians 1:18

Sir Bjorn and Sir Jonathan continued down the winding path. They were not even sure they were on the right trail. The pair was still shaken from the encounter with the enemy. Jonathan shivered as he remembered the sight of the pit leading down to who-knows-where and the piles of bones and armor. He was not sure if the deceptiveness of the enemy or the violence of the attack unnerved him the most.

The woods were quiet and the knights were alert. They rode single file, looking from side to side. They would not underestimate the forest or the enemy again. Bjorn held his shield a little higher than before.

As they came around a corner in the trail, the woods seemed to lighten some. Here and there streams of sunlight made their way through the canopy. The fog had lifted. Perhaps they were coming to the end?

Then the woods fell silent. Not even a leaf rustled.

Sir Jonathan turned to look at Sir Bjorn. They both nodded in unspoken agreement and reached for their weapons. Sir Jonathan pulled his shield around for a better grip and readied his lance. Sir Bjorn moved his shield to cover his back and freed his arms to use his bow. He slid an arrow from his quiver and was just about to nock it when they both heard something move in the bushes ahead.

Sir Jonathan called out much more confidently than he felt.

"You, there in the bushes! Stand and greet us as loyal to the King, or stand challenged to combat!"

"And if we choose not to be recognized?" answered a voice that sounded both defiant and slightly amused.

Sir Jonathan lowered his faceplate and gripped his lance. He moved the lance into position and brought the shield forward. Sir Bjorn drew back on his bow and readied to shoot.

"Prepare to loose, Sir Bjorn," he called out.

Several laughs erupted, then Sir Jonathan was sure he heard the gruff voice of Sir Seamus call out to others.

"I think we should come out while we can. I believe he aims to attack us all if we don't surrender right away," he bellowed. "Do not attack us, Sir Jonathan the Slight! We are loyal to the King and to our good friends," yelled Sir Seamus as he came into view with giant smile.

The knights emerged from hidden positions around the trail. They were laughing and smiling and happy to see Sir Jonathan. They hugged and exchanged greetings and handshakes. Sir Robert approached Sir Jonathan and put his hand on his shoulder.

"I knew you would be along, Jonathan. And who is this?" he asked, motioning to Bjorn.

"Sir Robert, this is Sir Bjorn. We rescued him from the dungeon in Felwood. Don't you remember?"

"Ah yes! Now I remember. You were looking less knightly then, and sicklier. How are you now, son?" asked Sir Robert warmly as he shook his hand.

"Sir Robert, I was hoping I would get a chance to meet you and thank you in person. I am much better now, thank you," replied Bjorn.

"And you are a knight?" smiled Sir Robert.

"Yes, sir. I was very early in my training when I was captured in the forest. I was just assigned to the 2nd Regiment, King's Heavy Horse Cavalry. I was tricked in an ambush and was in the prison for some time. Actually I am not sure how long before your group rescued me. While resting in the city I realized, with the help of Sir Jonathan, that I did not want to stay at rest but fulfill my vows. I would like to ride with you until I find my unit. Would that be okay?"

"Welcome to His Majesty's Mounted Light Rangers. We are part of the 5th Cavalry Regiment," said Sir Robert with smile and a hearty handshake.

"Well, Sir Seamus is a Ranger, but he is not that light," laughed Sir Stephen. The whole group joined in the laugh, including Seamus. Seamus, while chuckling, scooped up a pebble and flicked it at Stephen, who ducked just in time. It flew over his shoulder and hit Lynd. There was a small "tink" as it bounced off her armor. She turned around and looked at them both. Seamus had quickly glanced away and appeared to be studying the tree line as if being vigilant. Stephen, still laughing, caught the blame. Bjorn snickered at them both. He was already happy to be part of the group.

Jonathan looked around and changed the subject.

Turning to Lynd, Jonathan asked, "Where is Sir Reginald?"

Sir Robert stopped smiling. He looked at Jonathan for a moment as if thinking about his words carefully. He finally cleared his throat and said, "He was wounded in the battle that followed after we broke open the trap door. His wounds were serious, and he was recalled to the City Beautiful to heal. He will not be rejoining us. But we will see him again when we have finished our work and the King calls us to the City as well."

"What a great day that will be," said Lynd with a smile.

They spoke for a few minutes with the anticipation of children about to open a wrapped gift. Soon they too would be home for good and they would see those like Sir Reginald again.

"Let's move on. This forest is not safe. There is still an evil in these woods that is deceptive and deadly. We are not even sure what it is exactly," warned Sir Robert. "We only have sketchy reports and wild rumors, which leads me to believe few escape to tell the tale."

"Sir, I believe we know what it is now," said Sir Jonathan. As they moved down the trail and out of the forest, the two knights related to the others what had happened and how narrowly they had escaped. It was not pleasant to recount but it did help the others. Each time an enemy was faced, valuable information was gathered.

"Hmmm. That has to be one of the most deceptive evils we have encountered. Remember, the enemy knows he is no match for the King's weaponry. His most effective counterattack is deception. It sounds like the tactic almost worked on you both, too. It is obvious she has slain many strong knights."

"That's absolutely true. The door of her 'house' led to a pit full of death and horror. The deception was so vivid, it almost pulled us back in the very moment we were free," said Bjorn. With a shiver he said to himself and everyone around him, "I will never forget the piles of abandoned armor on the edge of that abyss."

The knights followed the trail out of the forest, and soon they were on the slopes of a rugged mountain range. It was noticeably colder. The mountains themselves were covered in forests except for the snow-cloaked tops. Lakes and rivers cut paths through the area. Jonathan thought it would be beautiful country, except for the dark forces he knew were waiting to attack him. They learned from their maps and briefs that it was crawling with the enemy. Still, Jonathan could not help thinking of how pristine and majestic the area must have been before the great rebellion against the King.

"Gentlemen," said Robert to the younger knights. "Those mountains are the beginning of the contested territory the King has sent us to scout—the Great East. We must not fail in our mission.

Beyond them lie countless dungeons where his people are bound in slavery."

It was a foreboding sight. The formidable mountains looked dangerous. Bjorn glanced at Jonathan and tried to smile, but the reality of the situation muted his effort into more of a grimace. Jonathan chuckled at Bjorn's face.

They continued across a meadow into another forest at the foot of the mountains. It was obvious to the young knights something big was underway and they were part of it. The whole group moved quietly and with purpose.

After a short ride, the party came to a camp near a stream. The giant trees in the forest meant that darkness came rather early. The camp was laid out in a defensive half circle with the stream to the back. Jonathan noticed the guard was doubled. Fires were built in pits to mask the light but allow for cooking and warmth. Weapons were stacked outside of the tents for quick access. There was no question—they were both dangerous and in danger.

As the knights prepared to rest, Jonathan found Robert sitting on a log by the fire looking at a map. The younger knight was still thinking about things he had experienced over the previous few days. Robert sensed that Jonathan needed to talk.

"Yes?" asked Robert with a grin. "Where would you like to start?"

"How did you know?" laughed Jonathan.

"I can tell by looking at you. It is obvious you have questions. So, where would you like to start, my friend?" continued the wise knight.

"Your friend, Captain Tanganye, referred to you as a 'Royal High Ambassador.' What is that position? What exactly is an ambassador?" asked the young knight.

"An ambassador is someone who goes on behalf of the King and presents his terms of peace. It isn't the ambassador's offer; it is the King's offer," he responded. "But it is the ambassador's privilege to go."

"Does the position have something to do with our current orders?" asked Jonathan.

"In a way, yes. You see, all of us have a place in which we were called to serve. Every citizen trades the rags of a slave for the coat of arms of the King. Each one is given a life of purpose, and though they differ in nature, they are equal in importance. I love what the King has asked of me. It is the highest of honors to have orders from the Crown. And it doesn't matter where the place of service is exactly, only that you are where your King has sent you. The sentinel on the wall of the refuge city is every bit as important as the knight serving in the inn and the long-range patrol deep behind enemy lines. And every citizen is rescued with the orders to be an ambassador; to go on behalf of the King. It is a great honor and a fulfilling life."

"I do understand that now. Battle scares me, Sir Robert, but the carrying of the King's colors into those battles has been worth it. I feel . . . useful. Obedient. Loyal. It's rewarding," continued Jonathan.

"Yes. Yes, it truly is. There are those citizens who are missing out by not marching with their King at the first opportunity and on until their last opportunity. It is the greatest tragedy of the citizen's life—to miss the march to battle and watch the King work. Remember this: there will never be a time when a citizen is not a citizen of the Great City, but there will be a time when that citizen is no longer at the front or able to serve the way that we are."

Jonathan frowned. "What do you mean? How can one no longer serve?"

"I did not say they would no longer serve," smiled Robert. "But when you are called to the City Beautiful it will be a permanent removal from the rigors of battle. There are some ways to serve, to honor your King, that can only come to you during this time in your life. Your time is precious and limited. You must invest it well. I am determined to not lose a minute. That is why I carry the title of Ambassador. I was called to press the attack into the frontier of the Great East and, eventually, into the Great East itself. It will be exceptionally difficult. Already the enemy is moving and maneuvering to resist. Tomorrow's battles will not be like any battles we have fought yet."

"I understand. I am ready to go. I just want to be where the King wants me. I saw a knight summoned to the City Beautiful from a place he was not assigned. He was resting in safety when he had orders to serve elsewhere. It was both happy and sad to see. He was happy to see his King, but . . . ."

"But he recognized the loss of not serving the King as he was called. Yes, I have seen it before. It is the greatest loss a citizen can suffer. I am determined not to ever experience it firsthand," said Sir Robert with great conviction.

"As am I," agreed Jonathan.

"As an Ambassador, my task is to press ever farther and farther into the areas the King has claimed but his armies have not yet reached. The King was relentless in assuring I would hear of his pardon. It is my mission with my remaining days to see to it I am just as relentless as he is. But . . ." Sir Robert's voice trailed off.

"But, what?" pressed his apprentice.

"Well, the area is so fiercely defended and so vast. Yet, the knights that are responding, while brave and tenacious, are fewer than what is needed. And it is fewer than what was commanded as well. I am afraid our casualties may be high, and I wonder who will carry the colors even further?" said Sir Robert as he gazed into the fire and poked at the logs with a stick.

Jonathan could tell it weighed heavily on him. The desperation to reach the imprisoned and the urgency to follow the King brought the recent events into sharp contrast. Yes, this is why the unit was pressing so diligently and moving so quickly. He was thankful to be part of it all, but at the same time he felt like a very small part.

"I don't know what I can do, as I am so slight and small. But, Sir Robert, regardless of what happens in the coming campaign, I will not leave or retreat. I will carry the colors right behind you. I will not give up either," said Sir Jonathan the Slight resolutely.

Sir Robert the Wise smiled. It was the kind of smile he was famous for; warm and genuine.

"I know, Sir Jonathan, King's knight. You are fast approaching the end of your apprenticeship. I do not know all the King has planned for you, but I am glad you are bearing arms with us in these borderlands of the Great East. I am pleased—no, honored—to draw swords in the King's name with you," said his friend.

They sat for a few minutes thinking before the next question came.

"And if we all fall in battle and you are alone?" asked Robert. "What will you do?"

Jonathan had never thought of that. The knights, his family, had always fought with such success that he had never pondered the thought of them falling in battle, or being too wounded to continue the campaign. What would he do?

"I have not thought about that too much," answered the younger knight truthfully.

"And yet you must," guided the older. "It is time for you to consider how you will follow your King if you see the day when there are few with you. Or even if you are totally alone."

Jonathan did think about it. But he knew the answer. It did not take him long.

"Sir, I will follow the King. Wherever he leads. I am sure I am in the Great East for a reason. And if I find myself alone, I will continue until he tells me I am finished. I am here to stay," answered the young knight.

"Jonathan, my friend, you are slight only in stature. In courage and determination, you are anything but slight. Let us prepare to serve together for a very long time—but if not, it is good to know this territory will have another knight pressing the attack," smiled Sir Robert. "Only the King gives victory. Let's trust him for it."

Sir Jonathan and Sir Bjorn took the first watch, then slept well the rest of the night. It was good to be among friends. As they drifted off to sleep, they both commented on how comforting it was to have others on guard.

When they arose the next morning, Sir Robert had plans for the entire group. Everyone was already gathered around eating, talking, and laughing. Sir Jonathan was reviewing the Kingsbook and replaying the battle in Darkwood again. His self-reflection was interrupted by Sir Robert's booming voice.

"Good morning, all. Let's talk about our orders and how we are going to carry them out." He began while everyone gathered around the map table. "First of all, this territory is a little bit different. We have heard from High Command it is going to be heavily contested. Nevertheless, there are those in captivity throughout this land the King wishes to pardon. And pardons are only good news if they arrive before the day of execution. Therefore, our job remains the same. We will attack where we are ordered and offer the King's terms. That will be the general direction of this campaign. Questions regarding overall objectives?"

No one answered. It seemed pretty straightforward to Sir Jonathan. Fight their way in, deliver the pardons, then fight their way out with freed citizens.

"Sounds simple enough," said Sir Jonathan.

"Also, since we intend to stay in this area and reclaim it for the King, construction on a new refuge city has already begun on this ridge line," he announced, pointing on the map to a long narrow ridge with steep valleys. "It will be a difficult undertaking but it should prove to be fairly defensible," said Sir Robert.

Jonathan noticed the terrain was very rugged and mountainous. It would be beautiful if it were not crawling with enemy fortresses and armies.

"Our first mission is several hours from here. A squad of King's Mounted Reconnaissance has reported a fortified tower here at the base of the mountain. They believe it holds several cells with prisoners, and the King wants his terms delivered. Our plan is to move out just after dark and hit them at night.

"There is a rocky outcropping just above the west wall. We plan to send two knights up the mountain wall; then they will lower themselves onto the embattlements here," he said, pointing at the map, "and release the counter weights. This will raise the gate and lower the bridge. The rest of us will ride into the courtyard and search for the prisoners. We expect heavy resistance, so I sent out a request to any nearby units for assistance. Questions?" asked Sir Robert.

"Yes. Just one. Who are the knights making the drop into the castle?" asked Sir Jonathan, already dreading the answer.

"Oh, good of you to ask. Well, we were thinking about you and Sir Bjorn. And I would prefer it to be more of a lowering than a drop," smiled Sir Robert.

"We'd love to 'drop' in!" spouted Sir Bjorn before Jonathan could answer. "Thank you so much!" He grinned and looked at Sir Jonathan, who was feeling very slight at the moment.

"Excellent!" replied Sir Seamus. "Okay, well it's a plan, then. And a better plan than Sir Stephen had for you two, if I do say so. He wanted to use a catapult."

"It would have worked. And it would have been fun to watch," smirked Stephen. "From the ground, at least."

Everyone giggled and snickered—except Jonathan. He was not sure if Stephen was joking or not. Bjorn was half smiling and half contemplating if it would work.

Finally Seamus cleared his throat as he choked back a little laughter at the thought.

"Prepare your armor and weapons and make sure to get some rest. This could be a long night," instructed Sir Seamus.

As night approached, the knights went about their business as if it were a normal night. Shortly after dark, however, their fire was doused and they silently gathered their weapons, mounted their horses, and set off for the dungeon at the base of the mountain. Along the road, two knights dressed in very thick plate armor and carrying huge double-edged axes and long, iron lances joined them. The King's crest on their dented armor also had a shield outline behind it. They were Heavy Horse Cavalry.

"We are Sir Mathias and Sir Charles of the King's 4th Heavy Horse. We have been detailed to your mission tonight, Sir Robert. We are at your service," boomed the first night with a big handshake and a bigger grin.

"You are most welcome, friends," replied Robert.

"They are huge," whispered Bjorn to Jonathan, but it was still overheard by the two knights.

"You should see the other guys. They sent us because we are the smallest," laughed Mathias.

Everyone chuckled softly.

This brought their total number up to a dozen heavily armed knights. They fell in line single file and continued moving through the dark. Jonathan always liked the way it felt to be part of a troop moving out and riding together. He felt full of purpose and value. It was great to have a mission. He also thought about all of the nights he had languished in chains with no idea that determined warriors were on the march to his dungeon with his pardon. *Determined warriors sent from a determined King,* he thought silently.

Though Sir Jonathan was excited about rescuing others, he was also nervous. Every time he met the enemy, he felt a knot in his stomach. He did not know what to expect. Would they be goblins? Greys? Would they have a dragon? The thought of the dragon guarding the Great East (or any dragon, for that matter) made him shiver. He tried to focus on the mission and task in front of him, but he realized fear was always stalking him any time he took up arms. He wondered if the others felt the same way.

In the bright moonlight, he noticed Sir Bjorn ride up next to him. He leaned over to speak with Jonathan.

"Sir Jonathan, may I ask you a question?"

"Of course," whispered the knight.

"Are you a little scared?" came Bjorn's timid question.

"Yes. A little. I know I shouldn't be, because the King's weapons are far and above the enemies' abilities—but I am. But I know you aren't, Bjorn. Why would anyone who was nervous volunteer to drop themselves onto a castle filled with goblins and take his friend with him?" said Sir Jonathan with a smile. They both snickered quietly. Sir Robert, who was listening to them talk, smiled to himself.

"It was easier to volunteer than to go, I guess. As soon as we turned our horses toward the enemy I realized we are really headed for combat," confessed Bjorn. "It's different when we are ambushed. There is no time to think, just to fight. Now we are riding into it. I guess it's different, that's all."

Neither spoke for a few moments. Robert wondered if he should offer wisdom and instruction on the subject. Then, before he could speak, the young apprentice whispered his own instructions.

"Trust the King. Trust his weapons. Follow the instructions from the Kingsbook. Regard his people with the same regard he has for them, and you will find both your courage and victory," said Sir Jonathan with conviction. "We were both slaves once, needing someone like you to 'drop in.'"

Sir Robert smiled again. His work with Sir Jonathan was nearing an end. He was not only applying his training but was helping to train another knight. He was young and had much to learn, but there was no denying it: Sir Jonathan the Slight was a King's knight. He was thankful to have him on the raid.

After some time, Sir Seamus came back and motioned the two younger knights forward. It was time to move into position. Sir Seamus nodded at the two and pointed to a small craggy trail that led up the ridge above the dark fortress. He then motioned to Sir Stephen and the rest of the knights. As they moved into position they could see the outline of the tower and walls with the ridges above. The enemy's fortress was easy to see against the night sky. It was a formidable, defensive position and their best hope was in the dropping of the bridge and rising of the gate.

Sir Jonathan and Sir Bjorn tied their horses to a tree and began to creep up the path. It was a perilous climb. The rocks were jagged and sharp. At times it was hard to move without dislodging gravel and earth. Each time they did they would stop and hold their breath, hoping the enemy was not alerted to the impending attack. Farther and farther they went until they were right over one of the walls. They could see the goblin guards walking back and forth. The knights took a few brief moments to gauge their patterns.

"Let's tie the ropes here," whispered Sir Jonathan as he pointed to an outcropping. His heart was beginning to race. He could feel the blood rushing in his head. He wanted to be anywhere but there in one way, and yet he did not ever want to be anywhere else but on a mission for the King. He thought about the King and smiled. In that moment, he remembered the one who had gone into a dungeon like this one to free him. And in that moment, he knew he did not just admire and appreciate his King. He *loved* his King. And then the knot in his stomach did not seem so big.

They checked their ropes and looked at each other. As Jonathan extended a hand, Bjorn grasped it tightly and gave it a shake. Then they grabbed their ropes with both hands and positioned their feet to push off of the rock face.

"For the King," whispered Bjorn.

Jonathan nodded before whispering, "Let's go."

Sir Bjorn, with his jaw clenched in determination, nodded and down they went. They let the ropes out slowly at first. It was cold and the wind was blowing, which hid the sound of their movements.

Two goblins passed under the knights. They were muttering as they hobbled along. One carried a torch and an axe and the other just a spear. The knights dropped behind them. Sir Bjorn's armor clinked against the stone and the guards turned with a start. The knights were close enough to take out the guards quickly, but not before one squealed.

"Oi! What goes on there, then?" shouted a goblin across the courtyard looking up at the wall. He had heard the squeal but could not see the guards.

The knights put their heads down and ran across the embattlements toward their objective.

"Hey! Anyone there?" the goblin growled.

The knights were getting closer to the huge ropes holding the bridge up and the gate down. Just then, in response to the guard in the courtyard calling out, a goblin sentry came around the corner from the gate housing. The glow of his torch gave him away, giving the knights a split second to be ready. As soon as he saw the knights, he opened his mouth to scream an alarm. But at that precise moment, a well-aimed arrow squashed the warning. As the sentry hit the ground in a heap, the knights realized they were running out of time.

"Great shot, Bjorn!" whispered Jonathan.

They ran for the ropes. There was no turning back now. Both knights drew their swords and raised them over the thick ropes.

"Ready?" asked Jonathan. Bjorn nodded.

"*NOW!*" said Jonathan. Their swords flashed together and the ropes shuttered under the blows. One more cut on Bjorn's and two more on Jonathan's, and the ropes frayed and popped. The bridge crashed down with a cloud of dust and a thundering roar. The counter weights of the gate fell next, and it flew up with sparks shooting into the night. Loud clanking and screeching of metal could be heard for miles.

As planned, Sir Bjorn dipped an arrow in the oil he had brought with him, then touched it to the flame from the fallen goblin's torch. He loosed the flaming arrow into the sky, then examined the woods.

Out of the edge of the forest, ten riders galloped down the trail toward the bridge and moat. The horses thundered and Sir Stephen blew a horn to add to the confusion.

A goblin in the courtyard below tried in vain to raise the bridge while another rang the alarm bell violently. Two goblins were trying to move a wagon to barricade the now open gate. Guards were waking up and arrows were beginning to fly everywhere. A half dozen goblins with pikes were running for the gate to buttress the barricade. They arrived too late.

The two lead knights were the Heavy Horse soldiers. As they stormed the gate, they lowered their shields and long lances. They barreled through the barricade and trampled several guards. Eight more knights rode in right behind them and began to fight the enemy. Orange flames rapidly lapped up the courtyard, and the sound of clanking steel and goblins' squealing filled the night.

Sir Jonathan and Sir Bjorn ran down a staircase to the courtyard, engaging a few guards as they ran. When they arrived at the bottom, the others joined them. Two more iron gates blocked them from descending into the bowels of the prison tower.

Sir Mathias hooked up a chain from the bars to the horses. With a loud scrape, he and Sir Charles pulled the gate off of its hinges. All the knights rushed down the staircase. Resistance was light in the main floor of the dungeon, since most of the guards were killed in the courtyard. Several cells were on the first floor and each was occupied.

A small voice shrieked in the darkness, "*Save me!* Help me, please!"

Lynd responded immediately by rushing over to the cell door. She called out to the occupant, "Who are you? Come forward into the torch light and be addressed. I bring a message from the King!"

The sounds and smells of the prison caused a rush of memories and emotions to flood Sir Jonathan's mind and heart. The mixture of mildew and filth caused his stomach to lurch. A guard broke his concentration and attempted to break his neck as well. A quick block from his shield, then the two began to trade sword blows. Sir Jonathan blocked an overhead attack, then successfully struck the goblin with a mortal blow. It screeched and fell to the floor, writhing and shrieking. It crawled toward a corner before disappearing through a trap door.

Sir Jonathan couldn't believe his eyes. *A trap door!* He called to Sir Stephen and Sir Bjorn. They all grabbed torches and found the lever that caused the door to fall away, revealing a dark staircase.

As more guards appeared out of seemingly nowhere, Sir Robert motioned for Sir Stephen to take the two other knights and follow the dying goblin.

The three men followed the circular staircase, their torches casting long shadows on the walls. The goblin had left a thick slimy trail that was easy to follow. Farther and farther into the bottom of the dungeon they raced until they emerged into a cave. Several cells were carved in the walls, but only one was occupied. The goblin they had been following was dead on the middle of the floor. Five more guards were crouched behind a table, yelling and cursing at the three knights.

"I'll watch these vermin, Sir Jonathan. Here," said Sir Stephen as he handed the young knight a cylindrical leather case. "Present the King's terms."

Sir Jonathan could not believe he had the honor of speaking for the King. He was speechless.

"*Me?*" he asked, almost shouting.

"Yes. And be quick before these slugs find their nerves."

Sir Jonathan walked up to the door of the occupied cell. He kept remembering his own dungeon and what a wretched thing it was to be a prisoner without hope. He smiled at the thought of how he would get to share this man's most wonderful day.

"Sir?"

"Who are you? What do you want?" asked a cautious voice from the shadows.

"I am Sir Jonathan the Slight, a knight in the service of the great King. I bring good news from the same. Because of your crimes against the throne you have been sentenced to this dungeon and to death. But the King has offered you a pardon and to grant you citizenship in his kingdom. Will you listen to the King's terms?" asked Jonathan expectantly. He was so happy to speak for the King that he had to try hard not to jump ahead.

"Hmmm. I think you have mistaken me for someone else. I am not guilty of all of the things said about me. The list of charges held against me is not entirely truthful, Sir Jonathan, King's knight," answered the slave confidently.

Sir Jonathan was taken back. He did not know what to say at first.

"You deny your treason and mutiny?" asked Sir Jonathan.

"Well, no one is perfect, but I meant no real harm. I do not believe I am guilty of all of these things on my list of charges. Besides, I have been a resident of these lands all of my life. As a baker—a really good one—I have served the community and donated much of my bread to the poor. It does not make sense that a good king, if he *were* a good king, would send me to the headsman's axe for a few indiscretions. I don't believe it. Furthermore, the chief goblin of this keep informs me I will have the right to dispute any charge and bargain for release. I don't believe I am in need of a pardon at this point."

Stunned, Sir Jonathan turned to see the goblins in the corner laughing and beginning to mock the knights. One tossed the prisoner another piece of moldy bread.

"How can you . . . but don't you see . . ." started Sir Jonathan.

"And why would I want to leave this place? I have a roof, I can go anywhere in my cell I please, and have all the food I want!" continued the slave, as he picked a maggot off of the goblin's bread then took a bite.

"You are mad," said Sir Bjorn before Sir Stephen restrained him.

"Friend," began Sir Jonathan, "even one of the charges of treason is enough to send you to the block. It is justice. What I bring you today is an offer of mercy to fulfill justice and free you forever. I, too, was once a prisoner of a dungeon such as this. One day the King offered me a pardon and I took it. He wrote his name on my accounts and canceled them forever. And here I am today, a free man. Will you not at least consider the King's terms?" Sir Jonathan was desperate to see the prisoner freed.

"I don't need it," said the prisoner between bites of the maggoty bread. "I am not guilty of these things—well, not all of them. I am a good man and valuable to these lands and towns. I am in no danger of execution, I assure you."

"You have been sentenced to death! Please, don't . . ." started Sir Jonathan, who was fighting back panic at the thought of not saving the man from his fate. The knight was desperate to see him pardoned.

"Enough! I need no pardon. Good day, King's knight!" spat the slave resolutely. And with that, he turned to the back of the cage and ate his bread.

Sir Jonathan turned his head at the sight. He was in shock. How could anyone reject so wonderful an offer? As his eyes moved around the dungeon he thought he saw a flash of movement on the stairs leading upward. He saw the trailing edge of a dark purple cloak.

"Duck!" cried Sir Stephen.

Without question or thinking, Sir Jonathan ducked his head as a hammer, thrown by a goblin, narrowly missed him. The goblin that had thrown it was already writhing on the ground, squealing from one of Sir Bjorn's arrows.

"Fall back to the staircase. We are finished here," said Sir Stephen as he blocked another missile hurled from the goblins.

Sir Jonathan the Slight was reeling from the slave's refusal. He felt dizzy and thoroughly sick to his stomach. Sir Stephen realized Jonathan was not thinking and grabbed his arm, dragging him to the staircase. Sir Bjorn was shooting arrows as quickly as he could, and another goblin screeched in pain.

Up the staircase they went until they emerged into the larger room of the dungeon. Several cell doors had been broken open and the knights were withdrawing from the keep. Sir Jonathan moved quickly with the others, stepping over debris and hopping over dead goblins.

"Looks like we made quite a mess, didn't we?" asked Sir Bjorn.

Sir Jonathan didn't answer. All he could think about was leaving the prisoner who would not listen. He was nearly despondent. His spirits were raised, however, when he reached the outside of the keep and reunited with his friends. There, on two horses with blankets covering them, sat two former slaves. They gushed with gratitude at the knights and talked excitedly about the King.

Sir Mathias held out a drink for each of them and Sir Seamus bandaged a wound on one of their legs. Sir Jonathan was grateful two were rescued, but he was nearly mad with fear for the life of the third. Lynd interrupted his thoughts.

"Sir Jonathan!" she said in the most serious tone he had ever heard her use. "It's Sir Robert; he has been badly hurt. Come quickly!"

CHAPTER 11

Under Siege

Sir Jonathan galloped down the trail behind Lynd. Their torches caused the shadows to dance eerily along the path. The others followed, but somewhat slower due to the weakened condition of the new citizens, Tabitha and Peter.

Jonathan was frantic to catch up to Sir Charles, who was escorting the wounded Sir Robert from the battle. As they rounded a bend in the road, he noticed Lynd slowing, so he pulled up on his reigns. There on the road ahead of them, Sir Charles had stopped the horses and had Sir Robert lying against a tree. Sir Robert was drinking water while Sir Charles examined a wound. As Sir Jonathan rushed over to them, he noticed two ugly black arrows still lodged in Sir Robert.

"Sir! Are you okay? What—what happened?" stammered Sir Jonathan, not knowing what to say. He knelt down beside his friend.

"That doesn't matter now. I'll be okay one way or the other. Were we victorious?" asked Sir Robert, locking his gaze on Sir Jonathan. Though Jonathan did not realize it, the older knight was still teaching.

"No. Well—yes, partly. But we did not get one. I couldn't . . . I—failed, Sir Robert. I failed," gasped Sir Jonathan. The events of the evening were nearly too much for the young knight to process. He had never felt so defeated, and it showed on his face. His shoulders were slumped, and his voice revealed how beaten he felt. And now he was worried about his friend.

"You failed? How so?" asked the wounded knight through a raspy cough.

"I did not rescue the third prisoner. I was unable to fulfill my orders," answered Sir Jonathan without making eye contact.

"What were your orders, Sir Knight?" asked Sir Robert through labored breathing.

"My orders were to rescue the prisoners," answered Sir Jonathan.

"No. No, they most certainly were not. Just as you are powerless to wield your weapons without the King, so you are powerless to rescue anyone. Even if you had the inclination, you could not break the chains of someone who has not received the King's pardon. Only the King can free someone. Your job, as it always has been and always will be, is to deliver the King's terms to everyone. Your duties are to fight any enemy wherever your Captain sends you and deliver his pardons. It is not, nor will it ever be, to do what only the King can do: to pardon. Do you understand?" asked Sir Robert.

"I think so, but . . . ."

"No. You *must* understand," Sir Robert inhaled a shaky breath. "You must realize the success of the mission you undertake is dependent on your obedience and faithfulness to go. It does not hinge on the pardons accepted, Sir Jonathan, only those delivered. Do you understand?"

"Yes sir, I do. My job is to fight any enemy and to deliver the King's terms. I am not responsible for releasing them. But," Sir Jonathan continued, "why then do I feel so badly for the slave who denied the pardon?"

"You feel badly for him because of what he chose to give up and what fate he chose for himself. I assure you, the King shares your regret and compassion for him. It is one reason you were sent into so dangerous and dark of a dungeon to present his offer," answered Sir Robert with a weak smile.

"Will it ever get easier to see someone deny the pardon?" asked Sir Jonathan.

"I hope it does not. If so, you have ceased to view the people as your King does, and in so doing will lose so much of what he intended, Sir Knight."

Just then Sir Seamus called out, "Riders approaching!"

"Form a shield line!" cried Lynd, who was already moving to stand between the sound of horses racing their way and their wounded friend. All at once the sound of swords being drawn filled the night air.

"Is it a counterattack?" asked Sir Bjorn, drawing his sword and herding Peter and Tabitha behind him.

As they were still forming, torches glowed through the bushes of the forest and cast long shadows from the trees. When the riders themselves came into view, the knights could see they were also knights—but they were no ordinary knights. They were Kingsguard. The lead knight carried a purple banner with the King's seal in gold and the crest of the City Beautiful.

"Greetings, Servants of the King!" called the lead knight.

"Greetings. Long live the King," answered Sir Seamus.

"Friends," continued the knight as he dismounted. "The King has sent us for Sir Robert. He was wounded tonight in battle and the King would like him to recover at the King's Capitol City under his direct care. He is being reassigned and we are here to escort him to the gates and to the King's presence."

The first Kingsguard turned to Robert.

"Sir Robert, greetings in the name of the King. It is time to go," said the Kingsguard sergeant.

"At last, I will see the City Beautiful with the King!" he exclaimed. "The King Himself!"

Though his body was broken, his smile was brighter than it had ever been. It seemed to rejuvenate Sir Robert to realize he was headed to see the King. Jonathan observed a deep joy on his face even in the midst of the shadowy forest trail and the events of the evening.

"Are you ready to go, sir?" asked Jonathan, thinking of the other knight he had seen reassigned who was also happy, but not quite ready.

Before Robert could answer, a Kingsguard looked at the elderly knight and chimed in, "When the King sent us to escort Sir Robert to the city, we asked where we would find him. The King said, *'If you would find my servant Robert, there is but one place you should look. Look for him to be on the King's business and on the King's battlefield. He was assigned a forward position. That is the only place you will find him.'* The King knows Robert is a knight of the City Beautiful, and he eagerly awaits your homecoming."

"I could ask for no more than that. I am quite ready, my friend," said Robert softly as he hugged his apprentice and friend.

Sir Robert embraced everyone the best he could with his wounds. They said farewell in a jumble of tears and smiles. Neither joy nor sadness was present without the other. They all knew he would be best cared for by the King, but they would miss his fellowship for a time.

Nevertheless, they all had the same ambition to be with the King in the City. It was hardest on Sir Jonathan, though he was thankful for the time he had been Sir Robert's apprentice.

"But how will I continue training?" asked the young knight. It seemed as if the night was only growing darker for Jonathan.

"Your training will continue in many ways, but you are ready for your next task without me. You have grown and learned so much. You are ready, King's knight," answered Sir Robert as he placed his hand on Sir Jonathan's shoulder and gave a firm squeeze. "You are ready to continue your service to the King."

"I wish we had more time, Robert," said Jonathan.

"I do, too. And we will, but it will have to wait until you arrive in the City Beautiful as well. I have something for you, my friend.

Back at camp, in my tent is a box with the King's seal on it. You will find a sealed letter with your name, and directly under it is a leather case. What you find is yours, and you will need it one day. Keep it safe and keep it at the ready. Dark and slithery days are ahead. Hold fast to your oath. I will see you again, Sir Jonathan."

A wide, genuine smile spread over his face as he continued, "We will feast in the King's hall and speak of these battles again. Until then, be faithful to your King and your vows. Treasure the Kingsbook and listen well to its instructions and warnings. The Great East and all those who are imprisoned there belong only to the One King. Never forget that. Long live the King," said Sir Robert.

"I will miss you, Sir Robert," said Jonathan.

"And I will miss you, but we will see each other again. My chief concern now is the unfinished task in the Great East. Who will press forward with the King's business?" asked Robert rhetorically as several Kingsguard helped him stand.

Sir Jonathan the Slight stood as tall as he possibly could and answered loudly, "My intentions have not changed, Sir Robert. I will continue the mission with the other knights. I will see the Great East opened for the King." He had never felt more determined to see the King's business done. Any doubt melted away as the last snow before spring. He would see it to completion whatever the cost.

A Kingsguard nodded when Sir Jonathan the Slight made his declaration and placed a reassuring hand on his shoulder. "Long live the King, Sir Jonathan. He is worthy of your fealty, your service, and your life."

"On the day the King sends you for me, you will also find me on the battlefield and under arms. Long live the King," Sir Jonathan repeated.

They helped the old knight onto his horse and began to form up to take him to the City. The formation reminded Sir Jonathan of a parade to escort an honored person—perhaps even a hero.

Sir Robert leaned over and handed something to Jonathan, whose eyes stung with the coming separation.

Sir Jonathan looked at the medallion in his hand. It was a silver design outlined in gold. It had the royal seal with a lion's head and crossed swords. On the bottom was a scroll representing a pardon with red letters. The words on the scroll read, *"Forgiven and Declared Just."*

"What is this?" asked the knight.

"It is the seal of a Royal High Ambassador. I want you to have it, if you would accept it."

"Yes," said Sir Jonathan timidly at first, then more resolutely, "Yes, I accept. I will serve the King as He commands."

"Very well," smiled the Kingsguard. Then he looked up at the others. "I would advise clearing this road quickly, Sir Seamus. The remaining guards have sent out requests for reinforcements to counter attack. This area is going to be won, but it is going to be a real fight."

"We are already moving. Good journey. Farewell, Sir Robert. We will feast with you soon. In the King's City!" declared the burly Seamus in a booming voice.

Too moved for words at their temporary separation, Sir Robert and his royal escort turned toward the City Beautiful and galloped into the night.

The ride back to the camp was a quiet one. Every now and then one of the new citizens would ask a question or request a drink of water.

"Where are they taking Sir Robert?" asked one of the rescued prisoners.

"They are escorting him away from these fields of battle to the lands without shadow, where the enemy can never go. There the City Beautiful, where the Great King lives, is waiting as Sir Robert's new home. And it is also now your home," whispered Stephen. "One day the King will call for you as well. It will be a wonderful day."

Sir Jonathan watched how caring and kind Sir Stephen was with the two. Even in the temporary sadness of the loss of their friend, everyone was encouraged by the rescue of new citizens. Throughout the ride, the knights cared for and encouraged their new friends. By the time they reached the camp, they were exhausted.

Sir Mathias requested first watch and Sir Bjorn joined him. The rest disappeared into their tents and soon fell asleep. But not Sir Jonathan. He had moved his things into Sir Robert's tent and gave his own tent to Peter. He crouched over the chest Sir Robert spoke of and lifted the lid. The chest contained many reminders of his friend and mentor. He was happy for Robert but at the same time missed him terribly already.

As instructed, he found the letter and package and lifted them out of the chest. He sat on the bed for some time before opening the letter from his friend.

Finally he turned it over, loosened the seal, and began to read:

Dear Jonathan: If you are reading this letter then it means the most wonderful of days has come for me. I am with the King. It is the goal of every knight to one day celebrate his service with his Captain and this is a joyous day for me. For you, however, there is more work to do. There are missions for you to undertake and battles to fight. I do not know what lies ahead, except that the way will be hazardous and full of the enemy. We are moving into the Great East and the enemy will be strong and vicious. Take heart and trust your King. At all times be on guard and never trust your own strength. Take neither a victory nor a defeat personally. I have entrusted a weapon to you that may be of use. It is unusual. You will know when it is needed and when you do, trust the King who made it and do not fear. Farewell, my friend. Be worthy of your vows and I will see you in the great city one day. Your Friend and Fellow Servant of the King, Sir Robert.

Sir Jonathan looked down at the package. It was heavy. He unwrapped it slowly and let out a low whistle when he saw the item. It was a lance point. No ordinary point—it was almost as long as his arm. The bright steel weapon had two twisting blades that came together to form an exceedingly sharp edge. It was a Kingforged dragon point with only one purpose: to penetrate tough dragon scales. Sir Jonathan shuddered at the thought of tangling with a dragon. But it was becoming clear that Sir Robert had intended to push far enough into the Great East that he would challenge the dragon that led the defense of those lands.

As his fingers wrapped around the weighty steel instrument, it seemed to Jonathan that it would fall to him to find a heavy horse knight or someone similar to use the point against the dragon. The knight was sure Robert had intended for him to find the right person to deploy it against the enemy. He tucked it away safely in his bags.

The exhausted knight lay back on the cot and reread the letter as he drifted off to sleep. All night his mind played back the events of the day. He was haunted by the slave's refusal of pardon. The transfer of his friend to the King's city comforted him, yet a lingering sadness remained. He remembered vividly the noise and confusion of battle. He imagined what he would feel like if one day he had to attach and employ the dragon point. He tossed and turned all night.

The next morning the knights met together to discuss what was next. It was time for Sir Mathias and Sir Charles to leave and go back to their unit. Lynd made sure they were well fed before they started their journey.

"We have not run into your unit where we are, Sir Bjorn, but you are welcome to ride with us if you would like," offered Sir Mathias.

"Thank you very much, sir, but I would like to stay with this unit for now. At least until I run into my other unit or receive different orders. I believe I have more to learn," replied the youngest knight with a nod to Jonathan.

Jonathan smiled as he thought about the weighty responsibility of training another knight to follow the King. It was a great honor, but a heavy duty as well.

After warm hugs and handshakes, it was time to say goodbye.

Seamus gave them each a sack of leftover food, and the two heavy knights rode off toward their own unit.

"I hate to see them go," said one knight. "They are really good in a fight."

"That's for sure. I would not want to be on the other end of their charge! Everyone here? Now, let's discuss our next move," said Sir Seamus. "Our map shows that three valleys stretch out from this ridge line. It is mostly unexplored. We have orders to reconnoiter and deliver the King's terms where possible."

"Perhaps we should split up for several days. Three teams, two days down the valley, then rendezvous at the new refuge city. That should be four days from now," suggested Lynd. "Thoughts?"

"Sounds good to me. What about the new citizens? They are not up to this," said Sir Stephen.

"The new refuge city is going up not far from here. Sir Bjorn and I will take them," volunteered Sir Jonathan. The idea of taking care of newly freed citizens encouraged the knight. He remembered the words of Sir Robert not long before about their importance to the King. He also remembered how at first he thought it a light and unimportant duty. Now he realized it was an honor and had its hazards as well.

"Good idea. Okay, they are yours. Take them and proceed to the refuge city. We'll meet you there. Long live the King." Sir Seamus rose to prepare.

The knights bid one another farewell and rode out in their separate directions. Sir Jonathan was happy to be moving with purpose again, but splitting up so soon after Sir Robert had left was difficult for him to do. He felt like he was leaving his family. He hurried to prepare so they could leave the camp before the others. He knew they were splitting up, but he did not want to be the last one in an empty camp. He thought it was strange to feel so sad after such a great victory and two rescued citizens.

Jonathan found himself battling loneliness. He began to wish they had all stayed together, but he knew it was not the best thing for the new citizens. He would fulfill the mission, but he began to think about being in the Great City and seeing everyone again, like Robert and Reginald. He liked the thought of dinner with his friends with no fear of a good bye or a midnight mission that would separate them again. *One day,* he thought as he tightened his saddlebags. *One day.*

He looked around at the happy faces of Peter and Tabitha. He was happy for them and remembered his own first day of freedom. They seemed hungry to learn about their King and what he and Bjorn had been doing since they had been freed. As Jonathan observed their eagerness, the knight remembered how important their task really was.

The mission must come first. I will see my friends again, Sir Jonathan resolved. And with the encouragement that comes from being obedient to the Captain even in small things, the King's knight steadied himself and mounted his horse.

Bjorn had similar thoughts. He was jovial and took every opportunity to encourage the two new citizens. At one point, Peter looked down and saw a nice gash in Bjorn's shirt—a souvenir from the night before. They talked about the close call and Bjorn recounted Sir Reginald's and Sir Stephen's antics about a mangled helmet—a story that had been told and retold around the fire. Then Jonathan chimed in and said he had actually seen the act on his first day of freedom. All four laughed at the memory.

Jonathan also smiled as he thought about how much Bjorn had grown over the short time he had known him. He watched as the younger knight shared all about life serving the King. His enthusiasm was contagious. Tabitha had so many questions and Bjorn seemed ready for them. As they moved along, a vigilant Jonathan rode out ahead to watch for enemy patrols while he listened to the conversations they were enjoying.

Soon they reached the city under construction and were warmly greeted by the guards and the construction detail. The city was simple, but it was going up fast. The guard towers were already manned. Patrols were going in and out of the city. What used to be enemy territory now lay under the fluttering banners of the King.

Crossing under the fortified gate, Sir Jonathan asked for the captain of the city. He was directed to an exceedingly friendly knight named Samuel. The energetic captain was directing builders, greeting patrols, and designing defenses. On several occasions he led patrols himself. Even though the city was situated high on a ridge and very defensible, Samuel was taking no chances. They were taking back enemy ground leading to the Great East and everyone seemed to know they would meet fierce resistance.

"Sir Samuel? My name is Sir Jonathan. I am with the 5th Mounted under Sir Robert—I mean, Sir Seamus. I am glad to meet you."

"Sir Jonathan, is it? The pleasure is mine. Welcome to the King's refuge city! And who did you bring with you?" he asked, smiling and stretching out a hand to Tabitha first, then Peter. Peter shook his hand but Tabitha passed on the handshake and gave him a solid hug. They all smiled at the sight.

"Meet Peter and Tabitha. The King has recently freed them from their dungeon. We have brought them here for rest. We are also going to rejoin our unit. They are scouting these three areas here," said Jonathan, pointing at the map Samuel was already studying.

"I see. Yes, those would be the best approaches to the area. I am sure you are aware we are supporting the push into the Great East. It is going to be tough to accomplish, but the King has ordered it. The enemy is strong, but he is unable to resist the King's weapons and power," said Samuel passionately. Jonathan could see why he was a good choice to captain the defenses of the new city. Even under the darkening sky and snow-filled clouds, he seemed cheery and optimistic. Sir Jonathan felt somewhat refreshed just being around him. In fact, Jonathan realized he was in need of rest as much as Peter and Tabitha. Samuel helped him feel rested quickly.

For the next few days, Jonathan and Bjorn spent time helping

Peter and Tabitha rest and recover. When they were awake, they spent hours explaining their new lives as they helped build the city defenses. (Bjorn had suggested they work while they talk to help the walls go up.) It was exciting and rewarding for all four of them to teach and learn and be together. From time to time, other citizens and knights would join in the discussion. Tabitha remarked that it was like having family she had never met. Jonathan felt the same way and realized he would do anything to protect them.

After a few days, the rest of the knights arrived with their scouting reports. They had not seen a lot of action, but the information they gathered was a gold mine. There were towers and dungeons all over the area, and while they were heavily guarded, they were not impregnable.

Sir Stephen's group had news that was somewhat more concerning. While they did not make direct contact with the enemy, there were signs all over the forest of massive troop movements. Apparently a large enemy force was on the move. But where could it be going?

The captain rubbed his beard while he listened. "Sergeant Khalil, assemble a patrol and scout the area leading to the bridge over the gorge. We need to know if they are on the march."

"Yes, Captain. Long live the King!" And off he went.

"I don't like the sound of that," said Seamus, as Lynd and Stephen nodded in agreement. "That much sign without direct contact? It smells like a sneak attack."

"Not only that, but a lot of sign with little contact could mean the enemy troops are massing for a major assault, and not just a sneaky raid," said Lynd while sharpening her sword. "Perhaps they are all in one area."

"Agreed. How long will you be here?" asked Samuel. "I could use everyone with a weapon until we know what we are dealing with."

Sir Seamus put his burly hand on Samuel's shoulder. "We will stay until your scouts return with news and we have a plan to deal with whatever shadowy mess they find. In the meantime, may we help with building defenses?"

"I am grateful. Yes, we could really use your help," replied a smiling Samuel. "I know it is only a matter of time before the counterattacks."

Jonathan and Bjorn had been chatting with the new citizens and knew they intended to talk to Sir Seamus about joining the fight. Both wanted to join with Captain Samuel to build and protect the city. They discussed it between themselves as they made makeshift beds in the stables. As the knights moved hay around, they talked about Peter and Tabitha's decision to join the King in service.

The walls and defenses are always built before the inns, so they would be sleeping on hay that night. But it did not matter much, as they were tired and would soon be asleep. With a bright fire between the group and warm blankets wrapped tightly, the knights drifted off.

Almost immediately, it seemed, after falling into a deep sleep, Captain Samuel and Sir Seamus shook them awake. Both of the young knights felt sluggish and slow as they struggled to wake up.

"Up, men. We have a problem," said the captain quietly. "Follow me." The emphasis on the word "problem" jolted them both awake. Problems on the front lines usually meant enemy troops.

It was still dark and Jonathan correctly guessed it was the wee hours of the morning. As they walked toward the temporary headquarters, they noticed soldiers, archers, and knights quietly assembling and moving toward their positions along the wall. Even the building crews were being armed and formed.

Jonathan looked at Bjorn. There was no need to discuss what they both knew. The city of refuge was under siege.

"You two are here because we have a problem and your captain says you have some experience that might prove to be useful," whispered Samuel as he lit a very small lantern in the command tent. "Sir Khalil's patrol did not come back last night. We were going to send out a second when an archer on the wall saw movement in the forest below. As soon as the sun went down, we noticed more and more movement. As it stands right now, we are surrounded except for the cliff face on our south. We are not sure how large the enemy force truly is."

"We did catch two teams of infiltrators trying to sneak in and get through the wall. They, of course, did not make it back, so the enemy has to know we are aware they are up to something," said a Sergeant at Arms.

"Do we know the enemy is still there? Have we made contact with the enemy after the infiltrators were intercepted?" asked Jonathan.

"Yes. Why?" asked the sergeant.

"Because if they are still there, they believe they are strong enough to lay siege instead of just a raid since they know they have been caught," answered Sir Seamus. He nodded and smiled at Jonathan.

"How can we help, sir?" asked Jonathan. He was trying not to let it show, but he was sure this was going to be a major action. The refuge city was not moving one inch and the enemy could not let them be so close to the doorsteps of the Great East unopposed.

"You have some rock climbing experience, I hear. We need two things, Sir Knight. I need you to climb down the south face and enter the forest below here," he instructed, pointing at the map. "Turn east at the tree line and follow the ravine. You will come across the enemy lines. We need to know what we are facing. Reconnoiter the enemy at the bridge crossing the ravine. Secondly, we want our patrol back. If you can find their whereabouts, I will be grateful. Don't attempt anything too risky, but if you can free them, do. Any questions?"

"No sir. We are ready to go now," answered Bjorn for both of them again. Jonathan forced a grin and nodded.

"One day I hope I get to volunteer you for something," said Jonathan to the younger knight as they left the tent. Both snickered.

"Please feel free to volunteer me for breakfast whenever you can," retorted Bjorn. The snickers turned into laughs.

They assembled their gear, armor, and weapons, and prepared

to go. Sir Seamus and Sir Stephen walked them to the cliff. It was a long drop, almost three times as far as the last one. They looked at each other and smiled nervously.

They had tied the two ropes to several of the large stones set aside for building more of the wall. Both prepared their gear to be quiet, but for their weapons to be easily accessible. Nobody knew for sure what they would face at the bottom.

Seamus gave the pair a few more words of instruction ending with the obligatory "be careful" that always seemed to follow when one entered a dangerous situation. The knights shook hands with their friends and started the long descent into the inky black night.

Slowly the knights were lowered down the cliff face. They were hoping for the moon to give them more light, but as soon as they began to descend it was obscured by clouds. At times Jonathan could not even see Bjorn, but they continued down. They could see neither the top nor the bottom. As they continued Jonathan thought he heard something and he stopped climbing. Apparently Bjorn heard it too, as he had stopped as well.

As Sir Jonathan peered down, he thought he saw something move. Did something really move? Or was it just . . . NO! *Something was moving.* Squinting and shifting his head around, he strained to make out what he was seeing. His chest began to heave and blood rushed to his ears. Then the moon escaped a cloud for just a moment and his heart almost stopped.

CHAPTER 12

Night Mission

Just for a moment, the moonlight revealed at least a half dozen goblins readying climbing gear. They were going to try to assault the city from the cliff! Sir Jonathan was only a short distance above the enemy climbers. The howling wind had helped hide the muffled sounds of their descent. If the moon were out any longer, he would be an easy target.

Jonathan looked around for Bjorn. He saw his friend for just a moment but it was long enough. He saw the alarm on his face and also saw him drawing his sword. Jonathan mouthed the words "*On three*" and Bjorn knew it was a countdown to attack.

Jonathan had no time to deal with the nervousness he always felt before combat. Though he tried to be ready at all times, the idea of fighting always made him nauseous.

Now in the darkness they counted to themselves. Each number counted was like an hour. Finally, the knights hit "three" and released the ropes they were holding.

The drop seemed much longer than either had anticipated. Again the moon helped as it appeared just in time for the knights to turn their drop into darkness into an attack from above. Both swords found their marks on the descent. In shock, the other four goblins froze for just a moment—a moment too long. Sir Jonathan and Sir Bjorn launched lightning-quick attacks and lunges that killed the other four goblins before they could respond. Not even a squeal was heard as the one-sided fight ended before it began.

"They are trying to climb the cliff," whispered Bjorn as he pointed to ten large coils of rope with grappling hooks.

"True. But look," Jonathan answered as he pointed at the dead goblins. "There are only six goblins and ten coils of rope. They are only the advance party. There is no telling when the rest will be along. We need to move quickly."

"What do you think we should do?" asked Bjorn, sheathing his sword.

"We continue the mission as assigned, but I have an idea that will cause a little trouble," said Sir Jonathan with a grin.

Jonathan articulated his idea and the two went to work. First they dragged the bodies over in plain view of the top of the cliff. Then they quickly coiled all of the ropes together. Once the ropes were all in one place, Bjorn placed tinder in the center of the pile. After a few minutes, sparks led to flames, which turned into a small fire in the middle of the coils.

High above the two knights, the captain caught a glimmer of light. "Do you see that?" asked Samuel. "What are they doing? They will give their position away!"

"No. Not those two. They are experienced men, despite their youth. Look at the fire! Look what is burning. What is it?" answered Stephen.

"It's rope. Go get the sergeant," said Samuel.

As the fire grew, it illuminated the bodies of the goblins. Seamus and Stephen traded concerned looks and began discussing what must have happened. It was apparent the night was becoming more dangerous.

"Well, one thing is for sure. They are still on their mission," said Seamus flatly.

"How do we know that?" asked a city archer who was already scanning the cliffs for possible climbers.

"Because you don't see their bodies and who else would start a fire with climbing ropes?" chuckled Sir Stephen.

Noiselessly the two knights slipped into the forest and began to move toward their objective. Even in the dark, the ravine was easy to follow because of its distinct jagged features. A small creek ran through the bottom and the noise of the rushing water covered their steps. The farther they traveled, the more confident they became. At least once they had to freeze and let an enemy patrol pass. The patrols were carrying torches and talking in normal voices, which was good for the knights. It meant they had not been discovered yet.

Gradually the creek turned into a stream, and the stream into a small river. The waters were flowing more roughly and they passed several small water falls. They were now climbing into the part of the forest the enemy had to be moving through. They slowed their advance and listened as they searched. It was only a few minutes before they saw lights in the distance through the thick forest.

As they moved closer and closer, they had to leave the cover of the stream and the ravine. The ravine was turning into a gorge and the stream was now a river. The lights they were creeping toward were moving. No. They were marching.

Jonathan's pulse quickened. He heard Bjorn gasp when he too realized the meaning of the torches moving. The closer they crept, the more they could hear the marching in cadence of the enemy army.

As they approached a road through the woods, they could see formations of goblins with torches and spears marching toward the city. It was a large force. There were wagons and even a few siege engines being pulled by hideous four-legged creatures with great horns on their heads.

"The refuge city is unfinished. A force of this size could destroy it. We have to warn them," whispered Bjorn.

"There isn't time and the advance party of their army is between us and the city," answered Jonathan. "It will take much too long to go back the way we came."

Just then, the goblin commander called a halt to the main body of the force just short of the bridge that spanned the gorge. It was a massive wooden bridge and seemed to be the only place to cross for some distance.

"What's going on?" whispered Bjorn.

"I am not sure, but it looks like the majority of their troops and heavy equipment has not crossed the gorge yet," answered the knight. They both looked at the enemy forces and the bridge and contemplated their seemingly hopeless position. They seemed powerless to stop the army from laying siege to the city and they did not even have enough time to warn or help. They were on the wrong side of the river gorge.

"Look! There is the captured patrol!" whispered Bjorn excitedly.

The missing patrol was sitting down on the ground. They were some distance from the bridge and being marched the other way before being tied to the trees along the trail. The knights could see the enemy soldiers laugh, mock, and spit insults at them as they marched past. Since the columns had been halted, the goblins closest to the captured patrol turned their attention to the King's scouts. They took turns kicking and hitting the bound soldiers. It was very hard for the two younger knights to stomach.

From their vantage point on an outcropping of the gorge, they could see the bridge and the lights along the forest road leading from the enemy territory toward the King's refuge city. On the bridge were several wagons with barrels. Sir Jonathan watched a goblin sergeant walk up to a wagon, dip a long stick in one, then light it on fire. The fire shot up the stick immediately.

"The barrel must be full of pitch. No doubt it is for the siege engines to rain fire down on the city when they get in range. This is not good at all," observed Jonathan. He had never felt so helpless or outnumbered since his rescue.

"What would the King want me to do?" he whispered to himself. *"What should we do?"*

In answer to the knight's question, an idea began to creep into Sir Jonathan the Slight's mind. It was reckless and a little bit far-fetched, but it might work. Sir Stephen would approve, but Sir Robert probably would have had a few questions. That thought made him smile on the inside.

"Sir Bjorn, it is time for me to volunteer you for something reckless," said Sir Jonathan with a serious tone but a wide grin.

He explained the plan to him, and they both thought it was crazy but it might just work. At one point Bjorn had to stifle a laugh, but then realized Jonathan was not joking.

They began to creep toward the road and the halted enemy columns.

It was obvious to both knights the goblins felt quite safe in the forests on the edge of the Great East. They were loud and seemed to be in good spirits, which is saying a lot for creatures so foul. Many of them had torches along the road, which cast eerie shadows all through the forest. Though the lighted columns looked ominous, it helped the knights navigate and hatch their plan.

When they were in range, Sir Bjorn pulled his bow and checked the string.

This might be the most important shot I ever make, he thought. From his quiver he removed an arrow with a long, pointed tip made for piercing armor. He nocked the arrow and waited for the right moment. Just before Jonathan moved toward his objective, he laid a hand on Bjorn's shoulder.

"Remember, the weapons are the King's. Trust him, not your own strength," reminded the knight in a hushed whisper. "He will see us through to victory tonight, brother."

Bjorn nodded in agreement without looking back. His mouth was dry, and he was shaking a little. As soon as the guards moved away from the center wagon, Sir Bjorn drew the bowstring tight and began to slowly release a breath. As he exhaled, he allowed his fingers to gently relax as he released the arrow.

With a familiar twang and whine, the arrow flew through the night air.

It hit the center barrel of pitch and sunk almost to the fletching. The wide armored tip made a gash big enough for pitch to leak out. Aiming at the fletching of the first arrow, he released the second arrow. It, too, slammed into the same barrel just below the first. The two arrows made a considerable hole in the barrel. Now pitch was pouring onto the wagon and seeping around the other barrels. It began to flow in black syrupy rivers down through the cracks in the wagon, forming puddles beneath the other barrels.

It was time to move. In order for the plan to work, Sir Bjorn had to wait in his position for Sir Jonathan to move over to the captured patrol. When he was close enough, Jonathan hooted like an owl. After the call, he drew his sword and crept even closer. And waited.

The goblin army, separated in units, lounged or stood in loose formations. They laughed and cackled and hooted and hollered. In all, they were a rowdy and raucous gaggle of fiends. Their noise covered the sounds of the impending attack.

Sir Bjorn nocked the third arrow of the night. Leaning against a tree, he readied his bow to shoot again. Then he saw his target. A rather portly goblin with a blazing torch was walking across the bridge inspecting the wagons. He would stop from time to time to cinch a knot tight or check the ropes on his cargo. When he reached the leaking wagon, he stopped. The sounds of drips and drops hitting the ground puzzled him.

Bjorn was tempted to shoot, but the guard was not close enough. With his heart pounding, he waited.

The greenish sentry placed his hand on the wagon and leaned over to look under the barrels. The knight could not have hoped for a better shot. The goblin's torch was only inches from the dripping pitch.

The knight drew quickly and held the bowstring just long enough to begin releasing a breath. He let go of the arrow and it flew straight into the back of the goblin. The sentry went rigid, dropping his torch. The torch fell onto the thick black puddle.

The entire forest lit up like a bright afternoon.

The torch igniting the pitch drowned the beast's squeal. In an instant, the fire was out of control. Flames licked up the streams of tar. The leaking barrel exploded. Several other barrels immediately incinerated and spread the fiery pitch all over the bridge. The cascading explosions thundered through the entire area. Everywhere the burning pitch landed, it started a furious fire. Both knights felt the waves of heat sweep through the forest.

The result was everything the knights had hoped for and more. The goblin formation closest to the exploding wagons was consumed by the fireball and simply disappeared. A flaming axe flying through the air was the only identifiable debris. All of the wagons of pitch detonated. The explosion threw fiery missiles in every direction. Two siege engines caught fire and were burning furiously. Enemy troops were running in every direction. Wounded goblins flailed everywhere. Confusion reigned.

As soon as the first barrel exploded, Jonathan began knifing through the ropes with a dagger. He told each knight to stay in place until they were all ready. Then, in the confusion of another tremendous secondary explosion, they melted into the forest and moved beyond the glow of the burning bridge.

"This way! Follow me," instructed Jonathan.

Just then an enormous crashing sound reverberated through the woods. The bridge had buckled under the stress of the explosions and the fire eating through the supports. The bridge was destroyed. It careened out of its place and down into the gorge. The night sky was aglow with fires and the flashes of secondary explosions. Everywhere a barrel of pitch landed, it exploded or threw fire in every direction.

There would be no attack on the new refuge city tonight.

They kept moving toward the ravine and Sir Bjorn.

"Keep moving," urged Sir Jonathan.

"Wait! Our sergeant is missing. Sir Khalil was taken down the trail by a goblin officer," gasped one of the knights, cradling her smashed arm.

"We can't leave him," said another.

"I'll go," said Jonathan. "One of you, come with me. The rest keep moving toward the ravine. You'll meet Sir Bjorn. Don't wait on me. We will make our way back another way. The forest will be crawling with the enemy soon and I don't think they will be happy."

Jonathan and another knight moved through the forest paralleling the road. Goblins shrieked with rage and pain and ran back and forth down the trail. Confusion and chaos spread much like the fires. The knights strained to see any sign of their brother. A few minutes later they saw Khalil tied hand and foot on the side of the trail. The officer beside him was shouting orders. Goblins were everywhere, but in complete pandemonium.

"Stay here," whispered Jonathan. He drew his sword and crept through the bushes toward the goblin officer. The goblin had just sent several sergeants away with orders and was waiting for the next volley of questions and reports.

In a rage, the goblin officer turned to kick the prisoner again, but instead of seeing one knight on the ground, he saw two. To his further dismay, one of the knights was not tied up awaiting a kick but had a drawn sword and a warrior's grin. The goblin's face went from rage to shock. He tried to yell for help but it was too late. Sir Jonathan's sword struck the goblin down in an instant.

Jonathan quickly released the patrol sergeant and they disappeared into the night. Moments later, shouts, squeals, and horns added to the confusion. The enemy knew their prisoner had escaped when they found the dead officer.

The other knight helped the sergeant move as Jonathan led them to the rendezvous. With every move they put more and more distance between the confusion and carnage of the destroyed goblin forces. They knew the siege was lifted before it even started.

Several more secondary explosions echoed throughout the river gorge. The three stopped to catch their breath.

"Wait. There is something you need to know," said Sir Khalil while grabbing Jonathan's cloak.

"What? What's wrong?" asked Jonathan.

"I heard the goblin guards talking about a cave not far from here. They say there is an evil in the cave they plan on using against the cities and the citizens. This siege is part of the plan to unleash it. If it is true, it must be destroyed. It has to be destroyed!" said the knight passionately.

Sir Jonathan thought about the knight's words. He tossed the thought over in his mind. He needed to return to the city, true—but shouldn't he scout out the report? In spite of the internal conflict, he thought he knew what to do.

"Keep moving in this direction, my friends. You'll find the rest of our men. Move out quickly," instructed Sir Jonathan.

"What are you going to do?" asked the patrol leader.

"I am going to find that cave," answered Sir Jonathan. "If it is part of a plan to attack the city, we have to know what it is and how to fight it. We have blown a bridge and routed an army, but they are not going to give up. But they will not let us move in unopposed. I am going to scout out their cave and its evil and see what we need for victory. I'll be back as soon as I can."

Unknown to the escaping knights, back at the refuge city, an observer on a tower saw a giant fireball mushroom up through the forest canopy.

"Cap'n! You're going to want to see this!" he called down.

Samuel and Seamus bounded up the stairs to the wall and then the archer's tower. Stephen was not far behind. Samuel looked and tried to imagine what caused the blast.

Seamus smiled from ear to ear. He knew. "That's my boys," he said softly. He turned to Stephen who was running for the wall. "That's our boys, Stephen!" he yelled. Then he let out the deep hearty laugh for which he was known so well. "They turned their recon mission into a bonfire!"

Sir Stephen ran up and stood beside them. He gazed at the rolling explosions and how the fire caused the low fog to glow orange. He sighed as he stroked his black beard and shook his head. "Next time, I'm going too, Seamus," he said forlornly.

"What could be on fire, sir?" asked an archer.

"It is the only bridge over the Reeking River. Without it, it will be hard to move any sizeable force. The river gorge in that area is jagged and steep. Whatever is on this side of the river is trapped," the city captain replied.

Seamus and Stephen quickly exchanged glances. A broad smile formed on Seamus's face and a quick grin spread across Stephen's.

"Well, if they have nowhere to go, it might be a good time to clean up. Stephen, looks like you will be in this one after all. Besides, it will be a good distraction if Jonathan is trying to lead the rescued patrol out," said Seamus.

"That's right!" exclaimed Samuel. "It's a great idea."

Seamus turned toward the stables and yelled, *"Rangers! To Horse!"*

In mere moments, the 5th Mounted was assembled with Sir Seamus in the front. They held lances and torches. Once everyone was formed up for battle, he turned and saluted Samuel, who returned with his own salute.

"For the King!" shouted the knights as Seamus led them charging into the wood line toward the fires that still burned brightly.

Some distance away, in the darkness of a forest crawling with angry goblins, Sir Jonathan the Slight began his search for a cave and an evil that would prove to be his most dangerous encounter yet.

CHAPTER 13

The Cave

"Pride goes before a fall . . . ."
– Proverbs 16:18

As Sir Jonathan moved parallel to the enemy-held road, he gradually crept beyond the sounds of the goblins' disorganized attempts to regroup. Fires filled the forest all night. It wasn't long until the darkness of night morphed into the grey of early dawn.

The knight came across a wide trail just before sunrise and decided to reconnoiter the area. He was unsure exactly what he was looking for, but the wounded knight had said the cave and the great evil lived in the vicinity. He suddenly felt certain he should have waited for more men, or at least for Bjorn.

In the early twilight it seemed as if the insects were getting worse. He kept waving at them, though he could not see them. Jonathan wondered how there could be so many biting bugs with the weather so cold.

He also considered the last few weeks. He had fought battle after battle and each one had led to a victory. He had escorted a number of the King's citizens to safety. He had just routed a large number of the enemy. He remembered the sight of the bridge falling in charred pieces to the ravine below. Everywhere he went, he was winning and prevailing.

I may be slight but I am teaching the enemy they had better not underestimate me, Sir Jonathan thought to himself.

As he was thinking these things, he seemed to have ridden into a large swarm of the biting insects. He could not see them, but he could hear their buzzing and feel the occasional bite. It did not matter. He was a knight and he was hunting something dangerous.

They have asked the right knight, he mumbled to himself. But the thought troubled him as well. Something was off. Maybe he was just tired? He had been up for some time.

Just then a slight path to the right appeared. It led uphill. He looked around cautiously, then began to creep up the path. When he reached the top of the trail, he saw a very small opening. It was a cave. He quickly fashioned a torch, lit it, and peered into the opening.

It was a very narrow tunnel. Cold air greeted him as he looked down. It was dark and smelled like death. *This has to be the creature's lair,* Sir Jonathan reasoned.

Should he wait? It was a very rare thing to try to attack the enemy alone. Only under very dire circumstances should it be considered. Jonathan knew this. He had counseled many knights to stand together against the enemy, and he had been counseled by many to do the same.

The insects buzzed angrily. Perhaps there would be fewer in the cave? "Ouch!" They were biting, too.

Something did not feel right to Jonathan. He was not sure if it was inside the cave or inside of him, but he felt a little off. He had conflicting thoughts of wanting to get help and wanting to go in alone to see what the danger truly was. He was even thinking things that were very un-Jonathan-like. At one point he caught himself thinking he really did not need any help at all. He tried to clear his head, but the incessant bugs were merciless. *I'll check it out and be quick about it,* he said to himself.

And with that thought, Sir Jonathan entered the cave alone. He had not gone far when he realized it was narrowing to the point one might need to crawl. His equipment and armaments were in the way, and the insects were still buzzing and stinging.

While swatting at them he began to think about leaving his sword. He had already left his lance and axe behind at the city. He carried his sword a little further, almost left it, then decided to take it with him anyway. He wanted to leave it, but in the back of his mind he felt uneasy doing so. He was surprised at the overwhelming desire to leave his sword and shield but the subtle alarm in his head would not allow him to consider it any further. He fixed his shield to his back and crawled onward.

The tunnel continued downward and gradually began to open. Finally, it turned the corner and he could stand again. He crept forward. His torch was the only light in the cave. He realized he carried only his leather satchel with the Kingsbook, a sword, and his shield on his back.

It doesn't matter, he thought while rubbing an insect sting. *I can handle this. I have handled more in the past.* Yet as soon as his heart uttered those words he vaguely remembered several embarrassing defeats. His head felt foggy. He was sure he needed some sleep and food.

As he walked further he began to see a light ahead. Then he heard something. He wasn't sure what it was, but he knew enough to be cautious. He slipped further down the cave and crept forward without a sound.

The light at the end of the tunnel was growing brighter, so he doused his torch to not give his position away. What was that sound? Was it . . . ?

It was breathing. Something very large was breathing.

The cave opened up into a very large cavern and down on the floor of the cavern, sleeping on a pile of bones, was a very large dragon. *A dragon!* That was the evil in this forest. Of course!

The dragon was greenish in color, striped like a lizard and probably the size of a dozen horses stretched nose to tail. It was also a fire breather. As it exhaled in its sleep, it emitted the occasional puff of smoke and the smell of sulfur. It had claws the size of short swords and its scales looked tougher than stone. Broken arrows protruded from different parts of the beast. Apparently others had fought with this dragon and failed.

Many people seem to have failed fighting this dragon. But I think I can kill it. They will probably call me Sir Jonathan the Dragon Slayer after today, he thought, but felt a twinge of shame almost immediately after thinking it. He waved a hand in front of his face to ward off the bugs buzzing around. *They seem to be attracted to the dragon,* he thought.

The knight looked around the cave. A ledge led around the rim. Sir Jonathan realized he could creep around the ledge until he was standing just above the beast. It would be a great place to attack.

Slowly he crept around the rocky outcropping. He would slide his feet a few steps, then listen. The dragon slept on. Its breathing was getting louder the closer he crept. The smell was also growing worse. Jonathan had always wondered what it would be like to fight a dragon, but the horrible odor was something he had not imagined. *The smell might be worse than the bite,* he thought.

Then the knight saw a long iron spear with a great broad point on it. The magnificent weapon was lying on the ledge just above the dragon.

I guess some poor soldier tried to kill the dragon and failed. He must have been an apprentice, not a true knight like me, thought the knight sympathetically. The guilt of thinking such a thought stung almost as bad as the incessant insects.

Leaving the sword his captain had given him in its sheath, he picked up the spear quietly and eased toward the edge. When he looked down on the dragon he realized he was standing just above its head. He had a twelve-foot drop or so to reach the creature. Then a plan formed in his mind.

He swatted at another buzzing insect as he pondered his plan. It was daring and might be his only chance. No, it would work, surely. And the dragon's bones would remain in this cave forever.

Jonathan gripped the spear with both hands and held it, point down, in front of him. He tiptoed up to the edge, then took a deep breath and held it. The dragon continued to snore, oblivious to the knight's plotting.

Then, with the spear gripped tightly, the knight jumped onto the head of the dragon.

When he landed, he used the full force of his fall to drive the spear into the neck of the dragon at the base of its skull. The spear pierced the neck and drove all the way down to the floor of the cave, pinning the dragon's head to the ground.

Sir Jonathan rolled to one side, hopeful it had worked. He came face to face with the big yellow eye of the filthy creature. It was wide with fright and terror at being attacked and hurt so badly. It could not even roar as it died.

"Now, who is the hunter and who is the hunted, dragon?" shouted Sir Jonathan, still breathing hard but already beginning to gloat at his victory. The knight's very uncharacteristic taunt echoed through the cavern.

The dragon heaved and gasped. One claw dug at the rock. Then it lay still. Black ooze ran out of his jaw and from one ear. It was clearly dead.

Sir Jonathan the Slight had killed a dragon.

"You aren't so big after all," mocked the knight as he kicked it with all of his might.

The dragon's eyes became glassy and its breathing stopped. Sir Jonathan looked around the cavern. It was larger than he noticed before, and at the top was an opening, which must have been how the dragon flew in and out. Then Sir Jonathan noticed a doorway just across from the dragon's head. He had not seen it before, either.

He walked over to the opening and read the inscription:

Enter ye who by strength the dragon slayed
And all of his plunder is thine to take away

Plunder? There is plunder? Sir Jonathan rubbed an insect sting and looked down at the doorway. He saw a gem on the ground. It was beautiful and reflected several different colors. He picked it up and looked at it against the opening of the cave.

While he was considering what to do with it, he looked through the doorway and saw even more. They were beautiful. And they were his! Two casks of oil for torches sat by the door of the cavern with a bundle of torch handles beside it. He grabbed a torch, dipped it in the thick oil, and lit it. The fire illuminated a hallway full of a treasure like the knight had never seen before.

I have slain this dragon myself. I will keep its treasure for myself, he thought confidently.

He entered and began to gather his newly found riches. There were diamonds and rubies and gems of all sizes. Many he had never even seen before. And there was gold! Stacks and stacks of gold coins covered the rooms that led off from the hallway. He surveyed the rooms first before grabbing anything. He could only carry so much and he did not want to waste his bags on less than the finest jewels a dragon slayer deserved.

Deeper into the hallway he went. He lit a torch from time to time on the wall to light his way. Everywhere the light of the torch went, he could see riches beyond his comprehension. The deeper into the cave, the more extravagant the riches appeared.

At one point Sir Jonathan saw a magnificent sword, much larger than his own. It was jeweled and the hilt was finished in a beautiful woodcarving—unlike anything he had ever laid eyes on. He felt it was a proper sword for a proper slayer of dragons. While still rubbing a fresh insect sting, Jonathan removed his sword—the one the King had given him—and laid it down. He picked up the dragon sword and fastened it to his waist.

A little further down he saw a gold shield with a silver dragon on it. It had dark gems for the eyes. It was breathing fire on the shield and the fire was a field of rubies. When he held it up against the light, the rubies glowed. He turned it back and forth in the torchlight, watching the rubies illuminate as if the dragon were breathing fire. He placed his shield—the one the King had given him—on a table next to some other discarded shields and carried the dragon shield on his back instead.

I bet no one in the refuge city has even seen so great a shield! Wait until they see this one. They will make me a leader of the city for sure! he thought.

Jonathan began to fill his pockets. He found sacks and began to fill them as well. Piles of gold and precious stones were now his. As he filled the bags, Jonathan notice that the air was cool, but he was beginning to sweat. Something was wrong.

I do not need the jewels; I am a King's knight, echoed a quiet but powerful thought through his heart. A King's knight.

Where did that thought come from? he wondered, scratching another insect bite. *Of course I need them. They belong to me. I earned them when I killed the dragon.*

He needed more space. He reached down to his leather satchel and removed the book. The Kingsbook. He held it in his hand briefly.

Ouch. Another fly stung badly. He swatted and scratched absentmindedly as he contemplated the Kingsbook.

Jonathan told himself he would return for the book. He tried to set it down on the table, but it slid off the edge.

The Kingsbook fell to the floor. As the knight bent down to pick it up, he saw that it had fallen open to a worn and familiar page. An underlined sentence caught his eye.

"Let the one who thinks he stands be careful lest he falls."

The knight thought about the words. He began to remember other words, too, about the King's power and the King's might. And there, kneeling on the floor of the cave, he felt foolish. His cheeks flamed red at the thought of trading the armor his King had given him. He was not the dragon slayer. He was the King's knight.

He had been foolish to think so highly of himself, knowing that no victory he had ever been a part of was from his own hand. He remembered in that instant the ghoul in the forest so long ago that had nearly crushed him with a hammer. He was ashamed and humbled. He slid the Kingsbook back into his satchel.

When Sir Jonathan the Slight stood up, he was shocked by what he saw. He was standing in a room with broken down furnishings. They were rotted and decayed. There were piles and piles of . . . rocks. Not jewels. There was no gold. But that was not what was most horrifying. The back of the room opened to a bottomless cavern. Skeletons lay around the room clutching bags of rocks, the very same that Jonathan had in his hands. He looked at his new shield and sword. Both were made of rotted wood and crawling with worms. They would be useless against weeds, much less against any foe he was likely to see leaving the cave.

But the worst part of Sir Jonathan's clarity was finding out what was biting him. There were no stinging insects. Flying around the room were dozens of filthy creatures. They looked like small winged imps with enlarged eyes and vicious mouths full of teeth. Each was about a foot tall and had a small crossbow. Several were feeding on the remains of a skeleton cast aside. It was macabre beyond belief. Death seeped from every dirty corner.

He was trying hard not to give away that he had been awakened by the words from the Kingsbook. The winged imps outnumbered him greatly. Jonathan knew he was in grave danger. It may already be too late.

Panic gripped the knight. He was deep inside of an evil lair and he had traded his weapons for junk. He calmed himself with the thought of knowing the truth. He pretended he was gathering more gold. Just then a flying imp shot him with another dart. He acted like he was swatting a fly and went back to gathering rocks.

But in that moment a thought crossed his mind.

But I did kill a dragon. Just then his handful of rocks shimmered ever so slightly with a goldish color, and the hovering imps faded ever so slightly . . . .

It is poison! The small crossbow bolts are dipped in poison. Sir Jonathan could now feel it playing with his mind. He had to stay focused.

My victories are the King's victories. I am the Slight; he is the Mighty One in battle, thought Sir Jonathan.

As soon as he thought about the truth of who he was and who the King was, the poison lost its power and things began to focus. Sir Jonathan tried to keep up the charade but panic was setting in. How much more could he take? The knight knew he was getting weaker. He glanced at a corpse as the imps feasted noisily on the bones. And an imp saw him grimace.

Sir Jonathan knew his time was short. Pretending to go from gold piece to gold piece he moved closer to his discarded shield and sword. He knew he was a dead man without the King's weapons.

Good. So long as I remember where my strength comes from, the poison of these vermin is powerless, he thought.

But the imp who saw Sir Jonathan grimace started chattering to the others. The buzzing of their wings became angrier. More and more hovered closer to Sir Jonathan.

Still whistling and collecting handfuls of rocks to deceive them, Sir Jonathan moved ever closer to his weapons and the door to the passage. He moved to a piece of rotted garment covered in worms. Though completely revolted, he pretended to hold it up and said, "Now this is worthy of a dragon slayer!" The filthy creatures seemed to be fooled for a moment. Jonathan inched ever closer to his weapons, which he knew were his only chance of survival.

They were within arm's length. Jonathan paused for a beat and a silent, steadying breath.

Then with a blinding speed born of desperation, he dropped the bags of rocks and the fake weapons and lunged for his own weapons. He scooped up the shield just in time to block a dozen tiny poisoned darts as they flew. He swung the shield around toward the wall and crushed an imp. It let out a final squeak and dropped to the ground in a heap. Jonathan swung his sword—the one the King had given him—and minced two imps with one blow. But the exertion was making him dizzy. The poison was still in his system.

The cave was alive now with angry imps. The chattering and shrieking and the sound of wings beating the air was deafening. Over and over the imps sent volley after volley of poisoned darts toward the knight. He blocked as many as he could but they were still striking him. Each time he tried to remember the teaching of the Kingsbook. Every time he did, it saved him from losing focus and perhaps even his life.

Stumbling through the corridor he kept repeating, even yelling, ". . . take heed, lest I fall!"

Finally, Sir Jonathan bounded up the stairs to the entrance. Several dozen imps were trying to roll a boulder across the doorway to trap him. Sir Jonathan ran and dove through the opening. When he turned around, he saw the passage full of the angry winged vermin flying at him. They were an evil flock of angry, toothy, pixie-like creatures.

He quickly kicked over the barrels of oil for the torches at the door. Then he threw a torch onto the slick and watched the flames fill the hall and cave with smoke and fire. At least a dozen imps were too close and were engulfed in the flames. The rest were trapped—at least until the flames died down.

Sir Jonathan turned to run while he could, but then was stopped in his tracks by a horrible sight. The green dragon was alive and right in front of him. But it was asleep. Snoring. How could this be?

Sir Jonathan kept his sword and shield ready and circled the beast. Then he realized the truth. The dragon was not real. It was part of the illusion. The evil enemy in this cave was pinned behind a wall of fire. The dragon was an illusion. He realized he brought the real enemy into the cave with him—pride.

Sir Jonathan considered this and knew he must run. But the poison was taking its toll on him. He was dizzy and nauseous and could barely move. He saw a staircase leading up to the ledge and stumbled toward it. Each step was agonizing but he had to make it to the top. Several times he stopped and wretched.

"Some knight I am! Slayer of dragons, indeed," he murmured between heaves. Yet, the admission actually made him feel a little better. He began to recount each time he was saved by the King and the King's weapons. The more he did, the more speed he gained. Then he recounted the story of the Shifter in the forest and how close he came to defeat. Again, his head cleared more.

He found the cave he came in through and began to retrace his steps. But there was a major difference. It was not the small cramped cave. He could walk standing up the whole way. At first he was unsure he was in the proper cave, but then he noticed his abandoned armor. He picked it up hastily as he went.

He was starting to feel quite sick. His steps were heavy and he used the cave wall to hold him up. A few times he stumbled and landed hard on sharp rocks. The rocks bruised and cut his hands as he went. He wretched again.

Just when he thought he could not continue, a shadow appeared in the light of the cave opening. It began to move toward him, but Sir Jonathan's eyesight had blurred, as had the line between friend and foe. He was raising his shield and sword when a pair of strong arms grabbed him and began carrying him out of the cave.

"Sir Knight! Are you okay? Come with me!" said his rescuer.

"Who are you?" murmured the knight.

"I am Ethan. Part of the 3rd Regiment Light Cavalry. You are with friends."

The knight pulled him out of the cave and down the trail. Seven other knights stood gathered around the trail. They all came to help except for two standing guard on the path.

"Lay him down here," instructed one of the knights, a lady with long brown hair. "Give him some water."

Slowly Sir Jonathan began to revive. He looked around at the friendly smiling faces.

"Welcome back, friend," said Sir Ethan jovially. "What were you doing in such a nasty place?"

"Learning an important lesson," answered Sir Jonathan while trying to regain his senses. As soon as he could breathe normally, Jonathan began to recount the events in the cave. He left nothing out, even though it was terribly embarrassing. In fact, the more he told about how badly he had been mistaken, the quicker his head cleared and his full strength returned.

"I have heard of these creatures before," spat Sir Ethan in unveiled disgust. Turning to his troops he continued, "Those demons require their victims to trust themselves and put confidence in their own strength. Then the poison they use is most effective. Without their prey deceived into thinking they are the source of their victory, they are quite powerless. That is why the illusion of a dragon waiting to be killed is so clever. Who would not be happy with themselves after killing a dragon?"

"What is the defense, then?" asked another knight, Riley.

"Remembering where one's true strength lies. Remembering the source of power for the knights' weapons. The knight wins battles when the knight allows the King's weapons to do the work. Do not trust the arm of your own strength, for to the degree that you do, their poison is potent," said Sir Jonathan quietly as he allowed the lesson to sink in.

"Here, a demonstration, then," said Ethan. "Sir Jonathan, how many victories have you won in battle?"

"None. The King has won them all. I am alive and victorious because of him," answered the knight solemnly with a renewed trust in his captain.

Just then, Sir Ethan pulled a dart out of Jonathan's shirt. It was still dripping with an orange-colored poison. He then rolled the tip around to make sure the poison stayed on, then stuck Jonathan's arm with the point.

"Ouch!" cried Sir Jonathan. "Whose side are you on?"

Sir Ethan laughed, "Now, what do you feel, friend?"

"Just a sting."

"How many victories have you won?" he asked again with his eyes locked on Sir Jonathan's.

"None," answered Sir Jonathan, then his face broke into a wry grin.

"You see? Remember who you are and many schemes of the enemy will never prevail," said Sir Ethan to his young knights. "Now, we would love to stay and talk, but we are on a mission. A city of refuge, which is under construction, was almost attacked. The goblin forces were routed but are regrouping in the forest. There is a castle keep not far from here where they are building their siege engines. Scouts suggest there are also citizens imprisoned there. We are on our way to rescue them and burn it to the ground. Will you go with us?"

"Yes. Yes, I will," answered Sir Jonathan, getting to his feet. All dizziness had left him completely.

"Good. I would like to ask you to lead the assault as well. Most of my unit is made of apprentices. I would like them to see experience at work," said Sir Ethan with a smile.

"Thank you, but no. I think I am completely unfit to lead today. Especially after my embarrassing defeat," replied Sir Jonathan.

"Oh, not at all. What did you learn today? I can think of no one better to lead an attack than one who has just reviewed so powerful a lesson. Your trust and reliance on your King has never been higher. How can we lose?" smiled his new friend.

"It was a humbling lesson for sure," rethought Sir Jonathan aloud. "Okay. I will lead the attack. Let's move out."

The knights mounted up and fell into a patrol formation as they moved down the trail.

Sir Riley had erected a warning sign on the road to tell other citizens of the dangers of the cave.

As soon as the knights were out of sight, a dozen flying imps flew out of the cave opening and tore the sign to pieces.

CHAPTER 14

Deception

"No man that wars concerns himself with the affairs of this life."
– 2 Timothy 2:4

It had been weeks since the incident with the "dragon" and the blowing of the bridge over the Reeking River, and there had been little time for rest or relaxing. Sir Jonathan the Slight was again on the move.

Light snow flurries swirled around him as he galloped down the path, frantically searching for signs of the wagon. He was sure the captives were taken this way. While Sir Stephen, Sir Bjorn, and the rest of their party scouted other trails, he had decided on the one that ran through a bog and then out onto a grassy plain. None of their scouting missions had taken them this far yet.

Every now and then Jonathan thought he saw the tracks of a wagon or the hoof prints of the wooly oxen the goblins used to pull their slave carts. Each time he would dismount and scour the area. Unable to find conclusive evidence, he would remount and continue on.

"We must find them soon," he thought aloud. Having seen the insides of many dungeons, he was repulsed by the thought of the King's citizens imprisoned one moment longer than necessary. He fought pangs of discouragement and a growing sense of desperation with each turn of the trail.

Routing the enemy's siege forces had only enraged the surviving goblin hordes and their commanders. After burning down the keep where the siege engines had been kept, Jonathan had rejoined his friends at the refuge city. But the way back had been dangerous. The woods were full of an enemy bent on revenge.

A scout had seen the filthy creatures ambush and capture a small unit of knights on patrol. Once they were in a slave cart, the enemy disappeared into the forest. Thankfully the scout went for help and the search was on. The rangers split up to try and find them as quickly as possible.

Around the bend in the road, the forest began to lighten so Jonathan could see patches of green through the gaps. He could smell the freshly cut grass and saw a bale of hay tied up in the center. Despite the overwhelming feeling of urgency, the sights and sounds had a calming effect—a fact that bothered him.

Jonathan ventured cautiously into the field. It did not feel right. It was all rather . . . pleasant. Yes, it was a comfortable pasture. It could have been a beautiful spring day.

But it wasn't. Not a few minutes before, he was in the woods and snow flurried around him. This was hotly contested battleground—how could there be farmland? How could anyone be safe planting and harvesting?

As he surveyed the fields, trying to make sense of it all, he noticed a rider on a converging path. He looked harmless, but the knight remembered where he was. Smoothly and effortlessly he reached across to grab the hilt of his sword as he sized up his potential opponent.

"That is far enough unless you intend combat. If that is your intention, by all means continue and I will meet you halfway," challenged Sir Jonathan as he turned his horse to intercept the rider.

"Oh, I mean you no harm and I carry no weapons," replied an old man.

Sir Jonathan instantly recalled his encounter with a beast disguised as an old man before. Though it seemed like ages ago the knight had not forgotten the experience and would not be fooled again.

"No weapons? In a war zone like this? You'll have to do better than that," replied the knight sarcastically as he unsheathed his sword in one fluid motion. Sir Jonathan the Slight prepared himself for a fight.

"I speak the truth. There is a treaty in this area and there is neither need for war nor violence. I am unarmed in compliance with this treaty," answered the elderly traveler as he held up his hands to show he indeed had no weapons.

"Interesting. I did not know there were treaties that would keep goblins out of these lands. Forgive me if I do not disarm as well," answered Sir Jonathan. He moved his head quickly from side to side, scanning the area for signs of an ambush. But all he saw was the wavy green grass moving in the pleasant breeze.

"How is this place so spring-like? Everywhere else around these mountains is cold, wet, and snowy this time of year," asked the knight suspiciously.

Jonathan had learned that if something did not seem right, it was probably a trap. Even as he thought about this, he was encouraged that he was so alert. He remembered reading the Kingsbook and realizing the more he followed the guidance of the King, the less susceptible he was to the deception of the enemy. In particular he thought about the enemy's constant search for a trap that would remove a knight from the battlefield, even if only for a while. After all, this was why he sought the missing knights of the 3rd Regiment.

"The terms of the treaty allow us favorable weather the whole year round—but enough of that now. We are traveling the same way it seems. Can we ride together? What are you doing in our fields?" continued the man.

Sir Jonathan sheathed his sword but not his guard. With the other hand, and out of sight of the traveler, he reached down and unbuckled a short battle axe slung by his saddle. The Kingsbook warned against complacency and Jonathan was determined not to be foolish ever again.

"I am looking for goblins hauling a cart full of citizens of the Great King. The enemy has captured them and I am going to find them. Have you seen anything? Can you point me in their direction?" questioned the knight.

"Indeed not, friend. There are no goblins or any of their allies on these lands or in the town just ahead. See it there? That is my destination," said the man excitedly.

The town sat a short distance away on a low hill. The town, though colorfully decorated, was walled with a large gate in view. Strings of ribbons fluttered in the breeze and gave the settlement the air of a carnival or festival. The gate was open and the road they were on seemed to lead straight to the entrance.

Jonathan looked at the gate and the bright decorations and then remembered an important lesson. The knight had learned that when a beautiful sight appeared it was best to pay attention to the flanks for ambush. He quickly scanned the right and left but saw only bales of hay and wagons of corn and other produce. As he searched, he thought about the man's outlandish claim of the absence of any enemy.

"No goblins? How is it you have been able to reason with them? The only way I have ever been able to converse intelligently with them is with a sword. They don't seem to understand things otherwise," chuckled the knight as he rode on.

"I have not seen a goblin on these lands after the treaty. And certainly not in town," mused the traveler.

"This town . . . is it a King's refuge city? I wasn't aware we had one established this far in the frontier yet. Perhaps some of the knights there have information on the goblins I am hunting," said the knight. But Jonathan knew there were no cities this far into the borderlands of the Great East. Every step forward seemed more like a trap.

"Most certainly not. It is no refuge city and there are no knights there. There may be a few there that are no longer involved in the war, but if there are, I do not know them firsthand. Perhaps it is time I tell you about the treaty, for after all, you will have to make a decision about it soon," said the man mysteriously.

As the two rode together toward the town in the distance, the old man began to speak.

"The treaty is simple. The founders of the city have voted to stay out of the war completely. With the help of a counselor and advisor from the kingdom of the Great East, they drew up a treaty of complete non-participation in the conflict. The treaty calls for no combatants of either side allowed on these lands. As such, no goblins—or knights, for that matter—are permitted entrance to the town or passage through the lands. The territory is small, but it is free of conflict as a result. An additional bonus was granted in favorable weather and all of the food we would need," said the man proudly.

"But what about the enemies of the King? They have enslaved the people of these lands! Their dungeons are everywhere and their atrocities are well known. How could you just deny it is happening?" asked Jonathan, more surprised than upset.

"Those *alleged* atrocities have not been happening here. We live in this town by our own choice; no one is a prisoner. In fact, we have seen reports that the injustice is on the King's side. Now, I do not know of any details, I am just saying what I have heard said from time to time on the streets. But the point is, there is no enslaving here. There is no war. So far—and we have no reason to doubt anything else would happen—the 'enemy' (as you call them) has held their end of the treaty," replied the traveler.

"And did the King sign the treaty? I wouldn't think he would," said Jonathan.

"Sadly, no. We were hoping for total peace in the area, but the King would not sign. His emissaries said the King lays claim to these lands and will not rest while his 'citizens' were being held as slaves. Furthermore, as these alleged 'slaves' might be held on the land in dispute, he would make no agreement precluding his campaign for their release. Even after we sent documents proving no slaves existed on these lands, he would not agree to a truce with the enemy in this area," sighed the man. He seemed genuinely disappointed in the King's refusal.

Every time he mentioned the "citizens" or "slaves" of the King he put a condescending emphasis on the word. It was beginning to irritate Jonathan.

"We were grateful the goblins decided to honor their side of the treaty, and we have been left in peace and provided with wealth and supplies as a result. We have neither permission to leave this paradise nor the need. Indeed, outside of these tolerant lands of rest there is only war. To be honest—and I mean no offense—only the goblins have acted in a way that preserves peace. Most of us have never even seen one. But I must inform you, as per the treaty, you may not enter the town with your weapons and armor. You must disarm and remove the Coat of Arms of the King to enter, friend," said the man with a toothy smile.

The knight had no intention of ever discarding the King's Coat of Arms, but it still sent a pain through his gut to consider such a move. Not in a thousand lifetimes could he imagine laying down his oath to the King and the honor and purpose he felt serving in his name. In that brief moment, Sir Jonathan recounted in his heart the oath of fealty and repeated under his breath to his captain, ". . . *all of my days, from this day until my last day.*"

No enticement of a city of rest, pleasure, and luxury seemed important at all at that point. The very idea caused Jonathan to think he might be on the right track. Everything he heard was the voice of the man but with the words of the enemy. He needed to see more of the city to know for sure. He needed to talk more to this stranger.

"Well, that is an interesting thought and request," answered Jonathan.

"I understand you feel compelled to serve, but before you say 'no,' please hear me out. The town is one of peace and comfort. It affords every luxury known to us. There will be no more nights of cold and days of travel. The sound of battle or the fear of conflict is unknown here.

"Before you decline, you must think of the welcome and opportunity here. Moreover, we need leaders with experience like you have. You have seen much and experienced much—I can see that from the scars on your armor. You would be respected and valued. You might even be made a city counselor. Would you not even consider this?" pleaded the old man. "You will not find a luxury like this anywhere else I have heard of in my life."

"Well, I am considering the situation very carefully, sir," said Jonathan. But he knew in his heart the stranger had no idea just how carefully he was evaluating what he was hearing. And plotting. The stranger may believe he is living in peace and safety, but the more Jonathan listened, the more he heard the words of the enemy.

As they rode along, the town came into better view. It was a magnificent sight. It did not look like the embattled fortress of a refuge city. It was pleasant and brightly colored. Even from a distance he could hear the sounds of laughter and smell the scent of delicious food cooking.

The smell of the food did cause Jonathan's stomach to growl. He realized it had been quite some time since he had eaten well. The activity around the city increased as they approached the outskirts of the town. Jonathan looked around, taking it all in. It did seem very restful. It was then that he realized how tired he was and the words of the old man began to sound enticing. During this enticement, he looked down and saw two distinct wagon ruts and a recognizable piece of cloth.

Enticement. Sir Jonathan had been there before. He did not like it then and he did not like it now. The warnings he felt were no longer obscure as they were in his early days. The enemy was every bit as deceitful, but Jonathan was picking up on it more quickly. As he thought about the trap, he acknowledged that without the training he had received and the truth from the Kingsbook, he would be completely betrayed by his own desire for a little comfort and rest. No, to Jonathan, this stranger's words sounded as much like the enemy as the goblin battle trumpet.

Now he knew for sure he was riding into a trap, but this is where the prisoners would probably be. So he rode on, but he was not riding into the ambush as a victim. He was advancing as a King's knight to where the battle was to be held. He was ready. With very little visible movement he readied his weapons.

The road led through a row of vendors before the entrance to the town. The vendors, who Jonathan assumed were townsfolk, were busy about their work, providing food and supplies to the other town people. They all wore cloaks and seemed quite burly for the ordinary shopkeeper. But everyone seemed so relaxed and peaceful. There was no hint of alarm, except in the knight's heart. As he rode past the first vendors, he became more alert. He, as only a veteran of battle could, had the feeling of being boxed in.

They passed a fruit stand on the side of the road. The vendor was loading a customer's sack with stacks of ripe fruit. The breeze carried the sweet smell right to Sir Jonathan's nose. But the smell was not completely sweet. Jonathan smirked to himself as he also caught the scent of goblin. He knew they were around. No one could ever smell a goblin and forget the pungent odor.

As he looked at the vendor, he noticed him staring back. Through a cloaked hood, the vendor looked at his armor and weapons and shot a quick glance across the road at the vendor with wagons and hay. The knight's heart began to beat faster. The vendor did not have a look of curiosity but alarm. Yes, he was in the right place. Jonathan looked back at the old man and started to say something. Then he stopped.

Wagons. The other vendor had wagons.

Loudly he answered back to the traveler, "Tell me, where would I put my weapons if I were to discard them and reside in your fine town?"

The overt comment had the desired effect, as the "vendors" seemed to relax a little. One even went back to tending the oxen.

"You are considering joining us then? Splendid! We would love a distinguished town's member such as yourself! One of the vendors ahead has a scrap metal shop where we can discard your weapons before we enter the town proper. You will not need them. Your days of war will be over. We must abide by the treaty, of course," exclaimed the man. He seemed genuinely happy at the news.

The loud conversation had just the result the knight was hoping to observe. Knowing glances were cast back and forth between the burly vendors. The knight smiled broadly and laughed as one hand waved at a shop keeper in a display of friendship while the other felt the handle of the readied battle-axe.

"Can we look at these wagons? I might need one if I help with the farming," said Jonathan as he was already guiding his horse over to the vendor's shack.

"Oh, I guess. I don't know why you would, though. No one needs to work in this town if they don't care to work," explained the traveler with a confused look on his face.

"Well, I have often wondered what farming would be like," said Jonathan loudly as he played the part.

When Jonathan neared the wagons he began to search for a clue while trying to not raise suspicion. The wagon wheel ruts around the shack were the same size. The oxen grazing in the pen were the same kinds of oxen that pulled the goblin slave cart, but none of this was proof enough.

Then a glimmer on the ground caught the observant knight's eye. It was a pin with a crest—the crest of the 3rd Regiment, King's Mounted Scouts. He had found them. He felt alarm, joy, and determination all at once while experience reminded him to keep calm and play along.

His face must have betrayed the look of recognition. The vendor, with his eyes fixed on Sir Jonathan's sword hand, walked out of his shack and approached the two riders.

"Who is this knight?" asked the vendor gruffly. "Why is he here? You know the treaty."

Surprised by the gruffness of the normally peaceful road vendors, the older man answered, "Well, he, uh, he is coming to join us. He is renouncing his orders to war and he is disarming. He will be part of our town."

Without breaking eye contact with the knight, the vendor slowed his advance as if deciding what to do next. Under his cloak his yellowish eyes seemed to be shifting back and forth as he thought.

Smiling from ear to ear, Sir Jonathan extended his sword hand to the large vendor and said, "What a wonderful place! I could use a rest from this awful war."

"What is your name?" replied the vendor as he stretched out his hand cautiously.

The knight grabbed his hand to shake it, then suddenly wrenched it toward him, twisting the vendor's wrist with great force. With a loud booming declaration, he answered the question, "I am Sir Jonathan the Slight, King's Knight and Ambassador! What is your name, *goblin*?"

And with that he kicked the vendor in the jaw. The hood flew back revealing the snarl of a goblin, but Jonathan had not let go. The other hand was already whirling around with the medium-sized battle axe he had already loosened. The goblin was squealing and writhing to get free but to no avail. It crashed onto the goblin's head and silenced him mid-squeal.

"What are you doing?!" screamed the old man. "How dare you break treaty on these lands!" He seemed genuinely terrified of the event and the chaos breaking out around them. Only then did Jonathan truly know the man was not a disguised enemy, but the enemy's prisoner.

Swinging around to face the other goblin-vendors, Sir Jonathan replied, "There is no treaty! You are a prisoner of this city! Look around! The vendors are goblin guards. You have been deceived! Ride for the woods, I'll meet you there. The King will set you free and offers you a pardon."

But the man hesitated. "No! We have peace here!" he exclaimed with a look of total bewilderment.

At that moment the vendors, now with long spears, were running at the knight. One goblin stumbled out of the fray and blew a trumpet. Another goblin lashed the old man with a noose around his neck and began to drag him to the town gates. He looked at the knight and grinned maliciously. "He's mine, King's filth!" he spat.

Sir Jonathan the Slight had his hands full with the six or seven guards that were surrounding him. Still on his horse he was able to maneuver around the uncloaked enemy and deal deadly blows with his axe and sword. He took comfort knowing the battle did not depend on his strength. With a weapon in each hand, he rode into the advancing enemy.

He threw his axe at the oxen pen and split the gate, causing a stampede. The confusion was exactly what he wanted. Animals ran in every direction, trampling guards and knocking over vendor stands.

With the illusion melting away, the enemy had no reason to hide its intentions. Nearly every vendor uncloaked to reveal a goblin. The brightly colored walls and decorations of the town fell away to reveal the town was no more than a fortified dungeon. Goblins began to beat the townspeople who were just outside of the gate as they brutally herded them back in the walls.

Sir Jonathan saw the grim sight and realized he would be unable to help those in the dungeon town for now. He turned to block a blow with his shield, then counterattacked with his broadsword. The goblins were still running and squealing in confusion, but some were starting to form a defense. He would not be able to stay much longer.

Just then a few stampeding oxen knocked the corner of a vendor shack completely off of the foundation. It crashed with cloud of dust to reveal a cage. Inside of the cage were seven knights bound and gagged. He had found them!

A pair of goblin guards came running at Sir Jonathan. He blocked one blow, but the other caused his horse to stumble. The knight was thrown from the saddle. Landing in a heap on the ground, he rolled to his feet and parried another blow. Backing up to the cage of knights, he fought off one attacker after another.

"Go! There are too many. Get out while you can!" ordered a knight who had managed to work her gag free.

"No! I'll not abandon friends to a goblin's chain," answered Sir Jonathan the Slight.

But he knew they were right. As the goblins were beginning to form they were moving in and surrounding the cage. Jonathan knew it wouldn't be long.

Just then all of the combatants and prisoners alike heard a thundering horn above the sound of fighting. Looking toward the road from where Jonathan had traveled, they saw a line of knights galloping toward the town.

The knights were in battle formation and in a full advance. Sir Stephen was in the front with his shield tucked just under his chin, leaning into a long, shiny lance. The horses' hooves were thundering now and the King's banner whipped in the wind. The knight with the horn continued to sound the attack.

A dozen goblin guards running toward Jonathan saw the line in full charge. They turned and fled into the fortress. One even dropped his axe as he ran.

A goblin with a crossbow ran to one side and was attempting to fire flaming bolts at the prisoners in the cage as Jonathan tried to block them. Sir Bjorn broke formation and ran the archer down with his lance.

"To the keep!" screeched a goblin sergeant. The enemy retreated in mass chaos toward the city. Enemy archers on the dungeon town wall rained flaming arrows down on the road approaching the fortress.

Sir Jonathan turned and opened the cage, setting the prisoners free. Unbound they began to move back toward the forest. Sir Stephen halted the squadron of knights and encircled the captives in a protective formation.

Jonathan was torn. On one hand they had rescued the knights from the 3rd, but on the other, the so-called town was nothing more than a cleverly disguised dungeon. Moreover, it was so well-fortified it would take more than the squadron of knights to take it with the guards alerted.

"Were you going to take the enemy on all alone?" asked Sir Seamus.

A very out of breath Bjorn added, "Would it be too much to ask to involve us in your adventures?"

"Yes. You, sir, need to learn to share," joked Stephen as they moved away from the fortress.

Jonathan was far too out of breath to answer back. He just laughed and enjoyed the thought of surviving the encounter.

"What are we going to do about the dungeon fortress?" asked a knight from the 3rd while rubbing her wrists where her bonds had left red welts.

"We will report it to the commanders of the area and begin to look for a way through the defenses," answered Seamus.

The knights, both on foot and horses, moved toward the friendly lines in a loose formation. Stephen led the way and Jonathan and Bjorn rode at the rear.

The green fields and gentle breeze had already changed. The fields were a muddy brown and the skies were overcast with a dark grey. There was no promise of spring in the air; the illusion had been replaced with reality. It was a wintery battleground.

"Are my eyes deceiving me or did this entire place just take a turn for the worse?" asked Bjorn to the other knights.

"No. It did not turn. It was always the enemy's ground. The enemy has deceived a dungeon full of people into thinking they were at peace in a wonderful little town," answered Jonathan while looking over his shoulder at the town. "The promise of peace and safety and comfort apart from the King's freedom only leads to slavery. They were having the highest of times in the illusion of freedom but were deep in the reality of slavery. There are slaves in the dungeon and probably captured knights as well."

"That seems worse than death to me," said Bjorn solemnly.

"Indeed, brother. Indeed," answered Jonathan.

CHAPTER 15

The Stranger

"The Lord is my Shepherd . . . ."
– Psalm 23:1

As night began to fall, so did the snow. It was already dark, and now the snow made the visibility worse. The road through the forest was winding and rough. It was the kind of forest that was more foreboding than beautiful, at least these days. Even in daylight the woods were dark and the trees crowded in on each other, making it dense and difficult to traverse. The wind was beginning to blow the snow flurries sideways. Sir Jonathan had searched for an alternate route, but this road was the only way he could search this area of the woods.

It had been several days since his search to find the captured knights. Now a desperate cry for help had gone out from a unit moving through these woods, and knights from his group had split up to find them. The frontier of the Great East was living up to its reputation of danger and excitement.

This is going to be a long night, Sir Jonathan thought to himself as he pulled his cloak a little tighter.

The knight ached from long days that had become long weeks. He was more than weary. He was exhausted and sore. Jonathan was thankful he was riding instead of walking, though. Sores on his feet had gradually turned his stride into a limp when he walked beside his horse. He was also hungry and could hear his stomach growl above the wind. Reaching into his satchel to see if there was anything left to eat, he found only crumbs. Maybe he would find some berries or a small rabbit in the morning. He could wait until then, he thought. He fought off the temptation to feel sorry for himself by considering the danger the other knights were in and what he was asked to do.

He looked around at the shadows his torch made on the trees and the trail. "This would be a great place for an ambush," he thought out loud. He fastened his cloak around his sword so that it gave him some protection against the biting wind but did not hinder a quick draw of the weapon if needed. Sir Jonathan considered stopping for the night and resting. His mission was important, but it was becoming hard to travel and stay alert.

As Sir Jonathan looked for a safer place to rest for the night, something down the trail caught his eye. He immediately drew his sword. Just a few dozen paces ahead he saw a tall figure with a dark cloak pulled around him. Quickly Sir Jonathan looked right then left for any sign of ambush. He then wheeled around to briefly study the trail behind. When he turned back around the stranger was still standing there with a torch in one hand and his other raised. It was obvious to Sir Jonathan that he was armed but had not drawn his sword.

The stranger spoke, "Good evening, Sir Knight. It is a nasty night to be on this road. Is all well? What is your business?"

"Good evening to you, sir. All is well as far as I know and I am on this road on the King's business. Are you also for the King? Tell me the truth, please. It has been a long day, so if you are not for my King let's fight now so I can continue on my way," said Sir Jonathan rather brashly and perhaps even a bit rudely if it were not the middle of a war.

The stranger laughed softly, "Oh, I am no enemy. On the contrary,

I wish you well in your journey since you are on the King's business. In fact, I have a small camp, a warm fire, and some extra venison stew, all of which you are welcome to share, if indeed you ride for the King. Will you join me?" And with that, the stranger turned his back and began to move in the direction of his camp.

Sir Jonathan felt slightly embarrassed that he had challenged the man so roughly. He thought for a moment about the stranger. Was it a trap? No, there was something about his answer and laugh that immediately put the knight at ease. When the stranger turned, Jonathan spotted a royal seal on his cape. Whoever he was and whatever his mission, Jonathan was sure he was no foe.

"Yes, I will join you. And I am grateful for the invitation. I apologize for my lack of manners."

"Nonsense. There is a war on. This is a dangerous road and these are dangerous times. It is refreshing to meet someone who keeps business to the point and remains on alert," responded Jonathan's host.

They both laughed as Sir Jonathan dismounted and limped beside the stranger. Just around the next turn in the road there was a small camp off to the right on a tiny clearing. Large boulders and a rocky outcropping provided walls and even a roof over part of the camp. The fire in the middle radiated heat off the boulders, which also blocked some of the wind. A pot of thick stew simmered on one side of the inviting fire. As soon as Sir Jonathan saw the camp and smelled the stew, he couldn't help himself from smiling at the sight. He also noticed several large, thick blankets and animal skins arranged under the outcropping. It would be the perfect place for some sleep if he could rest for a few minutes, or even a full hour.

Sir Jonathan finished tying up his horse next to the stranger's mount. It was a very large and powerful horse and his looked quite small in comparison.

"Please sit down," the man invited. "Tell me, what is your name and what is your business in this dark forest?"

Jonathan walked over to the fire and set his things behind him. Wincing, he sat down on a log and positioned his feet by the coals. He warmed almost instantly.

"I am Sir Jonathan or Sir Jonathan the Slight if you ask some of my friends. As you can see, I am rather small for a knight," he chuckled.

"I have been assigned to scout this area for signs of the enemy moving against our forces and to find a few of our friends," Jonathan answered. "We are preparing for a push into the Great East as our Lord Sovereign has commanded us. Part of a unit is missing and we have become worried. My job is to scout this forest for signs of a dungeon, then rendezvous with the other knights. Then, together, if we find them in time, we will free the captives."

After listening to his story, Jonathan's host announced, "I have heard of this dungeon you are scouting for and will tell you what I know after you have eaten and rested."

As he spoke he filled a large wooden bowl with heaping spoons of venison stew. He handed the bowl to Sir Jonathan, then picked up a fresh bread roll, tossed it back and forth in his hands to cool it slightly, and tore it in half. When he did, steamed poured out and he handed half to the hungry knight who had already started on his stew.

Each bite was amazing. The stew had big chunks of meat that fell apart as he chewed. It was the best Jonathan had ever tasted.

"Mmm, this is wonderful," Sir Jonathan gushed between mouthfuls. "'Toothsome' as my friend Robert would say. Unbelievably wonderful." The stew warmed him directly, body and soul. "It's wonderful. Simply wonderful," he repeated.

The stranger's laugh warmed Jonathan as much as the stew.

"You like that word, don't you? I am glad you like it. It is my own special recipe," replied the stranger as he poured hot apple cider into a big stone mug and handed it to the knight. He chuckled softly as the knight sighed again at how delicious the food tasted. He slurped loudly.

Except for Jonathan's slurping and muttering of "wonderful" after every other bite, they ate in silence for a few minutes and listened as the wind blew through the tall trees. The snow had begun to fall more steadily now and the flakes were becoming big and wet. The rocky outcropping gave some shelter and it seemed to Sir Jonathan that the snow was only falling outside of their camp, not on them.

Sir Jonathan began to wonder who the stranger was but their cloaks were pulled tightly against the wind and falling snow. "Sir, may I inquire as to your business in this dark forest?"

"Oh, my work is very similar to yours in many ways. Let's just say we are working for the same goal. More bread?" And with that the stranger gave Sir Jonathan another piece of hot bread. Jonathan used the bread to scoop up the last few bites of stew.

They ate in silence for a few more minutes before the host broke the quiet.

"I noticed a limp when you approached the camp. I believe you have some type of foot injury. Is that true?"

"Yes, I have a few blisters and sores that have not healed properly. I can manage though," replied the knight.

"I am well known for my ability in medicine and taking care of blistered feet. Will you let me take a look?" offered the cloaked stranger.

Sir Jonathan could not believe what he was hearing. "Really?" he exclaimed, excited at the thought of a remedy. "Yes, please, if you don't mind."

Sir Jonathan had finished his first mug of cider, and he couldn't eat another bite. He began to remove his boots. As he tried to pull them off he became aware of how bad his feet really were. The sores, blisters, and cuts were sticking to his socks and every move caused him to wince with pain. Jonathan rolled his eyes in frustration and embarrassment. *"A soldier really should take better care of his feet,"* he remembered Robert telling him.

"Allow me," said the stranger as he reached down to assist the knight. Carefully, he pulled the boots off and set them to one side. Then, very gingerly, he pulled the stockings off. Jonathan's feet were a mess and the caring stranger shook his head with genuine compassion. "It's no wonder you have been limping. I have just the thing for this."

Reaching into his bag, the stranger pulled out salve, bandages, and a few small brown bottles of liquids and powders. As the knight sat back the stranger began to clean and apply a thick layer of ointment to the sores on each foot. Amazingly, the knight's feet felt better almost immediately. They were warm and dry and the ointment took the pain away at once. Then the stranger looped some bandages around Jonathan's feet. The knight smiled to himself as he looked up at the snow falling through the tops of the enormous fir trees. His stomach was full, he was warm, and his feet were already feeling better. What a night this was turning out to be.

"Tell me, Sir Jonathan, how did you come to be a knight?"

Very solemnly Sir Jonathan looked at the hooded stranger and began to tell his story.

"I was a prisoner and held in a dark tower for my crimes against the King. I was sentenced to imprisonment and death, and rightly so, as I was a traitor and rebel. The King secured my pardon at no cost to me so that I could be free. He signed my pardon and destroyed my chains. If that wasn't enough, the King offered me an opportunity to help advance his kingdom and free others. I pledged my service and he has equipped me as you see. It is the greatest joy of my life to carry the King's standard into battle and to have served him these years."

The stranger listened as he sipped on a mug of cider. After a few moments of silence, he asked the knight, "And if your King were here, what would you say to him?"

Sir Jonathan poked the fire and without looking up said very seriously and quietly, "I would thank him. I would tell him he is my King and Captain and I will follow him and serve him all of my life. I have never known anyone like him."

"So you are friends, then?"

"I did not say that. No, I would want to be very much, but he is the King! Don't misunderstand me, though, I would love to have him call *me* friend, for I certainly consider him mine. I have never had a friend like him. It's just that I have not even been to the City Beautiful, and I have only seen him on the day of my release. I would not want to presume," replied Sir Jonathan. "But I cannot imagine anyone who has been more of a friend to me than the King. And I would want him to know that. My Captain deserves to be revered as the only King, and I do, very much, pledge my fealty to him. But more than just respect and obey him as King, I love him as well." Jonathan's voice trailed off a little. He was silent for a few moments and then continued, "He is the One King. He is my King. I'll have no other all of my days."

The wind howled through the trees as they sat around the fire in silence, thinking about what the knight had just said. Both of them sipped on their cider for a few minutes without talking.

"Jonathan, you mentioned the City Beautiful. Did you know that the King has a great hall there where his knights are invited to dine with him? When he welcomes a warrior home they feast in that hall together with all of the other knights who have already returned home. He has a place for every beloved citizen he has rescued in that wonderful city, but the hall is special and reserved," said the stranger.

"Really? Reserved for whom?" The exhausted Jonathan sat up straight. Instantly he awoke and his mind filled with questions and excitement.

"It is reserved for those who take up the call to live and fight as the King has commanded. It is a special place for ordinary citizens who simply obeyed and became the knights they were rescued to be. There is a special order of knight there as well. It is a place like no other, Sir Jonathan. Like no other, indeed," said the stranger.

Sir Jonathan looked at the cloaked stranger in near shock. Then he said evenly and seriously, emphasizing every word, "I have heard of nothing that I want more than to be invited into that hall by the King to eat with him and his knights! This is what I want above all now. How can I be sure to receive an invitation, friend? Please tell me what you know."

"You were called to be a knight and you have taken an oath to serve the King and the King only, right? Well, then, fulfill that oath. But you do not have the power to win, do you? Your Captain does and has provided you with everything necessary. Be faithful, Sir Jonathan, even in the face of certain death. Trust your King."

"I will. I want to, at least. I want nothing more," the knight said over and over.

They both looked into the fire for a while longer. Sir Jonathan poked a few coals with a stick and could not stop thinking about the Great Hall in the City Beautiful where the King (*the King himself!*) feasted with his citizens. His mind swam with thoughts about eating with the King and being an invited guest.

The stranger again broke the silence with another question. "You have told me what you would say to your King. Now tell me what you would want your King to say to you, if he were here at our fire."

Sir Jonathan did not hesitate to answer. He already knew what he would say.

"I would want him to tell me I am faithful. I would want to know above all else that he is pleased with my service to him. And I would want him to know that the greatest honor of my life is to bear his name as my King and his coat of arms on my armor. I seem to fail almost as much as I succeed, but I have no other ambition in this life. I would want him to tell me I am needed."

The stranger nodded slowly and seemed to affirm Jonathan's sentiments. Jonathan saw him smile. They sat for a while and both seemed to be thinking about the knight's words. Then it became obvious the stranger had something to say. He stroked his beard, stirred the fire, and cleared his throat.

"Sir Knight, would you really want the King to need you?" he asked with a depth in his words. Every syllable dripped with meaning.

Jonathan stopped and thought about it for a moment, perhaps for the first time. He felt much like he did when Robert or Stephen would ask a question that made him think.

"Well, I think so. What could be better than to be needed in battle for the King?" he asked, with growing confidence in his thought process.

"Indeed. What could be better?" asked the stranger. But the way he posed the question caused the knight to grow less confident. The stranger paused for quite some time and stirred the fire. Jonathan was dying to continue the conversation.

Finally the stranger spoke. "Suppose your friend, Sir Robert, had a journey to go on. An important mission that could not wait. In fact, you both knew it would be the journey of a lifetime. But the load Robert had to take on the journey was twice as much as he could bear. He needed help and you were the one he asked. How would you feel?" asked the stranger, turning just enough for Jonathan to see a smile in his thick snowy beard.

"Needed. I would feel needed and I would be glad for it, I suppose."

The stranger paused for some time and then continued, but his voice had taken on a deeper, richer tone.

"But suppose Sir Robert came to you on the eve of this great mission, this critical journey and he had no burden. There was nothing to carry. He did not *need* your help," the stranger paused for effect and sipped his mug of cider. "But, he invited you all the same. He asked you to join him. He did not need your help, but he desired your company. Now tell me, how would you feel?"

Jonathan thought for some time. Then, in a realization that would change his life for all time, he looked up at the hooded stranger. The knight's eyes revealed surprise and indescribable joy. He could barely speak, but he whispered the truth the stranger had just led him to ponder.

"*Wanted*," he gasped. His mind reeled with the idea.

"Do you think the King, mighty in battle, the only one who could defeat the enemy and all of his forces, *needs* you to 'help carry the load,' so to speak?" asked the stranger. His words were pointed and direct, but his tone was fatherly and gentle. "No. The King does not call for aid, for he has never needed rescue. But he has invited you, Sir Jonathan the Slight, King's knight. He has invited you on this journey. What does that mean to you?"

"Dare I answer what my heart tells me is the answer? I believe it can only mean I am wanted on this journey. I am more than a servant. I am a companion," muttered Jonathan, scarcely able to believe what he was learning. He was overwhelmed to the point of near dizziness.

The stranger took a long drink of his cider, then spoke again. "To be needed in time of trouble is good, but to be wanted for companionship is far greater. The King has no need of rescue, but he certainly desires and invites companionship. *Your* companionship, Jonathan."

With cloaks pulled tight against the cold, the two sat in silence around the fire for some time before the stranger spoke again. "I could not help but notice that much of your armor and weapons bear the marks of vigorous use. Some of it could use repair and sharpening. I am skilled in this as well and would offer my services to you. May I help you?"

Sir Jonathan sighed and said, "I wish that you could, but my armor and weapons are Kingforged from the City Beautiful itself. Only the King has the skill to make these weapons, and I doubt that anyone else can repair them. But you are very kind to offer and I am grateful."

This time it was the stranger that smiled, though Sir Jonathan could only see part of the smile under his hood. In a very kind but confident voice he replied, "Of course they are, but trust me when I say I am also skilled in this and you might be surprised. If not, nothing is lost but time spent with a friend around a warm fire."

Sir Jonathan was amused but also knew his things needed repair and sharpening. And this stranger had done wonders with his feet and the stew. He handed his sword and shield to the stranger along with other pieces of well-worn armor.

The stranger began with the King's Coat of Arms. He polished it on the hilt of the sword until it gleamed brightly in the glow of the fire. Then he started in on the sword. He pulled out of his bag a bluish stone and began to sharpen the blade. The stone looked like a jewel to Jonathan, but the stranger seemed to use it as a sharpener. Stroke after stroke he moved the stone back and forth. Small purplish sparks flew off. Sir Jonathan was amazed. Then the stranger reached into a leather bag, pulled out a few tools, and began to work on the handle and hilt. In no time the bits of scrap leather that Sir Jonathan had wrapped around the hilt were replaced with a proper handle. When he handed the broadsword back to Sir Jonathan, the knight was astonished. It still had the nicks and scars of many battles, but it was as sharp as the day he received it—maybe even sharper. The new handle was perfect and seemed to have been made for his hand.

"This is amazing work!" exclaimed Jonathan.

"And I am not finished," replied the stranger with a grin. The shield was next. For a long time, he worked on the pieces of armor, but Sir Jonathan was unable to stay awake. The warm fire, the comfort of his feet, and a full belly made his exhaustion sweep over him like a giant wave. Several times he trailed off in mid-sentence. Once, having begun to dream while sitting up, he began to babble as if the dream were real. The stranger chuckled when Jonathan realized he was sleeping and talking.

"Please, lie down and take advantage of a warm bed by the fire. I'll finish this while you sleep. You can't continue on your way if you fall out of the saddle and break something."

Sir Jonathan protested, "Yes, thank you, but I cannot sleep. One of us must stand watch and you have been so hospitable and generous. I'll take the first watch."

Laughing jovially the stranger replied, "Ha! There is no way I would let you stand watch when you cannot even stand. You must stay off your feet while the ointment sets, you are exhausted, and your weapons are being repaired. I'll finish here and stand watch."

"Thank you, Sir. I'll take the next watch. Wake me in a few hours?" he asked.

"I'll wake you when I am finished watching and not before," he answered firmly but warmly, chuckling as he emphasized "*not before.*"

"As you say. Thank you again."

"Sleep well, Sir Knight. Sleep well and rest. I am on watch."

The knight realized he was in terrible danger. He was backed against a stone wall and the dragon was coming closer. Half walking and half slithering, the dragon approached. Every time he opened his great mouth, smoke poured out and the knight could see rows of sharp fangs, each the size of a dagger. The jagged fangs dripped with venom and rage. The knight reached for his shield but it was broken into pieces. He drew his sword but it too was shattered, just shards of metal. There was nowhere to run and nowhere to hide. It was truly the end! The dragon laughed and slowly began to inhale a mighty breath. Even the yellow eyes of the beast seemed to be mocking as he brought his head around to exhale the fiery end of the knight . . .

"Sir Jonathan! Sir Jonathan! You are fighting a battle instead of sleeping as you were instructed," joked the stranger as he squeezed his shoulder. "Go back to sleep. There are no dragons here tonight. Rest."

Sir Jonathan was relieved to see the stranger and not a dragon. "My apologies. I hope I didn't yell too loudly."

"Even a yell would be quieter than your snoring," laughed the stranger.

As the stranger turned around to continue his watch, Jonathan laid his head back to sleep some more. Almost an inch of snow had fallen and the stranger's cloak had a fine, powdery coat. As he was drifting off, Jonathan saw the stranger lean back on his sword. *"I have seen that sword before,"* thought Jonathan, but he was so exhausted he was having a hard time focusing on his thoughts and memories. Before he could think more about it, he was asleep.

Sir Jonathan awoke with a start. Where was he? What was happening? Slowly he realized he was comfortable under several very large and warm furs and blankets. The woods were a dull misty grey from the early dawn. The fire was still large and roaring. He looked around and saw the stranger still standing watch. It was as if he had not moved from the post all night. He was covered in snow.

"I missed my watch! You didn't wake me?" accused Sir Jonathan through a yawn.

The stranger turned to stir a pot and laughed, "I said I would wake you when it was time for your watch. It isn't yet, hence you were not awakened. Sleep well?"

"Incredibly well. Thank you very much." Jonathan looked at his armor stacked neatly at the foot of his makeshift bed. It was still scarred and dinged, but it was repaired. His weapons were sharpened and his armor was ready for battle. Even a boot had been repaired.

Slowly Sir Jonathan swung his legs around to put his socks and boots on. That is when he noticed his feet. The bandages were loose and the sores were all gone. There were no open wounds. A few places were purplish from the healing, but the blisters were completely healed. Astonished, he turned to the stranger, who was pouring them both a mug of hot tea. "My feet . . . they are all better! How did you do that?"

"I told you I have seen wounded feet before. It is good ointment for beautiful feet," smiled the stranger as he handed Sir Jonathan the tea. Jonathan sipped the tea and looked at his feet. He would not be limping today. He was overcome with gratitude.

Sir Jonathan sat down in front of the fire and the stranger handed him breakfast—a fresh roll of bread with leftover stewed venison from the night before inside, and a hunk of cheese. It was incredible. As Sir Jonathan ate he began to think about everything that had happened in the last twelve hours. He began the evening exhausted, tired, and hungry on a dark road through a dark forest. Here he was now with a kind friend, healed feet, a full belly, repaired armor, and a great night's sleep on a warm bed.

"I cannot begin to thank you enough for your kindness and help. I am not sure I would have even been successful in my mission without your help, Sir. May I inquire as to your name, friend?" asked Jonathan sincerely.

"My name? Soon enough, but first, while you eat let me share with you the information about your mission."

As Sir Jonathan ate the bread and meat, the stranger unfolded a map and began to give him directions on which trail to take to the enemy stronghold. He then followed up with enemy troop strengths and weaknesses to their defenses.

"That is a lot of enemy troops. I might need to return to the camp and gather some reinforcements," said Sir Jonathan, looking at the map.

"There is no time. All indications point to the enemy moving the prisoners soon—maybe even today. You need to ride now and strike soon to assure success, Jonathan," replied the stranger evenly but with great authority. "I have already sent for the remainder of your unit. They will be along soon."

Sir Jonathan realized the man was correct. It was time to go. "You are right. But there are a lot of enemies between us."

"Sir Jonathan, never forget your armor and weapons were forged by the King for the King's business. The number of foe you face cannot be compared to the power the King has and has given you," the stranger encouraged.

Sir Jonathan nodded and knew he was right. He stood up quickly. It was time to move. Again he was aware of how rested and healthy he felt. Everything seemed new and strong.

Hurriedly Sir Jonathan gathered his things and dressed for the battle ahead. Just before mounting up he turned to the stranger, "Dear Sir, you have been so kind to me. I am grateful beyond words. I sincerely hope I see you again."

The stranger grabbed Sir Jonathan's shoulders, "You will, Jonathan. I assure you we will see each other again and eat another fine meal together. Ride hard and fight courageously and you will be successful today."

Sir Jonathan mounted up but now more than ever he was beginning to think he had met this man before. His brain was shouting details at him but he pushed those thoughts to the side to mentally plan for the battle ahead.

"Sir, thank you so much, and I look forward to our meeting again. Long Live the King!" And with that, Sir Jonathan spurred his horse and galloped down the snowy trail, still thinking about his encounter with the mysterious stranger. It was not but a few minutes later when he abruptly halted his horse.

All of the details came together! *Could it have been him?* It had to have been the King himself! Only the King could have repaired his armor. Only the King carried the sword that he saw. Now he remembered the crest he saw on the stranger's sword—it was the same sword and crest he saw the night the King freed him from the dungeon. It had to have been him!

Jonathan wheeled the horse around and galloped the short distance to the camp. When he arrived, the stranger was gone. The camp was also gone. All that was left was a smoldering campfire and a leather pouch with the King's seal on it. It had a letter on it addressed to Sir Jonathan. With trembling hands Sir Jonathan broke the seal and opened the letter.

It was handwritten and read, "Fight courageously today, Faithful Knight. We will enjoy another meal again soon." With the letter were three apples and three round loaves of bread that were still warm to the touch with meat and cheese packed inside.

Jonathan was overcome with emotion. On the night he needed the most help and guidance, the King himself had appeared and helped him. His feet were better and his armor was repaired. He was rested and not starving. What an amazing King! With sincere love for the King and gratitude for his time with his Captain, Sir Jonathan wheeled his horse around and galloped toward the waiting enemy.

CHAPTER 16

Orders Received

"Be strong in the Lord and in the strength of his might . . ."
– Ephesians 6:10

Sir Jonathan flew down the trail, still pondering his encounter with the King. Though the snow fell thickly, he was warmed by the thought. The wind howled and visibility was dropping quickly. But the knight did not care. He had just spoken with the King and was on a mission of his own direction. He was happy to be exactly where he was at the moment.

As he approached a crossroad, Jonathan slowed his horse to a trot and began to survey the area. All of a sudden he was surrounded. Filthy goblins, Greys, and a very large trollish looking creature encircled the knight. The troll was three times the size of a man and carried a giant club with a spike.

"Well, well, what do we 'ave 'ere?" bellowed the largest goblin the knight had ever seen. He was undoubtedly in charge.

"Out of my way! I am on the King's business. I am in a hurry and I haven't time to kill you all. Clear the road," said Sir Jonathan evenly without any emotion.

But it was an act. He was surrounded and he knew it. The familiar knots that appeared in his stomach before a battle returned.

The enemy soldiers laughed and scoffed. They also moved closer. Swords came out and axes shifted from hand to hand. There was no mistaking their intent. They wanted to pull him apart.

"You're a lit'le short in th' saddle to be speaking so rudely to me an' my men. One way or the other, hard way or not, you're finished," snarled the goblin chief, pointing a green bony finger at Jonathan. He flashed a mouth full of jagged teeth while readying a nasty-looking axe.

"But if you dismount, yield your weapons and armor and tell us why you are trespassing in our homelands, perhaps we will spare your life for a while. Perhaps," he continued.

Snickers and laughs echoed through the enemy ranks. They knew they had the smaller knight cornered. He would be an easy kill.

Jonathan looked around and realized there was nowhere to go. They had closed in behind him. He had been in tight spots in the past, but not like this. The troll-looking creature was as big as the beast from the first dungeon. This could be the end.

At the same time Sir Jonathan the Slight began to remember his time with the King. The King had encouraged him to not see the number of the enemy as much as the power of the King. He thought about the promise of victory the King gave him. He slowly reached across and wrapped his mailed hand around the hilt of his sword. He looked at the still-scoffing enemy and smiled. Not a fake smile, but a genuine confidence that spilled over into a joy to be exactly where he was—preparing to do battle for his King.

And then he saw something in the goblin chief's eyes. Just for a moment he saw a flicker of . . . fear?

Yes, it *was* fear!

It hit Sir Jonathan the Slight and he realized a timeless truth. The enemy knew what he sometimes forgot: they are no match for the King's weapons wielded in the King's power. They could not win, and Sir Jonathan could not lose.

Without another word, Sir Jonathan dismounted. He locked eyes on the chief and unsheathed his sword. He began to walk steadily toward the enemy captain as if the other enemy soldiers did not even exist. The look of shock on all of the goblins' faces confirmed Sir Jonathan's original thought. They really expected him to run or yield. Several on the periphery began to slink away.

The troll stepped forward, also surprised at the knight's steady pace toward the chief. The confident advance threw the ugly thing's timing off. He attempted to raise his club for a mighty blow but at that instant the knight darted forward with a burst of speed. He jumped up and stuck the sword straight through the creature's throat. It died before it could howl. More goblins melted into the forest.

"How dare you . . ." began the goblin chief, but he never finished his sentence. The sword in Sir Jonathan's hand was lighter than it had ever been. Just as the King had said, it was amazingly powerful. As soon as he had withdrawn the sword from the troll's throat he spun around and with a two-handed blow decapitated the goblin chief. The enemy captain and the enemy champion were defeated.

The goblins and Greys began to screech, curse, and howl as they saw both their champion and chief cut down so quickly and easily. Some ran away while others charged. Sir Jonathan counterattacked. The sword felt lighter and sharper than ever before. His shield felt stronger. There were enemies everywhere but they seemed to be so slow compared to what the knight expected. He realized the difference was the confidence he placed in the King. A giant mace crashed down on him, but with a swat of his shield it shattered.

Within just a few short moments, it was all over. Dead goblins and Greys lay everywhere. Many others had retreated. Thick, oily black streaks in the snow from the wounded trailed off in every direction. Jonathan could still hear them yelping as they tore through the forest.

Jonathan looked around, then yelled as loudly as he could, *"LONG LIVE THE KING!"* The knight's battle cry echoed on the wind and blowing snow.

He quickly mounted and raced down the path right in front of him. He needed to hurry now since word of his presence in the woods would surely spread to the enemy fortress. He rode as fast as he dared in the blinding snow.

Eventually the snow and fog lifted slightly. He continued around the winding paths, ready for the next enemy to jump out.

Through one stand of trees, he found himself in an opening in the forest. In the wide clearing he saw a black and awful castle keep. On the drawbridge were two wagons full of prisoners. Goblins bustled around, preparing to move out. It was clear the enemy was not expecting his arrival. They had not even posted a guard. Perhaps they were expecting the enemies in the woods to protect them?

The King had been right; he had to strike now or they might lose the prisoners. There was no time to waste. The knight lowered his faceplate and readied his shield and lance. He planned to charge right up the middle. He counted at least twelve goblins.

Then to his right he saw something move along the tree line. It was a horse with a rider. No, it was King's knight. He looked over at the knight and saluted. The knight lifted his faceplate to reveal it was Sir Bjorn. With a grin he saluted back.

Sir Jonathan was ecstatic to see his friend and one-time apprentice. He had been missed. On the other side was another old friend, Sir Stephen, who also saluted.

As they rode up to Sir Jonathan, the commotion alerted the goblins. They saw the knights, shot several arrows that fell harmlessly short, and ran for the castle door. The goblins slithered in and bolted it fast.

The knights exchanged very quick greetings and galloped toward the wagons. The captives inside were grateful to see the knights.

"Oh, thank you!" cried one.

"Greetings," said Sir Stephen. "In a bit of mess, are we?"

"It would have been much worse had it not been for you three. They were about to take us deeper toward their headquarters for questions, I'm afraid. They said we were going to feed the dragon. We are all very glad not to be going there," shivered one knight.

Sir Jonathan drew his sword and split the cages open. Everyone piled out, visibly relieved.

As they moved out of bowshot of the towers, both Sir Jonathan and Sir Stephen noticed something peculiar. All of the captives were knights and seemed to be in very good shape. They did not have the look of those who had been in captivity long. Furthermore, they all bore the insignia of the same unit. This was very strange.

They led them into the woods and out of sight of the tower. Finding a clearing in the woods surrounded by boulders, they built fires for warmth.

"What do you think of our new friends?" asked Stephen, out of earshot of the rescued.

"I have never seen an entire unit captured before. I would like to know what happened," answered Bjorn. "I'll take first watch, but tell me what you find out."

Sir Bjorn climbed up on a house-sized boulder and stood watch. The snow began to fall again, which could hide a counterattack. Bjorn removed his bow and began to survey the forest in front of him.

Sir Stephen and Sir Jonathan approached the group. They were growing more and more curious.

"May I ask a question? Who are you? You don't seem to be citizens or individual wayward knights but part of the same unit. How were you captured?" asked Sir Stephen.

"It is very embarrassing, but you deserve the truth. I am Sir Riley and we are all part of the same unit as you observed. Or we were. While we were headed for the front, our commander, who was quite young, sometimes gave us commands that did not make sense to us. At times we did not understand why he and his junior officers chose one path over another."

"I see. This is more common than is necessary, I am afraid. What happened next?" asked Sir Jonathan.

"Along the way we were joined by a Sergeant at Arms from another unit. He said he had been separated from his command in battle on a faraway front. He asked to ride with us. At first he was very helpful. He always seemed to be friendly and he could cook very well. We began to trust him. He always spoke of battles he had been in and victories he had won. But he never mentioned the King."

"That should have told us everything we needed to know," interrupted a knight sadly, a Sir Ander by name.

Riley shook his head and put his hand on the shoulder of the other knight. He took a deep breath and continued. It seemed to Jonathan and Stephen that his words were painful to say.

"One day our commander, Sir Nevin, gave us orders to march in a certain direction. He had chosen the most difficult route. The sergeant overheard our discussions and joined in the dissent. Always with a smile, but he dissented nonetheless. As the days passed, the sergeant always seemed to know what to do. On several occasions he pointed out right where the enemy was camping. But they always slipped away. We blamed it on our commander Sir Nevin, but always credited the knowledge of finding them to the sergeant."

"How convenient that this sergeant knew where the enemy was," mused Sir Stephen while looking from Riley to Jonathan.

"Yes. It was convenient. Blinded by discontent, we could see no good in our commander and no fault in the sergeant. He claimed to know a better way to accomplish our objectives without nights in the forest," Sir Riley said, then paused, looking down.

"Go on, brother," said Sir Stephen.

"In direct violation of our vows and honor and loyalty, we abandoned our commander in the night. Over half of our unit came with us," said Riley slowly.

Several of the knights looked away. One put her head in her hands and sobbed quietly.

"We followed the sergeant to this castle and attacked. It was a trap. The sergeant was a very cleverly disguised enemy and we were caught and imprisoned two nights ago," finished Sir Riley.

No one spoke for a few minutes. The heaviness of the failure seemed to weigh the knights down. The only sound was the wind blowing through the giant, snow-covered fir trees as each knight thought of his or her own betrayal.

"Well, you are safe now. And on the road to rejoining your unit, I suppose," said Sir Jonathan encouragingly.

"No. No, we aren't. And that is the most horrible part. When we abandoned our commander they were left with less than half of their forces. They were ambushed the next night. Many were wounded terribly. Some were killed. The unit had to turn back and to our knowledge, the mission we were on could not be completed. We caused our unit to fail. We failed our King," lamented Sir Riley. The weight of their short-sightedness was sinking in. Jonathan could empathize and felt genuine sorrow for their commander and the rest of the unit.

Stephen opened his mouth several times to attempt to encourage them, but he could not find the words. The sadness of a commander abandoned in the field was overwhelming.

"How did you come by this information?" asked Sir Stephen.

"The 'sergeant' told us the night they went out to ambush the unit. Then they returned with pieces of armor and things left behind," answered Sir Riley. "Among the trophies was our commander's bloodied saddle."

"What did this sergeant look like?" asked Sir Jonathan. His anger was growing.

"When not disguised, he was a very ugly goblin and bigger than most. He has a troll with him who is a fearsome monster," replied a knight.

"The band that attacked our unit was mixed with Greys as well," said another knight. "He disguised himself with some kind of power. He is a very rotten enemy, indeed."

"Was," said Sir Jonathan resolutely.

"Excuse me, Sir Knight?" inquired the lady with her head in her hands. She lifted her head in hope, straining to hear. "What did you say?"

"He *was* a very rotten enemy. I relieved him of his exceedingly ugly head. And just shortly before that, I killed the troll. Most of his cutthroats ran off, but those that didn't have their carcasses scattered along this trail," answered Sir Jonathan. "He will not be deceiving anyone again."

Sir Stephen grinned. "You have been busy."

"Well done, sir! Did you see any sign of our unit?" asked Riley, his face showing relief.

"No. I am afraid not, my friend," answered Sir Jonathan.

"What was your mission?" asked Sir Stephen, changing the subject.

"Just beyond the frontier, a large enemy force is blocking the entrance to the Great East territory. If that force can be defeated or driven back, there will be a way into the territory. The King's army is massing for an invasion, but the entranced is blocked for now. Forward scouts report it is the largest enemy force yet, possibly an entire army. Some say they have a dragon, too. A large red and black fire breather named Apateon. We have been marshaling a great force to join the battle. Our unit was told to move through these forests and the mountains to our east and gather all available units. I still have a copy of the orders hidden in my boot," answered Sir Riley.

He pulled the parchment out and unrolled it. The King's seal was on the top and the orders were quite plain. All available units were to report to the front. The enemy was to be attacked head on immediately, and slaves were to be rescued.

"There is no mistaking the orders. It includes us as well," said Sir Stephen. He let out a low whistle mimicking a bird—the signal for Bjorn to join them.

Bjorn left his post as over watch and ran toward Stephen. Bjorn could tell by the look on his face that Stephen had serious news.

"Gentlemen, we have only option: to obey. Agreed?" asked Stephen.

"Agreed," they said together.

"I will ride for Seamus and the rest of the unit. They were to meet us back at the camp after these trails were scouted. I will relay the orders to them, and we will ride for the front and attack immediately as instructed. Sir Bjorn, will you escort the knights to the refuge city on the outside of the forest? Rearm the knights and lead them to the front. Sir Riley, will you follow Sir Bjorn?" asked Sir Stephen.

"Yes, but we are not worthy to continue to the front. We will stay at the city," answered Sir Riley, ruefully refusing to make eye contact.

Sir Jonathan began to protest, but Sir Bjorn interrupted him.

"What you did was treasonous, to be sure. But will you now add disobedience and dishonor to that mistake? Did you learn from your errors?" asked Sir Bjorn.

"Yes. Yes, we have." All of the knights nodded and moved closer to the three.

"Then forget the past and fulfill your vows. Do not forget you have sworn to follow the King, who bought you and sealed your pardon. Do not let your rebellion on the field be the last thing you do as his soldiers. Remember who you are. If our King did not forgive and restore, you would still be in your dungeon cells. But he does. Awake in yourselves the desire to please the One King. Will you ride with me to the front to obey his commands?" asked Sir Bjorn passionately.

"Aye. We will ride with you, Sir Bjorn. We will follow you into battle as captain," they answered. "And none of us will turn back as before."

"And that leaves you, Sir Jonathan. It seems the orders are urgent. We cannot delay," said Sir Stephen.

"Agreed. I will ride directly to the front and inform the

commanders you are on your way. I'll gather any soldier along the way and bring them to the front as commanded. The orders are to attack immediately, so I will be needed there. If Apateon is there, I have something to give the officer in charge that may affect the outcome. I cannot delay. I trust I will see you all in a few days, brothers," said Sir Jonathan with a bright smile and a firm handshake.

"Oh, one more thing," added Jonathan. He reached in his bag and tossed them each an apple and a roll with the meat and cheese inside.

"Where did you get these?" asked Stephen incredulously as he swallowed a bite. "We are starving."

"A friend of ours sent them. Enjoy," answered Jonathan, who was amazed and encouraged that the King had known he would see his friends and that they too would need food. What a wonderful King!

The knights mounted and traded words of encouragement and laughter while the rescued knights formed up on the snowy road to march. Then they all shook hands, shouted *"Long Live the King,"* and rode off in their separate directions. Jonathan couldn't help but wonder if it was for the last time.

CHAPTER 17

The Charge

"Suffer hardship with me, as a good soldier of Christ Jesus."
– 2 Timothy 2:3

Sir Jonathan the Slight's mind raced as did his horse through the forest toward the King's armies. Fallen branches snapped and scattered beneath the hooves of his horse. Normally he would have taken it much more slowly, but the orders were urgent. The icy wind whipped his face and reddened his cheeks as he galloped on toward the meeting point. The enemy's resistance grew stronger as they moved closer to the front. It was full of the King's subjects who needed to hear his terms. Danger or not, they had to keep pressing the attack.

Jonathan remembered the gift Sir Robert had given him some time ago. While galloping through the forest he reached around and felt the saddlebag. His hand closed around the hard steel. Yes. It was there. Hopefully the officer in charge would give it to the best heavy horse knight he had to take on the dragon. Apparently, Sir Robert had known all along this would be a great and terrible battle.

Just then three soldiers with long lances stepped out of the bushes. One held up a hand.

"Halt! Come forward slowly and be identified," challenged the sentry.

"Sir Jonathan the Slight, a knight of the King's 5th Cavalry Light Mounted Rangers and Royal High Ambassador. I am responding to the orders to assemble for battle in the Far Valley, entrance to the heart of the Great East."

"Greetings in the King's name then, Sir Jonathan. You'll find the forces entrenched just a few leagues down this trail. Godspeed," called the sentry.

Sir Jonathan removed the hood from his cloak but left the chain mail in place. He looked at the sentry. Surely he heard him wrong.

"Sir, did you say the King's army was *entrenched*?"

"Yes sir. They have thrown up earthen works along the ridge on the edge of the forest. It is very defensible. They have a great view of the Far Valley," answered the sentry.

"But the orders were to attack. Not entrench. I am confused. Why aren't we attacking?" asked the knight.

"Well, some did attack as the orders stated. But they were driven back. Some were killed and many were wounded. They have a dragon, you know—Apateon. He isn't the biggest dragon, of course, but he is the biggest any of us have seen."

"Well, he isn't as large as *Thanatos the Unbeaten*, that is for sure," said another sentry. The rest nodded and agreed.

The first sentry continued, "And they have a frightful array of troops. They hold the high ground on either side of the valley. The enemy is incredibly strong. I don't think we have enough troops. That is my opinion," answered the soldier.

"It has never been, nor will it ever be about our number or the strength of our arms, my brother. We have orders. We obey. We trust the King and watch *him* win," said Sir Jonathan passionately. The thought of an army entrenched instead of advancing caused Sir Jonathan's stomach to turn.

The sentries didn't answer. They just looked around at each other. One kicked at a rock with her boot. Nothing more was said on the matter.

Sir Jonathan bid them farewell and rode on. How could they be entrenched? It was not the order of battle to entrench. *No ground is gained that way*, he thought. The knight was troubled. He had not expected this at all.

After a few leagues he saw it was true. All along the ridge line that separated the Far Valley from the forest, the King's army had entrenched. Long wooden spikes formed defenses and the soldiers stayed safely behind them. Sir Jonathan looked down the line and saw all manner of soldiers and knights and archers. A few looked wounded and exhausted. Most were resting and carrying on the daily duties that accompanied an army at camp.

Then Jonathan looked behind the King's forces to the valley beyond. It was an awful sight.

Out over the valley, in the far distance, he saw the enemy forces. They were arrayed in legions like six large black boxes of insects. In the middle slithered a dragon, black and red and striped like a lizard. It shrieked and howled and blew big fireballs into the air as if to warn all who could see what death awaited them if they ventured out. Jonathan shivered at the sight.

Then he saw something that made his stomach turn. The enemy, in an insult to his King, had brought out cages of slaves to parade up and down the lines. They were taunted and mocked. Some, it was evident from the broken cages, had already been executed or fed to the dragon. It both angered Sir Jonathan and filled him with desperation to see them rescued.

His fury at Apateon grew.

Jonathan needed to speak to the commander in charge immediately. He looked around until he found an officer who pointed him in the right direction.

He rode over to a tent with banners flying the King's seal and the standard of a heavy horse mounted unit. All of the horses were unsaddled and tied in the woods where the dragon could not see them and be tempted to devour them as a snack. He dismounted and walked into the tent.

"Greetings. Long Live the King!" said Sir Jonathan confidently even though he was the shortest knight in the tent.

"Long Live the King!" they all replied.

"Sir Jonathan the Slight, King's 5th Rangers, reporting as ordered. Who is in charge here?" asked the knight.

"I am." A man stepped forward and extended his right arm in greeting. "Major Justin, Commander 11th Heavy Horse. How may I help you?" asked the Major jovially.

"I am wondering where to go and what element to join. I have more from my unit coming, but it may be a few days. When is the attack planned?" asked Sir Jonathan.

"Attack?" the Major repeated. The tent grew uncomfortably silent. After a pause, in which all eyes turned to Jonathan to size him up, the Major spoke.

"We already tried that. It was not pretty. We are defending this area now. I know of no attack scheduled," he answered, looking back down. His answer wasn't as jovial as his greeting.

Jonathan's mind was spinning. He knew what the orders were and he saw the desperate condition of the slaves. Yet, at the same time, he was in the presence of officers more experienced and decorated than he. His stomach was in knots. Standing among those who were not following the King's orders was more uncomfortable than preparing for battle. He wanted to back out of the tent and disappear. He wished his friends were there; they would know what to do. Then, he heard himself speak.

"Sir. With all due respect, it is my understanding that we are to attack immediately. The prisoners are in danger and the orders are clear. We should not even delay another hour. With the King's power the victory will surely be ours," replied the smaller knight.

One knight laughed softly and turned back to his papers. The Major looked up with a sour expression that turned to a faint smile.

"Yes, the orders say attack. But we can't right now. We aren't strong enough. We will be defeated," said the officer. "But I admire your courage."

Jonathan was feeling sick. How could this be? He spoke again.

"Sir, I apologize if this seems impertinent, but we weren't told to attack only if victory was assured. We were told to attack. I saw the orders myself. There! They are on your own map table. How else can we read them?"

"I know. But we are too few. Maybe if more troops arrive," offered Justin weakly.

Softly the knight replied, "It isn't about numbers." Shaking his head, Jonathan turned to walk out of the tent.

"Where are you going, Ranger?" asked the Major.

"I am sorry, sir. But I have no choice. Please excuse me," said Sir Jonathan the Slight quietly.

"And what are you going to do, Sir *Slight*?" asked a burly lieutenant, emphasizing "slight" in his question.

"I am going to obey my King. It is all I have and it is all I care about," answered Sir Jonathan politely but firmly.

"You will die today, then," said the burly lieutenant flatly and in a matter-of-fact tone.

"Maybe. But that is not my concern. A knight does as he is commanded, when he is commanded. That is the vow. The King decides when and how that vow is fulfilled." Jonathan turned to leave.

Then, he stopped and wheeled around. His hand reached down and grabbed the hilt of his sword. He looked at all of them and they looked back at him. When everyone was quiet Jonathan spoke again.

"I do not know you but I want to trust you are all followers of the King and citizens of the City Beautiful. But you would do well to look after one another. The lies of the enemy are in this tent." Jonathan exhaled and then began again, "Excuse me for saying so, but if we think of our safety, if we consider our chances at success as more important than battle orders— then we have lost the battle to a lie." His strong words then echoed in the silence, "We must remember who is the King and who is the soldier." He paused and looked at them sincerely.

Then Sir Jonathan the Slight reached into a pocket on his tunic and pulled out one of his most prized possessions—the ancient parchment with the Oath of Fealty. He instantly remembered the day Sir Robert gave it to him. Part of him wanted to keep it, but he knew there were those in the tent that needed it more. He opened it slowly and carefully, as if it were nearly too delicate to handle. Without another word he walked back over to the map table and carefully laid it next to a copy of the orders for all to see.

"Godspeed, friends. Long Live the King," saluted Sir Jonathan before striding back to his horse.

As Jonathan left the tent the other knights looked at each other silently. His words had stung, but not cruelly as if they were malicious. The burly lieutenant looked down at the ancient writing for a few moments. Then he stood up, nodded to his Major, and walked out of the tent.

Jonathan rode his horse over to an outcropping and surveyed the enemy lines. He had a clear view of the lines of both sides. The sight was even more sickening from there. The dragon shrieked at the King's lines again. Jeers of enemy goblins mingled in sick song with the cries of the slaves in cages. It was too much. He remembered the night of his own rescue. He remembered the incredible acts of his King.

Jonathan retrieved the orders from his bag and reread them. They were clear. If he were to obey, he needed to charge. He could not delay.

He pulled the leather satchel out and retrieved the dragon point. He looked at it for some time, and he began to realize the truth. It wasn't going to be carried by a heavy horse knight in the future. It was going to be used by a light mounted ranger today.

"I am not adequate. I am not up to this. But I know one who is," said the knight under his breath.

With great care and shaking hands, he fixed it to his lance then covered it with a piece of leather to hide it. He then retrieved another prized possession—the King's banner. It was bright, but also ragged. The ends were frayed from use and a blackish hole marred the top portion. He tied it to his lance so it would fly like a pennant as he advanced. From a distance, it would not look like a lance at all, but a flag bearing the King's standard.

A soldier or two had come up to see what he was doing. They watched him as he unpacked his heaviest armor and began to dress for battle. They gathered around him for a few minutes before one had enough courage to ask questions.

"Sir, what are you doing?"

"I am preparing to follow my orders, friend. I am going to charge," he said confidently, though his insides were completely knotted. The old feeling of pre-battle jitters had returned.

"Charge?! That would be death! There are so many!" squeaked one.

"Maybe. But I have sworn allegiance to the King who pardoned me. All along he has taken care of me, guided me, and given me victory. Today he has ordered those slaves rescued. It is my honor to obey. I care not what happens next, but I intend to obey my King," said Sir Jonathan. The more he spoke about his King the more confident he felt.

"Understood. But sir, you should know, they have a dragon," offered a knight.

"Yes, but I have a King. I may not survive this charge—that is true. But, by the King and his power and weapons, their dragon will not live to see another day, either," said the knight resolutely. "He will never feast on another slave."

"Are you going alone?" asked another.

"No. He will not be alone," boomed another voice. The burly lieutenant from the command tent was trotting up on his horse. He was wearing the solid plate armor of a heavy horse knight. He had a broad axe and a long silvery lance. His heavy armor was dented and well worn. He no longer looked like a knight in camp but one dressed for battle and spoiling for a fight.

He walked up to Jonathan confidently and put huge hand on the knight's shoulder. Sincerely and warmly he addressed his new friend.

"You have reminded me of what matters most, Jonathan. I am going with you. I'll follow you down the middle if you will let me. I am Lieutenant Morgan, King's Heavy Horse, 1st Battalion," said the hulking knight as he stretched out his hand to Jonathan.

Jonathan reached for the large knight's hand and replied, "Jonathan. Sir Jonathan the Slight, friend of the King."

"Of that I am sure. Your words in the tent made that clear as do your actions now," smiled Morgan.

"Let's go kill a dragon," said Jonathan, shaking the burly knight's hand.

"We will help you prepare, Sir Knights," said one of the soldiers. He immediately began to help the two check their equipment and arms. Any baggage not directly related to the impending attack was discarded. Any item that would slow an advance was cast aside.

The knight affixed plate armor around his horse and dressed himself in his heavy battle armor. He checked and rechecked everything until he was sure it was all ready.

It was time.

"Long Live the King!" shouted the soldiers who helped him mount.

"Long Live the King!" answered Sir Jonathan the Slight. "You too have orders, my friends. Follow them. Follow me down the valley for your Lord and King. The battle will be his whether we are many or few."

Several of the soldiers nodded and quickly ran off to gather their gear.

Sir Jonathan the Slight, King's Knight and Royal High Ambassador of the Kingdom, guided his horse onto the Far Valley of Shadows, the gateway to the Great East. He moved out in front of the ridge line where all of the soldiers in the trenches could see him and where he could see all the enemy arrays. The lieutenant guided his horse next to him and lowered his faceplate.

The dragon saw them and beat the air with giant wings. It bellowed and the sound reverberated through all of the King's army. The enemy soldiers began to jeer and chant and howl and mock. Many called for them to come closer.

The encamped soldiers looked on.

Jonathan smiled as he thought how much Sir Stephen would approve of his plan for the dragon. It was time to move. He looked to his left and checked the lines for any sign of Bjorn or the rest of his friends. He knew they would be here eventually. Then he looked to his right, and high on a rocky outcropping he saw an amazing sight.

On the rocky outcropping, far above the lines, was a cloaked rider surrounded by Kingsguard. The Royal Banner was flying on the lance of the Kingsguard closest to him. It was the King. It had to be.

"Sir Jonathan! Look!" exclaimed the Lieutenant.

Sir Jonathan raised his lance and saluted his Captain and King. And then the King drew his great broadsword and returned the salute to the knights.

"If only the other knights and soldiers would leave their safety and move out toward the enemy they would see their Great King!" exclaimed Lieutenant Morgan. "They are missing this." With his mailed arm, he gestured back to where many hid, never taking his eyes off the King. "I almost missed this, Jonathan."

The sight of their great and powerful King come to fight alongside them was overwhelming. In that instance the knights did not think of the danger but were overcome with thankfulness. The familiar knots in Jonathan's stomach were gone. The knight was overtaken with a profound sense of gratefulness for his freedom, life, and mission.

And it was time to complete the mission.

Sir Jonathan the Slight turned toward the enemy lines for the last time. There would be no turning back. He lowered his cross-shaped visor and readjusted the grip on his shield and lance. He then said out loud with Morgan following along:

"I am the weak one. You are the strong one. This is your shield. This is your armor. These are your weapons. These are your knights. And this is your battle. Long Live the King."

"Long live the King!" echoed the lieutenant.

And with that, to the howling of the enemy, Sir Jonathan guided his horse to a trot and then to a gallop. He aimed their attack right at the dragon and spurred his horse to run the fastest it had ever run.

Faster and faster the horses ran until the only sounds the knights could hear were the thundering of hooves, the clinking of armor, and their own breath inside of their helmets. Occasionally, they heard the shriek of the dragon. It seemed to taunt them and welcome them forward, but they did not feel intimidated.

The two horses galloped in sync. Behind them, blowing a trumpet and carrying a banner, three soldiers had formed and began to charge far behind the advancing knights.

The two knights approached the center formation of the enemy. Faster and faster they galloped. Closer and closer the enemy loomed.

Then something resembling a black fog rose above the heads of the goblin battle lines. *Arrows!* Hundreds of enemy archers had unleashed a deadly volley at the knights. Some were even on fire. Their shields blocked most of the arrows and the King's servants continued to ride on. Jonathan could feel the arrows slam into his armor, but they couldn't penetrate the thick plates. Several hammered his shield but bounced off.

They were close enough to inhale the putrid stench of dragon now. The dragon bellowed again and Sir Jonathan heard it above the sound of the horses' hooves thundering across the ground. A great fireball ignited over the head of the enemy as it expelled a flaming blast.

Then Sir Jonathan saw something that warmed his soul in the middle of the cold battlefield he was crossing. He saw one of the faces of the slaves—a little girl. And as he galloped closer he saw something in her eyes that put a smile on his face. *Hope.* She looked at the King's charging servants and had hope.

Sir Jonathan the Slight turned his horse in an oblique as if to attack the enemy commanders assembled to the right of the dragon. This move caused the dragon to move slightly to reposition for a strike. It began to draw in a great breath to immolate the knights. Its lips curled back into a wicked snarl.

Then at the last minute Sir Jonathan pulled the leather strip that held the cover on the dragon point. It fluttered into the breeze, revealing the twisted blades and long narrow point. The dragon saw it as well but it was too late. Sir Jonathan turned his horse to his true objective and aimed the point right at the dragon's lower jaw. The knight actually laughed out loud and shouted when he saw the terror in the beast's eyes. Lieutenant Morgan continued on toward the assembled commanders, determined to trample them under his horse. He held his lance tightly in one hand and had now pulled out the enormous battle-axe with the other.

The filthy Apateon turned his head upward to avoid the blow but the knight was too fast. It slammed into the dragon's head with the force of a lightning strike. Flammable fluid from the dragon's throat began to spew out of the wound and ignite upon mixing with the air. The dragon shrieked as its head disappeared in its own flames.

The knights slammed into the enemy lines with tremendous force. The sound was like thunder that echoed up and down the King's lines.

What the attacking knights could not see was the effect their charge had on the King's army. Almost as soon as they were half way across the valley on their attack, soldiers and knights began to form up and march toward the enemy lines.

At first it was just a young, wounded soldier on foot. He had one arm in a sling and a bandage over his left eye. He picked up a King's banner and began to march by himself across the field toward the enemy as if he were leading an entire battalion. More and more soldiers left the entrenchments and started across.

On one section of the line, an entire company of soldiers followed their commander forward. They lined up and began to march. All along the line, the troops formed and moved out. In one area, twenty apprentices with shining new armor followed their mentor out onto the field. (It would be the last time any of the twenty would ever wear unspotted armor again. Soon they would be known as the Mangled Twenty, but that is another story.)

Almost near the end of the line, a formation of knights emerged from the woods. The horses leaped over the trenches and earthen works. In the lead, carrying a banner with the King's seal and the insignia of the mounted cavalry was Sir Bjorn. Behind him were the remains of the unit they had rescued days earlier. Each was rearmed and mounted. The recently rescued knights did not hesitate or question their new captain. As soon as they were free of the tree line they galloped toward the enemy behind Sir Bjorn. They nearly overtook him in their excitement to prove they had learned from their mistakes.

Each formation aimed for the center, where a dark, oily smoke was rising from the burning carcass of a red and black dragon.

CHAPTER 18

Thanatos the Unbeaten

"The last enemy that will be abolished is death."
– 1 Cor. 15:26

Slowly Sir Jonathan the Slight blinked his eyes open to see that he was on his horse. He was awake and riding and aware of riders with him. He looked around and saw six Kingsguard.

"Good morning, Sir Jonathan," said one.

"Good morning, sir," answered Jonathan. "Where are we going?" Sir Jonathan asked in one hopeful breath. He thought he knew.

"We are on our way to the King's City Beautiful, Sir Jonathan. Your wounds need treatment under the King's care. Furthermore, he has recalled you. Your transfer is permanent. Congratulations, brave knight," beamed the Kingsguard. "You are going home."

"Home." The word coursed through his heart like a cool drink on a hot day. He had never had a real home. Well, he had, but he had never been there.

Sir Jonathan could hardly believe his ears. He had read about the City and heard about it from Sir Robert. He was ecstatic. The long days and nights on rough trails and mountains were over. The long years of warfare and deprivation were at an end. *Home.* He was going home at last.

But as wonderful as the City was itself, what excited Sir Jonathan the most was seeing the King. *"The City is called the City Beautiful because the King is there,"* Sir Robert used to say. Finally, he would be with the King. He could not wait to see Him. Thoughts flooded his excited mind. He had so many things to ask the King.

Jonathan's thoughts turned toward the battle and the slaves.

"Friends, may I ask about the battle? How did it go? Were we successful?" asked Sir Jonathan.

"Yes, but at significant cost. The charge rallied the King's army. It formed and attacked as it was ordered to do. A well-placed lance dispatched a very large and ugly dragon. The army charged and the enemy was routed. Actually, they are still in full retreat to the mountains," answered a Kingsguard joyfully.

"And the slaves?" asked Sir Jonathan earnestly.

"What slaves? There were a great number of citizens rescued, but there were no slaves," responded a Kingsguard with a big smile. "Some are being escorted to a refuge city and some have already taken their vows as knights. A building party has just begun on a refuge city on the very spot the dragon died."

Sir Jonathan smiled and turned his face toward the sun. It was warm and golden and reminded him of his first sunrise after his last day as a slave. This was a wonderful day.

The path they were on wound along bright green fields. A cool, clear stream ran next to the path. Several times Sir Jonathan stopped to drink and was refreshed. Fruit trees also grew along the path. It was calm and restful. It seemed as if the long years of warfare were so far removed that they had never even existed.

As they rode along, the Kingsguard told him more and more about the City and the people there. It is full of citizens who have been rescued by the King. They are free from attack and deception there. It was wonderful to think about the people he would meet. He had many friends there as well.

They came around a corner in the path, and the knight's face froze in terror. The smile had disappeared. Quickly he drew his sword and raised his shield.

There in the road, lying down so as to block their way, was the largest dragon he had ever seen. It was nothing like the smaller dragon he had killed on the battlefield. This was a gigantic creature. Only one dragon could be that big: *Thanatos the Unbeaten.*

"Shield line! Shields and lances!" shouted Sir Jonathan to his companions. *"Dragon!"*

"Sir Jonathan, we will form if you command, but you must know that we maneuver on a defeated foe. This dragon is a rotting ruin. It holds no danger for you," assured a Kingsguard.

"It's a trick!" answered Sir Jonathan. "This is *Thanatos the Unbeaten.* It cannot be defeated. It's a trap!"

"No, Sir Jonathan. It *was* called Thanatos the Unbeaten in ages past, but it is no longer a threat because it is no longer unbeaten."

"How? Who could have killed it?" questioned Sir Jonathan franticly, still ready for an attack. His eyes never left the dragon.

"This dragon was slain by the only one who could kill such a monster. Go and see for yourself. It is quite harmless," answered a Kingsguard.

Slowly Sir Jonathan dismounted and moved closer to the mammoth beast. It was gigantic to the knight. The head alone was more than double the size of his horse. Its mouth was twisted in an ugly snarl. The dark red eyes were lifeless.

Cautiously Sir Jonathan walked around the carcass. He was ready for it to spring to life at any moment. He looked at a front claw and saw spots of bright red blood.

"That's not dragon's blood," he thought.

Then on the other side of the front arm he saw the hilt and handle of a great broadsword. It was buried deep in the dragon's heart. Thick black blood had oozed everywhere.

"Now *that* is dragon's blood," he said out loud.

The sword was very familiar to the knight. He took several steps forward and then recognized the crest instantly. It was the King's sword. There was no mistake. The same sword that destroyed the door to his cell so long ago and watched over him that night in the forest was up to its hilt in the heart of the most fearsome beast to have ever lived.

"For ages this dragon has stood between the King's city and the people he loves, but not anymore. The King himself killed this beast with his own hands, though at a significant cost. Now the only threat this foe poses to the citizens of the City is in its once fearsome reputation. Citizens who do not realize it is only a carcass can be afraid, but in effect, it has no power," explained a Kingsguard.

Just then, squeals of laughter rang out. Jonathan looked up at the tail of the dragon. Several children from the city were chasing each other. Without any fear of the dragon, they leaped over its lifeless tail in pursuit of the leader. To them, it was a minor obstacle in their chase. Even the smallest of them, a little girl who was laughing the loudest, climbed over the carcass and continued on without a second thought.

"Victory," said Sir Jonathan. It was the only word he could manage.

"Total and complete victory," continued a Kingsguard. "There is nothing left for you to do but enter the gates. The King has made that so."

It seemed like only an instant, but there he was at the gates of the City Beautiful. Jonathan dismounted and walked with his escort up to the door. The walls were towering and seemed to go on in either direction without end. The sounds of laughter, rejoicing, and peace permeated the air. It seemed almost too good to be true. But it was true. The knight was home.

The Kingsguard called out in a booming voice to the sentries.

"Open the gates! One of the King's own citizens and a knight of the Kingdom has come home!"

A loud cheer emerged from the walls. Sir Jonathan did not know he had so many friends. He could hear them singing and calling out, "Long Live the King!" "Welcome, knight!" He was home and he knew it.

He turned around and looked down the mountain at the valley below and the lands he had just come from. Past the body of *Thanatos the Rotting* (as it was now called) over the hills he could see smoke rising from a distant battlefield. Far in the distance he could see the snowy forests and dark swamps he had left. He took a deep breath and remembered.

It was the King who rescued him from his dungeon, signing his own princely name to the death warrant and setting him free. It was the King who offered him a place of worth and meaning in service to the Kingdom. It was the King who had equipped him for success and guaranteed it with his own power and weapons. It was the King who had watched over him and guided him to victory. And here at the end of everything and the long years of his life, it was the King who had defeated the undefeated. And now it was the King who had called him to his own City. From beginning to end, it was all the King.

With a grateful heart and great anticipation, Sir Jonathan the Slight, King's Knight and Royal High Ambassador of the King, turned and entered the City Beautiful.

Chapter 19

The Armory

"His Lord said to him, 'Well done, good and faithful servant . . .'"
– Matthew 25:21

The King's City Beautiful felt like home to Sir Jonathan the Slight. It was beautiful, majestic, and full of family he had never seen. Hugs, handshakes, and the warmest of greetings came at him from all directions. It was wonderful to be home, though he had not been there before. All of the toil and battle from a few moments ago faded quickly into a memory.

A very pleasant guide approached Jonathan.

"You may sheath your sword, Sir Jonathan, King's Knight. There are no enemies here." He greeted him warmly and explained he was to show him through the Armory to the Great Hall where he could remove his armor and hang his weapons. They would no longer be needed, the Guide explained. It was then the knight realized he was still in armor and carrying a very heavy shield and various other weapons. He wiped a blackish stain off of the blade with the bottom of his cloak as he had countless times before and sheathed the great sword.

Everywhere, smiling and laughing citizens greeted him. The

knight knew some of them but not all, though no one was a stranger. The mood was peaceful and freeing.

Jonathan followed the Guide down a large corridor and approached two very large wooden doors with ornate carvings on the front. The carvings were scenes of famous battles that he recognized instantly. The knights on the front of the doors were well known and admired. Jonathan touched the Kingsbook in his worn leather bag as he remembered reading about them on so many occasions.

As they continued on, the doors swung open and an awesome sight greeted the Knight. On multiple racks in many rows hung some of the brightest and shiniest armor the knight had ever seen. There were shields of various sizes that looked like they were fresh from the blacksmith. Few scratches, if any, could be found on most. A large red cross was on every one. Some of them reflected the sunlight that was streaming through the windows and cast a myriad of beautiful colors around the room.

Sir Jonathan had never before seen such an array of perfect shields—round, traditional, square. All of them were beautiful and seemingly untouched. As they walked he noticed that they went on for quite a way. Hallways branched off with more and more racks of the glimmering perfect shields. To the knight they seemed as if they were waiting on a great army to come through and retrieve them for battle or a parade. They reminded him of the great day when he swore fealty to the King and received his own armor. He had a bright new shield at one time, too; every bit as bright as these on display.

It was then the knight looked down at his own shield. He was slightly embarrassed by what he carried. His traditional-styled shield was not shiny anywhere. It was worn and beaten, though the red cross and the King's coat of arms were distinct and as bright as those on the racks. He noticed several large nicks out of the edges. One jagged scar almost went through the entire shield. A dragon's claw had nearly demolished it and the evidence of that encounter was ugly and raw. Three small arrowheads from crossbow bolts stuck in a tight group on the lower left corner of the shield. All of them were black and powdery with ash; they were on fire when they hit. The knight remembered that encounter with a shudder. He self-consciously ran his hand over multiple dents, dings, rips, and spurs.

"My shield does not belong in a hall full of these gleaming bright shields," he thought to himself.

He shifted his arm ever so slightly to hide it a little from the Guide. "Shall I lay my shield with these? Maybe in the back?"

The Guide turned and smiled faintly, "No. This certainly is not the place for a shield such as yours."

Jonathan nodded and tried to will his cheeks not to flame red. He knew his worn and beaten shield did not belong with these untouched trophies. Maybe there was a closet or corner somewhere for shields like the one he carried. Or maybe he needed to take it to the blacksmith first for repair.

After a long walk down the Hall of Shields, they came to another wing of the Armory. Hanging on the walls and standing in large groups on great wooden racks were some of the largest, most beautiful broadswords the knight had ever seen. There were jeweled hilts and intricately carved handles on the brightest blades. The edges looked razor sharp and the tips like they could split stone. He had never seen more grandeur in a sword—not even when they were new from the smith. It looked as if entire blocks of the city were full of the swords of kings! He asked the Guide if he could possibly hold one of them. The Guide gave him a curious look as if the very thought of him wanting to hold one was oddly out of place, almost improper.

Jonathan looked down at his own sword and thought he understood why. His sword was neither bright nor kingly in its appearance. The jewels in the hilt had long since been knocked out and lost on his journey. The knight replayed battle after battle and could remember crushing, teeth-rattling blows that could have easily dislodged a ruby or an emerald. Though still very sharp, there were nicks out of the blade as well. Some of them were severe and would require serious work at a forge.

It might not even be reparable, thought the knight. At one point he even wished he had a new sword like the ones he saw lining the walls. Part of the hilt of his weapon was cracked and bound tightly with leather and cord. The carvings were scratched and faded. The red cross on the hilt was still present and bright, but all around it the details were subdued. His sword, though fully trustworthy and a true treasure, was not like these beautiful pieces at all. The realization made him slightly embarrassed. He thought about asking where to put his sword, but then he remembered how the Guide had reacted to the same question about his shield and he swallowed the question.

They continued on into an area containing beautiful suits of armor. Some of the helmets had decorative plumes and ornate carvings. Some were simple and some were intricate. All were shiny and seemed untouched. There were not any dents like the ones he had. He was quite sure at one point he recognized one suit in particular. He could not be totally confident, but he thought it had belonged to Sir George from the refuge city so long ago.

Without being conscious of his hand, he had run his fingers across the top of his helmet under his arm. Grooves, dents, dings and cracks were all over the top. He could remember when and where he received most of them. Each memory was accompanied by the hideous snarl of battle and the earsplitting clank of weapons and shields. Memories of the encounters were woven in with the scratches and dings.

He shivered as he remembered several incidents where he was sure he was finished, but his armor had held. He remembered the hideous mouth of some beast that bore down on his helmet and would have crushed his head had his helmet not been so sturdy. But the giant fangs left ominous punctures as evidence of the great battle. It now bore the scars of those events and he was sure they did not belong in a room with this fine armor.

He remembered his helmet had once looked that way many years ago. He recalled how often he had to use his armor and was sure there was nothing he could have done to keep it from being damaged and dirtied. He remembered long treks through snowy mountains and marching through swampy bogs. He did as he was told, but it took a definite toll on his armor and uniform. Still, it was a little awkward to be around such fine and ornate helmets. In some ways he felt as though he had arrived at a royal event severely underdressed.

As he walked and remembered, he saw complete sets of armor—most of which had no blemishes. No dirt. No blood. He did not need to look down to realize what a sight he must be. He had seen the dents and dirt so many times. He was sure that a dent in the back could never be repaired—it was just too massive. He was not even going to think about asking the Guide where to set his armor. He was sure it would not be among these princely pieces and helmets.

The Guide noticed that he had finally stopped asking where to place his knightly equipment. He had also noticed the somber look as he gazed around at the spotless suits.

Finally, the Guide spoke. "There is a good reason you are not permitted to store your arms among these pieces, Sir Jonathan, King's knight." The Guide paused and studied him while stroking his long gray beard before asking with a lilt in his gruff voice, "Do you know why?"

Their voices echoed down the lengthy stone hallway. The stillness of the corridor made the Guide's pause seem much longer than it was.

After a slight hesitation the knight responded, "I believe it is because mine are soiled and scarred. Perhaps they are not worthy. My weapons looked like this a long time ago; when I was young and had just met the King. But now . . ." Jonathan's voice trailed into silence as he inspected his uniform.

The Guide was quiet for a few moments before saying, "Well, Sir Jonathan, what happened to them?"

"He offered me a place to serve him. He is the King, so I followed.

The battles were tough and the mountains and valleys treacherous and full of enemies. These paths provided me with no lack of ambushes and attacks, some of which I foolishly walked into without thinking. He gave me quests to complete and beloved charges to take care of through these battles and to escort to safety. Sometimes I fell into trouble from the enemy or myself and the armor was all that kept me from disaster. I was designated an Ambassador as well as knight, and it seemed as if I was always fighting. My armor and weapons are damaged and worn because of my work, sir," the knight defended pleadingly.

The Guide did not respond. The hall was quiet.

The knight sighed. "I am worn. As a result of all this, I am very worn. My armor has faded. My weapons are dented, pitted, and scarred. My apologies for making excuses, but dressed like this, I am not ready to see the King. I am quite underdressed."

The Guide shook his head slowly and smiled. "It is always the same with Knights of your Order."

Sir Jonathan looked up. "Order? What Order, Sir? What do you mean?"

"It would not disgrace this hall to lay your armor here; it would be a disgrace to you. And the King. You are one of the Overcomers. You cannot lay your armor here for it would be a shame. But not for what you are thinking. It would be a shame for *you*—you were given quests and battles and challenges and trials. And though not perfect, you chose to fight for and serve your King. When you were called, you answered. Your armor *is* dented and bruised and scarred—but from the King's business. It is the weaponry of an Overcomer; the dress of a friend of the King—not one to be ashamed of before the King.

"The armor and weapons of these halls are not meant to be trophies; they are not on display as a glory but as reminders of a wasted life. Though called to battle, the knights who owned this armor refused to go, or ran when the horrors of battle appeared.

Some decided the life of ease outside these walls was more important than the command of the King from within these walls. It is a hall of missed opportunity, of squandered life. It is the King who forged all of these weapons and armor and they could withstand any assault. It is the King who called their owners to battle and provided the strength and means to overcome. All they had to do was trust the King and follow Him into battle—as you did. But they did not. They did not answer their call fully; they did not overcome."

Very warmly he put his hands on Jonathan's shoulders and said to the knight, "But you, slight as you are—you were different. Though afraid, you trusted him. Though weary, you followed. You made mistakes, but you followed your King. You are to be taken through that door to see your beloved Captain. And by order of the King himself, you are to store your armor in his hall."

The Guide pointed to an ornate doorway with a sign over it. The sign gave the knight a rising hope and joy. Inscribed above the door were the words, **_Enter, Friend of the King_**.

"Though all in this city are citizens and beloved of the King, this door into the King's presence is a special entrance and not for all. It is only for those who are of the Order to which you belong—that of an Overcomer. Every citizen was called to take up his or her armor and follow the King. All were given armor and weapons equal to any quest or battle with the King as their guide. Some chose not to engage the enemy. For many reasons, none of which matter now, those, whose armor you saw in the great halls, failed to answer the King's call to follow Him completely. In doing this they failed to secure an invitation through that door. Their armor and weapons serve as a warning."

At that point another guide came up and said, "The King is anxious to see and welcome his friend. He has not stopped asking for him. You are requested in the Great Hall at once."

The knight looked down at his dented armor differently. The Guide's words were sinking in. He again ran his hand down his dented shield, but this time he smiled. *The armor of a friend of the King,* he repeated in his heart. His mind was racing.

Sir Jonathan the Slight said to his guide, "I'll wait for you here until your business with the King is complete. Is there somewhere I can rest?"

The Guide smiled and replied, "Sir Knight, **you** are the ambassador and friend on which the King is waiting. It is your return that has been anticipated. It is you he wishes to see. We will not keep His Majesty waiting. Come, the King is anxious to see you, Sir Knight."

Turning to the guards at the Great Doors leading to the King's Hall, his voice thundered, *"Open the Doors for the friend of the King!"*

The order to open the doors reverberated through the halls of stacked armor. It reminded Jonathan of a thunderstorm echoing off the mountains.

"Sir, shouldn't I change first? I am still wearing goblin-stained clothes and dented armor!"

"Not at all. He is a Warrior King who loves his warriors! It's time!"

The great doors swung open and it was a sight like no other. They had entered a great hall with expansive rooms all connected. The roughhewn stone walls had shields and swords of all sizes hanging on them. Tables lined the hall and were furnished with a great feast. Large fireplaces were roaring along the walls. Knights, almost without number, sat at the tables laughing, eating, and enjoying each other's company. At the front of the room was a long and massive wooden table.

There he saw him! *It was the King!* He was already getting up and headed to the knight with long, powerful strides and the warmest smile.

Though nervous, Jonathan approached the King almost at a run, then kneeled with his sword drawn in salute of fealty. He did not even want to look up. He was so honored to be in his presence and so thankful he was no longer a slave. The flood of emotions was almost too much. He had dreamed of this day for so long.

Silence fell over the room. There was a faint clink of armor as the King lifted him up and looked him in the eye for a moment with a broad bright smile. The King hugged him tightly and at that moment every tired muscle from long years of fighting was relieved. Jonathan's lifetime of suffering and deprivation seemed completely insignificant. The roar of dragons, shrieks of goblins, and hardships of the years melted away. The terror of sudden ambushes and fierceness of relentless attacks seemed to disappear. All in all, at that point the arduous life of a soldier seemed to be very light and short-lived.

He then heard the King say to him, "Welcome home! You have been a faithful servant. You have been a trustworthy soldier. You are my friend."

Then the King turned to the great hall. And in a loud, thunderous voice the King exclaimed, "This is Sir Jonathan the . . ." He paused and looked at the knight with a bright smile before continuing, "Sir Jonathan the Faithful. This knight is my friend! He is a soldier of the kingdom and a faithful servant! Welcome your brother and fellow member of the Order of Overcomers!"

The Great Hall erupted in a thunderous cheer so loud the knight thought his ears would burst. Sir Jonathan the Faithful saw it was full of men and women dressed as he was. Shields lined the walls and seemed to go on forever. They were pitted, scarred, and gashed—like his. Swords and axes and other weapons stood in rows along the walls. They were also scarred and bearing the marks of great battles—like his. The men and women in the Hall were standing at tables with a wonderful feast in front of them. An even louder cheer and shouts in praise of the King followed the loud cheer of welcome.

It had almost died down when another knight way in the back of a room thundered at the top of his lungs, "Long Live the King!" And the knights were back to their feet roaring in cheers, banging on shields, and raising their mugs high. Sir Jonathan the Faithful joined in with all of his might and raised his sword high in salute.

The King told Jonathan to hang his shield on the wall then come sit at his table for a meal. The Guide brought him over to a prepared place with the knight's name. On a gold plate was inscribed the following:

SIR JONATHAN THE FAITHFUL
KING'S KNIGHT AND AMBASSADOR

He hung his shield there and stacked his armor alongside other stacks of arms that looked like his. With a twinkle in his eyes the Guide then smiled and said, "This is where the armor of a King's knight goes, Sir Jonathan, friend of the King."

He was hugged and slapped on the back with greeting the whole way over. He saw many friendly faces, like Sir Reginald's. Some he recognized, some he didn't. All of them were dressed like he was—as a knight. He turned to walk back up to the King's table and saw Sir Robert standing in front of him, smiling broadly.

"Welcome home, brother!" exclaimed Sir Robert as he hugged him tightly. Sir Jonathan was thrilled to see his old friend. He hugged him but was unable to speak. "Hurry, now. The King is waiting. We'll speak again soon."

Jonathan pulled away and turned to the front of the room.

He approached the long table and was seated with the King. As he began to sit, the King stood and again called loudly to the hall of Knights.

"This is a Knight of the Order of Overcomers!"

There was another loud cheer. At that point he placed over Jonathan a new, finely woven cloak, whiter than the brightest snow. It was unlike any he had ever seen. On the back was a bright red cross. In one corner were a shield and a crossed pair of swords—the seal of the Order of Overcomers. The King placed a ring on his finger with the same seal.

The ring was beautiful beyond proper description, with jewels forming the crest of the Royal Family. But perhaps the greatest feature of the ring was not the jewels, but the inscription:

For all time, you will be identified as one of my knights, Sir Jonathan the Faithful. And, more than that, let this ring proclaim another truth: you are a member of my family. Always.

Jonathan was speechless. He had never imagined such a gift awaited him. He did not know whether to weep or shout.

Again the Great Hall echoed in thunderous cheers, shouts, and applause that quickly began to be directed to the King. The King sat down next to the knight and grabbed a loaf of warm bread. He pulled apart a piece and gave half to the knight and kept the other half. "Now," said the King as he dipped it in a familiar venison stew, "Let's talk about your journey . . . ."

Nothing in the long timeless echoes of eternity would ever dim the sight or experience of that moment; walking through the entrance as the King hailed Jonathan as a friend. Nothing he ever suffered on his journey could be compared to the welcome and homecoming he received.

And then the real adventure began . . . .

AFTER

The field was strewn with the brokenness that accompanies a tremendous battle. Spears, swords, axes, and all manner of debris littered the vast area. Grass was only visible poking up in shards and slivers between the metal armaments. In the center, vultures picked at the exposed ribs of the dead dragon. The only sounds above the wind were the greedy caws of the scavengers as they ate, and the construction of the new city of refuge that had just begun.

A small, dirty hand reached down to the ground and pulled up a silver and gold medallion. It was covered in mud and a few spots of dried blood.

The little hand began to rub the medallion to clean it. Slowly the symbols became legible. It was a lion's head with crossed swords. A scroll on the bottom had the phrase *"Forgiven and Declared Just"* in bold, dark red letters over gold.

A knight on a horse called to the young girl.

"What have you found, my dear?"

"A medallion. I have found a medallion. I believe it has the King's seal. Do you know what it means?" she asked as she placed it in his mailed hand.

The knight rubbed it in his fingers. He knew. He had seen it before many times. He nodded to the young girl who was adjusting her new belt. She had to tighten it around the new cloak, as she was small for her age. She did not want her King's seal to be distorted, so she constantly fidgeted with it.

"Yes, Lady Rachel. I do. It is the insignia of a Royal High

Ambassador of the Kingdom. This was worn by an ambassador and knight."

"Do you know him, sir?" she asked again as she mounted her new little horse. "Do you know the ambassador it belongs to?"

"I do. I know him well," he said as he thought about his friend. "Here, put this on," he said as leaned over and put it around her neck.

"But I haven't earned it. I . . . I . . ." she began.

"Will you serve your King as you have vowed?" he asked kindly.

"I will. I'm unsure how I will, but I want nothing more than to serve him. I will never forget what it meant to have the King shatter the door of my cage," she said ardently has she pushed her wild brown hair out of her face. "But I haven't earned this title."

"You will, young lady. You will. It is time to meet the others and move out," he said reassuringly.

"Yes, Captain. Where are we going?" she asked.

"Do you see those mountains in the distance? That is where we are going," he answered.

"No one has ever been there, sir. It is the Great East. Those mountains are enemy held," she said.

"Yes, they are. Today. And that is why we are going," answered the knight.

She nodded and pulled her pony around to follow the knight toward the others. A heavily armored column flying the banners of the King waited in formation to move out. As he approached he raised his hand to signal the column to move.

She is small. But so was I when I began, thought the knight. She reminded him of himself when Sir Jonathan had helped pull him out of a dungeon so long ago.

Sir Bjorn smiled to himself at the joy of serving the King and turned his armored column toward the mountains in the distance.

"Long Live the King," he shouted. The knights thundered back the same in response. Sir Bjorn, King's knight, rode to the head of the column and the company started into the heart of the Great East.

Lightning Source UK Ltd.
Milton Keynes UK
UKHW021429011220
374434UK00010B/509